Annie S. Swan

Aldersyde

A Border Story of Seventy Years Ago

Annie S. Swan

Aldersyde
A Border Story of Seventy Years Ago

ISBN/EAN: 9783337341565

Printed in Europe, USA, Canada, Australia, Japan

Cover: Foto ©Andreas Hilbeck / pixelio.de

More available books at **www.hansebooks.com**

PRINTED BY MORRISON AND GIBB, EDINBURGH,

FOR

OLIPHANT, ANDERSON, & FERRIER

LONDON: HAMILTON, ADAMS, AND CO.

A Border Story of Seventy Years Ago

BY

ANNIE S. SWAN

AUTHOR OF 'CARLOWRIE,' 'A DIVIDED HOUSE,' ETC. ETC.

New Edition

EDINBURGH

OLIPHANT, ANDERSON, & FERRIER

1887

TO

MY SISTER JANET

TENDER AND TRUE

BOOK. I.
THE TWA MISS NESBITS.

BOOK. I.

THE TWA MISS NESBITS.

CHAPTER I.

> ' Nae ancient name, nor high degree,
>   Nor mither wit, nor penny fee,
>   Can lengthen oot life's day ;
>   Grim, pitiless, and cauld, Death stands
>   Tae beckon us wi' ruthless hands,
>   An' a' maun gang his way.'

UPON a grey and cheerless winter afternoon Marget Drysdale was ironing in the laundry at Aldersyde. A pile of damp linen lay on one end of the board, and she was exercising her skill on the frilled bosom of one of her master's shirts. Everything about her was spotlessly clean. Her sleeves were tucked up to her elbows, and she wore a big white apron with a bib over her working garb. There was no part of her domestic duty of which Marget was so proud as her laundry work, and she had proved by experience that its success depended mainly on cleanliness. She was not a comely person, nor striking in any way. Her figure was short and ungraceful, her face broad, and rough, and red, but a very honest face withal, and one to be trusted. Her eyes, though small, were keen, and did not allow much to pass by them unobserved. They were red about the rims on this dreary afternoon, and more than once she had to dry them hastily, lest a stray tear might mar the beauty of her work.

A privileged person in the house of Aldersyde was Marget Drysdale. Ten years before, she had come, a raw, awkward, slow-handed lass of seventeen, to help in the kitchen, under the grim supervision of old Elspet Broun, who had served the Nesbits faithfully for fifty years, and, feeling herself beginning to fail, desired a recruit whom she might instruct in the ways of the house.

A very hard life of it had Marget, before she was able to please her unflinching taskmistress; yet when the time came, Elspet laid down her armour in peace.

'For,' said she, 'Marget's neither wasterfu' nor careless, but wull serve the hoose as weel, nay, better than me, for she's young and strong.'

The mantle of Elspet Broun's devotion had descended upon her successor, for Marget would have laid down her life willingly for the house of Aldersyde.

The Nesbits had fallen from their former high

place among the county gentry. The time had been when they had held their own among the Border families, and there had been gay revels in Aldersyde. From the beginning they had been an idle, careless, spendthrift race, and the estate passed from one scion to another, a burdened heritage which it was thought impossible to redeem. But when Walter Nesbit, thirteenth heir of Aldersyde, entered into possession, a change took place. To begin with, he departed from the way of his forebears by marrying a maiden of lower degree than himself, the daughter of the parish minister of Broomlee. What hand she had in it was never known, but within six months after their marriage all the servants save Elspet Broun and Tammas Dodds the coachman were dismissed, and the house, under the personal supervision of the mistress, was kept on the most economical scale. They had registered a vow that if it should please God to give them a son, he should enter upon an unburdened heritage. Years passed, two little girls came to make gladsomeness in Aldersyde, but the desire of their hearts remained unfulfilled, for they had no heir.

When the elder sister was fifteen, Mrs. Nesbit died, and from that time the Laird was a changed man. Never of a robust constitution, the shock utterly broke him down mentally and physically.

He had been accustomed to lean upon his wife, to leave all his concerns in her strong, prudent hand, knowing she would give them her first and best care.

Janet, the elder girl, had inherited her mother's nature; the younger, her outward appearance. Thus they might have been equally dear to the father's heart; but while clinging in his dependence to Janet, Isabel was the apple of his eye. She was a vain, frivolous, selfish thing, in whom all the gracelessness of the Nesbits had found a dwelling-place. She was the younger by five years, and Janet regarded her with almost a mother's tenderness. Next to Aldersyde, she loved Tibbie beyond any earthly thing. Aldersyde was first: she would have died for the place; and every tree, and flower, and moss-grown stone upon it was sacred to her.

After her mother's death, she did her utmost to follow in her footsteps, and add to the wherewithal which would one day redeem Aldersyde. It did not matter to her that, at her father's death, it would pass from them into the hands of a distant kinsman; in this, as in every other thing, Janet Nesbit was unselfish to the core. Ten years had passed since the death of Mrs. Nesbit, and now the Laird himself lay in the west bedroom sick unto death. Already Janet had faced the grievous certainty that ere very long Tibbie and she would need to say good-bye to their father and quit Aldersyde for ever. Marget Drysdale had faced it also, but not with the calm resignation displayed by her mistress. To her the leaving of Aldersyde seemed an unbearable hardship. That and other kindred gloomy thoughts distracted her attention from her favourite work, and she actually held down an iron on the delicate linen, till it was singed irredeemably.

'Confoond it!' she exclaimed in dismay, and set the iron down on the stone floor to cool.

Just then, a light step sounded in the kitchen beyond, and a quiet voice turned Marget's thoughts in another direction.

'Marget, ye'd better bid Tammas ride tae Aldershope an' tell Doctor Elliot tae come up immediately.'

The quaint phraseology, the sweet, clear, womanly voice, were in keeping with the outward appearance of the speaker. A very sweet and comely person to look at was Miss Nesbit of Aldersyde. She was about middle height, and carried herself like a young oak. Her face was long and inclined to be thin, her mouth grave and somewhat sad-looking with a determined curve in the upper lip which showed that she was a woman with a will. Her eyes were hazel, lovely eyes, which made the beauty of her face. They were fringed by long lashes, golden brown like the hair which rippled on her brow. She was faultlessly neat in her attire, and looked what she was, as pure and sweet a gentle-woman as eyes could wish to see.

'Is the Laird waur, Miss Nesbit?' asked Marget in a choked voice.

'He's comin very near the end, Marget,' said Miss Nesbit with the calmness born of habitual self-control. 'Bid Tammas gang immediately.'

Then she turned about quickly, and took her way up-stairs. It was a lovely old staircase, made of solid oak, polished like a mirror, and not disfigured and hidden by carpets or other covering. It ter-minated at a wide landing, where a door to the right opened into the drawing - room, and one on the left into what was called the west bedroom.

Miss Nesbit first entered the drawing-room, a long, low-ceiled apartment, the furnishings of which had been magnificent in their day, but were faded and shabby now to the last degree. A wood fire crackled in the high brass grate, and on the tiger-skin rug in front of it a figure reclined with a velvet cushion under her head in the very luxuriance of ease. It was that of a young girl, dazzlingly fair, with a face like an opening rose, and eyes as blue as the forget-me-not.

'Is that you, Janet?' she inquired without troubling to look up.

'Get up, Tibbie, an' come wi' me,' answered Miss Nesbit brusquely. 'Father's sinkin' fast.'

'Can I do any good, Janet?' asked Tibbie carelessly. 'It only vexes me to see him so ill. And you know he'll no bide me to do anything for him.'

'Tibbie! Tibbie!' said Miss Nesbit in low, wailing tones, 'oor father hasna many hoors, maybe no meenits, tae live.'

'You said that last night, Janet; I'll come by and by,' Tibbie made answer. Then without another word Miss Nesbit went out and closed the door after her.

The chamber where the Laird of Aldersyde lay dying was dim and darkened, and its stillness only broken by his uneasy breathing. Miss Nesbit crossed from the door to the bed with noiseless step, and finding that he had fallen into a light doze, went over to the front window and drew aside the blind.

A November storm was sweeping through Ettrick Vale. From her post Miss Nesbit could see the winding Yarrow rushing swiftly and sullenly between its banks, as if St. Mary's had overflowed and sent its surplus to swell the silver stream into a raging flood. A wild wind came roaring over the mist-crowned hills, and swept across barren stubble-fields and newly-upturned lea, till it bent the dripping alders and laved them in the stream.   The rain was weeping on the panes, but not more bitterly, I trow, than Janet Nesbit, though her eyes were dry.   Suddenly there was an uneasy movement at the bed, and a whispering voice broke the dreary stillness.

'Janet!'

In a moment she was by his side.

'Father, I'm here,' she said.

These words had been the text of her daily life since her mother died, and though he loved the younger better, he had leaned upon the elder with that dependence all weak natures lavish on the strong.   To my thinking, it is a pitiful thing to see a man depending on a woman, be she young or old. Is it not the order of things reversed?

'Raise my head, Janet.'

At once her arm was deftly placed beneath his feeble head, and raising him up, she supported him on her shoulder.   So close to each other, the resemblance between them was strongly marked. The wealth of brown hair, the deep hazel eyes, and straight well-shaped nose were characteristic cf both.   But the mouths were not alike, the Laird's being weak and undecided, an index to the nature of the man.

'I'm slippin' awa, Janet.'

'Ay, father.'

Her brow contracted slightly, but she showed no other sign of emotion.

'I wush ye had ha'en a brither, Janet, an' ye wadna hae had to gang awa frae Aldersyde.'

Miss Nesbit made no answer. On this subject she could not think, much less speak yet.

'Hugh Nesbit's the heir, ye ken, Janet,' continued the Laird feebly. 'I hinna seen him sin' he was a laddie. I wush he could hae been here afore I deid, so that I micht tell him tae be guid to my lassies.'

'We're no needin' Hugh Nesbit's guidness, Tibbie an' me,' said Miss Nesbit with quiet pride.

A silence followed, during which she cast her memory back to a long gone summer time, when her schoolboy cousin, Hugh Nesbit, had spent his holidays at Aldersyde. Isabel was a toddling three-year-old girl then, and the rude, cunning, cruel boy was the terror of her life. He would pinch her, and slap her when there was no one by, and upon one occasion Janet had caught him torturing and terrifying her with a pin. Then the hot blood of the Nesbits had risen within her, and with a strength which made her marvel, she had beaten him with her riding switch till he howled for mercy. In revenge he had drowned her kitten and tied a lighted paper to her cat's tail, for which Janet never could forgive him.

All animals and helpless things shrank from Hugh

Nesbit, feeling instinctively that he was their enemy. Janet remembered crying out in agony at seeing him cut out a sparrow's tongue, and how he had laughed at her and tortured the bird under her very eye. That was his first and last visit to Aldersyde, although he was its heir.

Ay, that boy grown to manhood was the heir, and soon would be Laird of Aldersyde. What wonder if Miss Nesbit's eyes grew dark, and a bitter, bitter tear trembled on the drooping lids?

'Whaur's Tibbie?' asked the sick man eagerly.

'In the drawin'-room ; will I get her?'

'No yet. I hae some things tae say tae ye, my lass. But draw up the blind ; it's darkening doon.'

The blind was up, and the room light enough ; it was the shadow from afar darkening the eyes of the dying Laird.

'There's Windyknowe, ye ken, Janet, gin Hugh winna let ye bide in Aldersyde. Bein' a sodger, he'll maybe bid ye tak care o' the hoose when he's awa. Oh, Janet, it's a cruel, cruel law that winna let a man leave his hame tae his lassies.'

Miss Nesbit bowed her head—ay, it was cruel.

'What money there is, ye ken whaur tae get it, Janet, an' a' that's in Aldersyde is yours an' Tibbie's. Hugh Nesbit gets only the bare wa s.'

True ; yet to call the bare walls of Aldersyde her own, ay without a sixpence in the world, Janet

Nesbit would have counted herself rich among women.

'If yer mither an' me hadna set oor hearts on seein' Aldersyde free, there wad hae been mair for Tibbie an' you,' said the Laird regretfully.

'Wheesht, father!' said Janet with kindling eye. 'Aldersyde an' the honour of the Nesbits is o' mair account than Tibbie an' me.' Then she added with a sigh, 'Maybe Hugh Nesbit 'll mak a guid Laird.'

'He hadna the promise o'd in his youth,' answered the Laird. 'Wet my lips, bairn, an' syne read frae the Book. Hae ye sent for Elliot?'

'Ay.'

Miss Nesbit touched her father's lips with brandy, then taking the Book from the table, began to read from the Revelation. The music of her voice lulled the listener into a doze, and fearing that he might awaken if she paused, she read on till the door was softly opened to admit the doctor. He was a tall broad - shouldered man, of middle age and stern appearance. His features were strongly marked, his eyes dark and piercing, his voice harsh and unpleasant. But he was a skilful man in his profession, and one to be relied on. Miss Nesbit bowed slightly and rose. Then the two noiselessly crossed to the window, and stood talking in whispers. The short winter's day was near its close;

already the shadows of the night were darkening down. The rain had ceased, and the grey sky was breaking overhead. A few minutes passed, then a movement at the bed caused the doctor to approach his patient, while Miss Nesbit proceeded to light the night-lamp on the side table.

'Janet!'

In a moment Miss Nesbit answered the eager, stifled cry, and was at her post. A change had come upon the Laird's face even in these few minutes—that terrible change all of us must dread, because it is not seen save on the face of the dying. Miss Nesbit cast her eyes imploringly up at the doctor's face. He slightly shook his head, and turned away.

Then knowing the end was at hand, she slipped her arm beneath her father's head, and pillowed it on her breast. There was not a ripple on the dead calm of her face, though beneath the plaited boddice of her gown her heart was breaking.

'Father, it's but gaun hame tae mother,' she whispered, and the words brought the shadow of a smile upon his wasted lips.

'Lay me doon,' he said with difficulty. 'I'm weary, weary, an' wad fain sleep.'

She obeyed him, and turned to the doctor.

'Wull ye gang for Isabel, Doctor Elliot? She's in the drawin'-room,' she said.

The doctor nodded, and was crossing the room, when the Laird suddenly held up his hand and spoke in tones of wonderful strength and clearness :

'The way's made plain for my feet even in the Jordan. Eh! but the Lord's guid, guid, Elliot.' Then casting his eyes full on Janet's face, he added solemnly, 'Tak care o' Tibbie.'

He turned upon his pillow, and being weary, fell asleep.

'Dinna gang for Isabel, Doctor Elliot,' said Miss Nesbit presently. 'I'll gang to her mysel''

'Very well, Miss Nesbit. Good evening,' said the man of few words, and went his way.

Miss Nesbit went away over to the front window when the doctor left the room, and stood there, her face showing ghastly white in the shadow. The leafless trees were swaying and bending in the wind, but above their dreary rustling she could hear the voice of the swollen Yarrow. From her post she could see the lonely Loch of the Lowes lying in the dark shadow of the silent hills, and a fitful beam from the wintry moon playing weirdly and uncertainly on its troubled breast. Turning to the right, her eyes travelled to the ruined chapel of St. Mary of the Lowes and the burying-ground surrounding it, where, ere many days were past, a grave would be opened among the straggling headstones to receive the remains of another Laird of Aldersyde. A shudder ran through Miss Nesbit's frame, and she swayed in momentary faintness; but it passed, and she quitted the room to seek her sister. She was still basking, all unconscious, on the tiger skin at the drawing-room fire.

'Get up, Tibbie,' said Miss Nesbit in a voice which caused Tibbie to spring to her feet, her eyes dilating with sudden dread. Then Miss Nesbit did a very unusual thing for her, being the most undemonstrative of women. She took her young sister in her arms, close, with a grip which hurt.

'Tibbie,' she said, and her voice shook, 'he's fa'n asleep, an' there's only you and me, twa hameless orphan lassies left in a cauld warld alane!'

CHAPTER II.

'Dear hands slip daily frae oor grasp,
  An' hearts are sundert sair,
An' e'en grow dim wi' bitter tears
  For them they'll see nae mair.'

ITH her own hands Miss Nesbit performed the last offices for the dead. Tibbie seemed to shrink from helping in the task, and would not even enter the room to look upon her father's face, which to Janet seemed only beautiful in its perfect peace and rest from pain. But she could be gentle with the weakness she could not understand, and bade Marget light a fire in the dining-room, so that Tibbie could be farther removed from the chamber she seemed to dread. After lighting the fire, Marget proceeded to set the table for the late tea. The regular ways of the house had been set aside during the long illness of the Laird.

Having finished her sad duties, Miss Nesbit retired to her own room to change her gown and make her hair smooth before she went to the tea-table. It was characteristic of her that even in the first hours of her grief she should be thus particular in observing such trivial matters. Even in her sorrow for the dead, she did not forget her duty to the living. As the clock in the hall struck seven, she came down-stairs. Just as she was about to enter the dining-room, there came a loud knock at the outer door, which sent echoes thundering through the silent house.

'Guid guide us a',' she heard Marget say as she came breathlessly up the kitchen stair, 'whatten a crater can this be at sic a time o' nicht?'

Miss Nisbet slipped within the dining-room door, and listened with bated breath while Marget undid the fastenings to admit the visitor.

'I am Captain Nesbit,' she heard a man's voice say. 'How's the Laird?'

'Gane,' was Marget's laconic response. Then the door was slammed with unnecessary force.

'Cousin Hugh, Janet,' said Tibbie, rising from the fire with brightening eyes.

Miss Nesbit nodded, her heart too full of bitterness to speak.

Yet why should it be? Was it not a right and fitting thing that the Laird of Aldersyde should

come to see to his own? It passed in a moment;
then she threw open the room door wide, and stepped
out into the hall. Beneath the lamp, a man was
taking off his overcoat. He was tall, but slender,
not like the broad-shouldered sons of Aldersyde, yet
he carried himself with a graceful and soldierly
bearing.

'You are welcome to Aldersyde, Hugh Nesbit,'
said Janet, striving to speak heartily as well as
sincerely.

He wheeled round immediately, and for a
moment they looked at each other in silence. After
that one steady look into his face, Miss Nesbit's eyes
fell, and her heart sank. It was a dark, passionate,
evil face, with sinister black eyes and long, thin, cruel
lips, partially hidden by a drooping moustache. He
advanced, smiling, with extended hand to the
graceful woman he had come to supplant.

'Cousin Janet! Am I right?' he said smoothly.

'I am Janet Nesbit,' she answered with some
stiffness.

'I am truly sorry I am too late to see my uncle.
Your excellent but somewhat uncivil domestic has
just given me the sad news.'

'Come in, Cousin Hugh,' said Miss Nesbit.
'Isabel is here, and we are just aboot tae hae oor
tea.'

Hugh Nesbit bowed and followed her into the

room.   Tibbie was standing on the hearth, the red glow of the firelight playing on her golden head and bright, expectant face.   Her cousin's eyes gleamed with admiration, and he bent low over the hand she offered him.

'Cousin Isabel, it was worth a sixteen-mile ride on a wretched night to see you at the end of it.'

The flimsy compliment pleased the giddy thing, and she smiled a satisfied smile.

'I'm glad you're come, Cousin Hugh,' she said in her sweetest tones.

'Have you any luggage wi' ye?' asked Miss Nesbit.

'Only a bag,' he answered.   'I shall not stay many days at present.'

It may have been her fancy, but to Janet Nesbit his last word seemed needlessly emphasized.

'I'll bid Marget tak it up tae the sooth room. I suppose it'll dae?' she said, moving towards the bell-rope.

'Any apartment you please, fair cousin; I am in your hands.'

Marget did not answer the summons with her usual promptness.   Several minutes elapsed before she entered, bringing the tea-tray with her.

'Marget, tak Captain Nesbit's bag up tae the sooth room, an' licht a fire, an' hing up the sheets tae air.'

'Humph!' said Marget, tossing her head; 'I've

jist ta'en doon the poke frae the cast bed-room lum ;
will it no dae ? '

'Make ready the south room as I desire, Marget,'
repeated Miss Nesbit gently, whereupon Marget
dropped a profound curtsey, cast a look of indignant
scorn upon Hugh Nesbit, and retired.

'Really, cousin, your domestic amuses me,' said
Hugh Nesbit. 'Is it the custom in this Border
county of yours to permit such licence in
inferiors ? '

'Marget is mair a freen than a servant, an' is
privileged to dae muckle as she likes,' answered Miss
Nesbit briefly, and seated herself before the urn.

Hugh Nesbit placed a chair for Isabel, and
drawing in his own, took his seat beside her.

Miss Nesbit asked the grace herself, surmising her
cousin would in all likelihood refuse. Then the
meal began.

'It is, let me see, twelve, fourteen, fifteen years
since I was here before,' said Hugh Nesbit, medita-
tively stirring his tea. 'We were not very good
friends in these days, Cousin Janet.'

'No,' she answered ; 'maybe ye can mind why.'

'I remember the thrashing you gave me for teasing Isabel. What a little fury you were ; I can
scarcely imagine you in such a passion now.'

'If I had the same cause, I'll no answer for the
consequences, Hugh,' returned Miss Nesbit quickly.

'Is not London a splendid place, Cousin Hugh?' asked Isabel eagerly. 'What a lot you must have seen!'

'Yes, I have knocked about plenty in my time; but I have been tied to Woolwich pretty tightly for months back. This Peninsular business keeps us on the alert. We were daily expecting orders to march. It was with the utmost difficulty I got leave of absence, when your letter reached me.'

'You'll leave the army now, surely?' said Isabel.

'Yes; I have decided to sell out,' he answered carelessly. 'Where is Uncle Walter to be buried?' he broke off suddenly, and looked directly at Janet.

'Where my mother lies, in the chapel of St. Mary's, Hugh,' she replied in a surprised way.

'I see. Who is to be asked? If you will furnish me with a list of names, I shall fill up invitations to-night.'

He had counted on his uncle's certain death, then! Miss Nesbit bit her lip, and rose.

'That's my wark, Cousin Hugh. I shall invite the folk tae my father's funeral.'

'Oh, very well,' said Hugh Nesbit, shrugging his shoulders. 'It was only to save you trouble. I am glad to be relieved.'

'Will ye come up the stair and see my father now?' she asked.

'Oh, well, there's no use; fact is, I'd rather not,' he answered.

A slight smile curled Miss Nesbit's lips.

'Maybe yer feared, like Tibbie?' she said.

'Well, not exactly; but I'm not used to such things. I'll wait till daylight, anyway. With your permission, I'll take a smoke, and join you in the drawing-room in a few minutes.'

'As ye please, Cousin Hugh. Come away, Tibbie.'

Tibbie rose reluctantly, and they quitted the room. There were no words between them till they entered the drawing-room and shut the door.

'That's the Laird o' Aldersyde, Janet,' said Tibbie, throwing herself into an easy chair.

'Ay, Tibbie.'

Miss Nesbit folded her hands on the low mantel-shelf, and bent her eyes on the fire.

'D'ye like him, Janet?'

'Marget disna,' said Miss Nesbit, not choosing to say ay or no to Tibbie's question.

'Marget!' echoed Tibbie wrathfully. 'My face got red at the way she spoke to Cousin Hugh.'

'If ye never get onything waur than Marget's honest tongue tae gar yer face grow red, Tibbie, my wummin, ye'll dae,' said Miss Nesbit drily, and for the moment Tibbie was silenced.

Miss Nesbit stood up straight and looked about the room, which was endeared to her heart by so many hallowed memories.   Her mother's work-table and footstool stood where she had left them in the front window, and close by was the spinet which in bygone days had responded to her touch, and filled the room with the heart-stirring melodies of the old Border ballads.   Never had the dear, homely place seemed so dear to Janet Nesbit as now, when reflecting how soon she would have to leave it to the occupation of strangers.

'We'll can mak Windyknowe like hame, Tibbie,' she said with an effort ; 'efter we get a' the auld things set in't.'

'What d'ye say aboot Windyknowe ? ' asked Tibbie, wakened from her reverie.

'Ye ken, Tibbie, we canna bide in Aldersyde noo,' answered Miss Nesbit with a break in her voice. 'Let us be thankfu' we hae Windyknowe tae gang tae.'

' It didna enter my head to think we would need to go away from Aldersyde,' said Tibbie.

Miss Nesbit smiled slightly.   If left in the world alone, what would become of this young sister of hers, who never in her life had taken a thought beyond the moment with her?

Presently a footfall was heard on the stair, and Hugh Nesbit sauntered into the room with his hands in his pockets. Miss Nesbit sat down by Tibbie, and her cousin lounged up against the mantel, and took a deliberate and critical survey of the room and its occupants.

'This place is exactly as it used to be,' he said. 'You used to sing and play on that thing with legs in the corner.   Do you ever do it now, Cousin Janet?'

'No' this mony a day,' answered Miss Nesbit.

'It is an awful place this to be buried alive in. Listen to that howling wind !   Ugh! it's enough to give a fellow the blues,' said the Laird of Aldersyde, shrugging his shoulders.

'The wind ?' queried Miss Nesbit in surprise. To her the tempest roaring over Bourhope spoke with the voice of a friend.

'I agree with you, Cousin Hugh,' said Tibbie, shivering. 'I hate storms and wind.   If it was always summer time, Aldersyde would be a pleasant place.'

'I think I'll have the trees thinned round the house,' said Hugh Nesbit, keeping his eyes fixed on Janet's pale face.   'Useless timber might with advantage be turned into cash.'

Miss Nesbit winced, but preserved a proud silence.

'The place needs many alterations which I shall have executed directly,' he went on mercilessly, knowing the pain he was inflicting.   'I shall have all that ivy stripped off the front.   It is a harbour for damp and insects, besides being opposed to all modern taste.'

'Tibbie, you an' me had better gang doon the
stair,' said Miss Nesbit in a strange, sharp way.
'Sic talk has nae interest for us.'

At that moment a loud and imperative knock at
the hall door caused them all to start. Miss Nesbit
rose at once, and motioning to Tibbie, they quitted
the room. Just as they reached the landing, a gust
of wind swept up from the open door, and they
heard the tones of a shrill, wheezy voice both
recognised at once.

'Janet Nesbit, whaur are ye?'

'Grizzie Oliphant as I live, Janet Nesbit!'
exclaimed Tibbie. 'What on earth brings her frae
Yair to-night?'

Miss Nesbit did not look particularly delighted;
nevertheless, it behoved her to go down immediately and bid her father's kinswoman welcome.
Tibbie remained on the landing and peered over
the balustrade to behold Miss Grizzie. In the
middle of the hall stood a tall, angular, bony woman,
past middle life, attired in a stiff black satin gown,
a filled-in plaid, and a towering head-gear of the
same material. She had several band-boxes with
her, and a black velvet reticule on her right arm.

'Weel, Janet Nesbit?' she said grimly, and her
restless black eyes wandered scrutinizingly over the
face and figure of her comely young kinswoman.

'How are ye, Miss Grizzie?' asked Miss Nesbit. 'This is a surprise.'

'It needna be, then,' snapped Miss Grizzie. 'I met Doctor Elliot yestreen in Yair, an' he telt me yer faither hadna mony hoors tae leeve; an' that ye were hoorly expeckin' Hugh Nesbit's son at Aldersyde. So as it wasna a fittin' thing for twa lassies an' a maid bidin' in the hoose their lane wi' a young man, I gar'd Tammas Erskine yoke the coach an' bring me ower. He'll bide here, of course, till I gang hame; but I'm gaun tae bide a bit wi' ye in yer tribulation. Has Hugh Nesbit come? an' whaur's Tibbie?'

'Yes; he cam' about twa hoors sin' syne; an' Tibbie's up the stair, Miss Grizzie,' answered Miss Nesbit slowly.

'Weel, bid that ill-mainnert maid o' yours cairry my things up tae the sooth room, an' cairry up a shovelful o' coal frae the kitchen fire tae air the sheets, or I'll hae rheumatism in my left leg.'

'I hae putten Cousin Hugh in the sooth room,' Miss Nesbit ventured to say.

'An' what altho'? ony room's guid eneugh for Hugh Nesbit's son, I'm thinkin'. He'll no hae lain on feathers a' his days, nae mair than his ne'er-dae-weel faither afore him,' quoth Miss Grizzie. 'Sae let Marget cairry his things oot, an' pit mine in.'

There was no help for it, Miss Nesbit knew. It

was the habit of Miss Grizzie to turn upside down every house she visited.

'Come up the stair, then, Miss Grizzie,' she said, and laid her hand on one of the band-boxes.

'Na, na; I'll tak that,' said Miss Grizzie. 'My best bannet's in ane, and my new kep in the ither. Tak that bag. It has my hoose goon, an' my shoon in it.'

Miss Nesbit obeyed, and led the way up-stairs. Tibbie fled into her bedroom at their approach. When they reached the south room, Miss Grizzie very quietly lifted Hugh Nesbit's portmanteau and one or two things off the dressing-table, and conveyed them outside to the landing. Then she proceeded to take off her travelling garments and get into her house gown.

'So yer faither's deid at last, Janet Nesbit. Weel, I houp ye see it's for the best,' said she.

'I'm tryin' tae think it,' answered Miss Nesbit, folding her quiet hands upon her lap, her habit when her heart was stirred.

'Ye *maun* think it. If ye rebel again' Providence, it's just tempin' Him tae send anither dispensation.'

Miss Nesbit remained silent.

'Hugh Nesbit gets Aldersyde, of coorse. What's left to you lassies?'

'My father's money, an' Windyknowe,' replied Miss Nesbit, knowing that she had no alternative but answer every question.

'Humph! it'll dae till ye get men. When are ye gaun to reign at Ravelaw noo, Janet Nesbit?'

Miss Nesbit's face flushed a deep red.

'What put that thocht i' yer heid, Miss Grizzie?'

'Dinna be a fule, Janet Nesbit,' retorted Miss Grizzie. 'Sandy Riddell wull hae been here the day, readily?'

'No, Miss Grizzie.'

To Janet's unutterable relief, Tibbie's entrance changed the subject. Miss Grizzie turned about, hair-brush in hand, and surveyed the bonnie Isabel from head to foot.

'Humph! ye're a weel-faured hizzie,' she said, offering her hand. 'I hope ye mind that beauty is vain, an' a virtuous wummin faur abune rubies, as Solomon says?'

'I didna ken he said that, Miss Grizzie,' said Tibbie in her cool, careless way.

Horror was depicted on the face of Miss Grizzie.

'I doot ye've hain a puir upbringin', lassies. I thocht yer mither, a minister's dochter, wad hae garr'd ye read yer Bibles; but, tae be sure, she was ower saft for the upbringing o' Nesbit bairns. They aye needit the rod.'

'What'll ye tak tae eat, Miss Grizzie?' inquired Miss Nesbit, knowing from experience to ignore such speeches.

'Naething.   Whaur's Hugh Nesbit?'

'He's in the drawin'-room,' said Tibbie.

'Ye seem tae ken brawly whaur tae find the young man, my wummin,' quoth Miss Grizzie, fixing her keen eyes on Tibbie's face. 'I dinna think Janet has the upper haund o' ye.   Weel, I'm awa in tae see Hugh Nesbit.   Ye needna come, lassies : I want a word wi' the young man mysel''

So saying, Miss Grizzie stalked away to the drawing-room.

Hugh Nesbit had thrown himself on the sofa, but sprang up at the opening of the door, and absolutely stared at the vision on the threshold.   She was now attired in a merino gown of scanty dimensions, a black cap adorned in a fearful manner with crape flowers and jingling beads, a black lace cape on her shoulders, and black silk mittens on her hands.

'Ye'll be Hugh Nesbit?' she said, stalking familiarly into the room.   'I'm Grizel Oliphant frae Yair, second cousin tae Walter Nesbit.   Hoo are ye?'

Hugh Nesbit managed to give the lady his hand, and make some sort of murmured reply.   Then she stood in front of him, eyeing him in a severe and critical manner.

'Humph! ye're a jimpy black body, no like the Nesbit lads, wha hae aye been stoot an' fair.   Weel,

I houp ye'll mak a guid heid o' Aldersyde, an' set an example o' a godly Laird in Ettrick Vale.'

Whereupon, whether dissatisfied with her company or not, Miss Grizzie very abruptly quitted the young man's presence, and retired to the south room ; nor would any asking induce her to leave it again that evening. The Miss Nesbits abode awhile with her ; then Janet said she was tired, and bade Tibbie come with her to bid their cousin good-night, after which they would retire to their rest.

Miss Nesbit had borne much that day, and strength of body was failing her under the long-continued strain. As Tibbie and she passed their father's room on their way to their own, she stretched out her hand and touched the door, as if that could comfort and sustain her.

No words passed between the sisters as they made themselves ready for bed. It was weeks since Janet had shared her sister's room : a sofa in the sick-room had given her the scanty rest vouchsafed to a nurse.

In a few minutes Tibbie was in bed, and asleep ; but Janet moved about the room slowly and heavily, removing her things with dazed, mechanical fingers. Once in the night a noise awakened Tibbie, and she turned round in affright. It was the sound of weeping—not gentle, healing tears, but a fierce, wild storm like the rushing of the wind-tossed Yarrow.

She was afraid and awe - stricken, and dared not move. Listening with bated breath, she caught the words:

'God tak care o' Tibbie an' me, an' keep Aldersyde. Amen.'

CHAPTER III.

THE next day many callers came to offer their condolences to the Miss Nesbits in their tribulation. Among the first were the doctor’s wife, gentle, delicate, little Mrs. Elliot, and her daughter Mary, whose fair beauty had won for her the name of the Lily of Aldershope. Hugh Nesbit was in the house when they came, and made himself particularly agreeable to Miss Elliot, claiming a right, he said, to renew the acquaintance begun at Aldersyde when they were children. Mary Elliot did not look as if she thought it a desirable thing to renew such acquaintance, which was very fresh in her mind still as an unpleasant memory. They did not stay long, but their silently - expressed sympathy, after the peculiar comfort administered by Miss Grizzie, was very sweet to the Miss Nesbits.

Mr. Bourhill, the minister of Aldershope, was also an early caller; but, upon beholding him coming up the avenue, Hugh Nesbit took himself off to the stables. Mr. Bourhill had ever been a dear friend and a kindly-welcomed guest in Aldersyde, and he mourned its Laird with the sincerity which was part of his nature. Like the Elliots', his sympathy, being true and deep, did not find its expression in a multitude of words. A close hand clasp for each, and a 'God comfort you,' spoken in rich, full tones to Miss Nesbit, told all that was in his heart.

Miss Grizzie having taken offence at Tibbie at the breakfast table, had shut herself into the south room, and was not visible when Mr. Bourhill came.

Very willingly would Tibbie also have escaped out of the room, as she never felt at ease under the glance of Mr. Bourhill's keen grey eyes; but civility demanded that she should remain at least a few minutes. But when Miss Nesbit requested him to come up to see her father, Tibbie went down to Marget in the kitchen.

I am not ashamed to write that tears came into the eyes of Mr. Bourhill when he looked upon the face of his friend. All great natures are tender of heart, and easily moved.

'Truly, He giveth His beloved sleep,' he said

more to himself than to Miss Nesbit. 'Looking upon such perfect peace, we cannot mourn.'

'No for him, only for oorsels,' Miss Nesbit made answer, and turned her eyes away.

Well that she did so, for there sprang into the face of Mr. Bourhill a something deeper than the mere expression of ministerial sympathy. He had loved Janet Nesbit long, but never in his life had he found it so hard a task to hide his love from her.

'Ye'll hae heard that the new Laird of Aldersyde cam' hame last nicht,' she said, craving his sympathy in this trial also.

'No ; who is he ? ' he asked in quick surprise.

'My cousin, Captain Hugh Nesbit, the only son o' my father's youngest brither.'

The minister heard in silence. It swept across him what a mighty change in many ways their father's death would make for the Miss Nesbits, and what a severing of the heart-strings was before them in the leaving of Aldersyde.

'May I ask, without seeming curious, what is to become of you and Miss Isabel ?' he said by and by.

'There's Windyknowe, ye ken,' she answered, and stopped abruptly.

Quick was the minister's ear to note the tearless bitterness in her voice. Again the longing, almost incontrollable, came upon him to take the sorrowing, desolate woman to his great heart, and comfort her in its love.   His face grew pale with the intensity of his emotion, and involuntarily he took a step toward her.   But the thought of where they were, in the very presence of death, checked him, and he turned away, just in time.   When Miss Nesbit brought her eyes back from the chapel of St. Mary, she saw only in his face the expression of sorrowing sympathy befitting a minister conversing with a bereaved member of his flock.

'The funeral is on Thursday, at twa o'clock.   We'll expeck ye awhile afore that, tae conduct the service i' the hoose,' said Miss Nesbit as he turned to go.

'I shall be there,' he answered gravely.

'It is ten years this very day sin' ye buried my mither,' she said with a wintry smile.   'Ye was newly placed in Aldershope then, Mr. Bourhill, an' I was but a lassie o' fifteen.'

'Time hastens on,' returned the minister in a constrained manner.   Then they shook hands, and he went his way.

Miss Grizzie having recovered her equanimity, now appeared in the drawing-room, and could not conceal her chagrin at missing the Elliots and Mr. Bourhill.

Miss Nesbit found the presence of her kinswoman anything but a comfort during the days intervening between her father's death and burial.   Courtesy demanded that she should keep her company, since Tibbie absolutely refused to do so ; and though never at any time did she relish Miss Grizzie's ill-natured, gossiping talk, in her present frame of mind it was almost intolerable to her. Miss Grizzie and the new Laird did not take to each other; and there never failed to be a war of words between them, at meal-times, or when they happened to be in each other's company.

Grey and cheerless over Bourhope crept the morning of the day on which the Laird of Aldersyde was to be carried to his rest.

Miss Grizzie spent the forenoon making an elaborate toilet, while Miss Nesbit was in the kitchen instructing Marget concerning the dinner to be prepared for the mourners upon their return from the burying-ground. Tibbie having dressed herself in her black silk gown, and adorned her graceful neck with a profusion of white net quilling, put a shawl about her, and went out with her cousin. The two were the best of friends.

At one o'clock the two Miss Nesbits, and Miss Grizzie, seated themselves in the drawing-room, while the Laird waited to welcome the guests below. Before a quarter past the hour, a carriage swept up the avenue, and Miss Grizzie stretched her neck round the window curtains to see to whom it pertained.

'Ye needna redden, Janet Nesbit,' she said maliciously. 'It's no Sandy Riddell yet, only auld Watty Scott o' Scottrigg an' his leddy-faced son, an' Chairlie Dooglas the lawyer frae Melrose!'

The personage whom Miss Grizzie mentioned with so little respect, was no less than Sir Walter Scott, eleventh baronet of Scottrigg and Tushiemuir. In his youth, he had paid some attention to Miss Grizzie, but in the end had deserted her for bonnie Katie Graeme of Mosslee.

To look at her now, one would not think Miss Grizzie likely to be susceptible to the tender passion; but in her young days Grizel Oliphant had been as romantic as any schoolgirl, and even yet regretted the lover of her youth.

The slim, handsome young man had developed into a portly old gentleman, with white locks and a rubicund countenance, which showed to advantage against his spotless shirt front. He had a loud, hearty voice, which even the sorrowfulness of the occasion which brought him to Aldersyde could not subdue; but the warm cordiality of the grip which he gave the Miss Nesbits left no doubt in their minds of his true sympathy for them.

Miss Grizzie rose and made him a dignified curtsey, inquiring at the same time for his health and that of his lady.

'She's weel, but failin', like oorsels, Miss Grizzie,' said Sir Walter. 'It's mony a year sin' you an' me were lad an' lass.'

Very wroth was Miss Grizzie, but the occasion forbade any exhibition of temper; so she turned to speak to the son, a pleasant-faced young man of modest, unassuming manner.

Mr. Douglas the lawyer, having made his bow to the company, retired into the eastern window, to look over sundry documents he had brought with him.

'So ye've gotten the new Laird hame, Janet, bairn,' said Sir Walter. 'What like a chield is he? I mind wild Hugh Nesbit the elder weel.'

'Did ye no see him doon the stair, Sir Walter?' asked Miss Nesbit. 'He was waiting in the dinin'-room.'

'Marget showed us directly up,' returned the baronet; 'so we didna see him.'

'He's a black sheep, Watty Scott, if ever there was ane,' cried Miss Grizzie shrilly. 'He'll mak ducks an' drakes o' Aldersyde afore anither Martinmas. Chairlie Dooglas, it shows hoo muckle's i' your lawyers' heids, that ye canna mend that ill entail law. I wad brawly like tae ken what richt a gomeril like Hugh Nesbit has tae tak Aldersyde ower the heid o' a douce young wummin like Janet Nesbit?'

Miss Grizzie had suffered from the entail law herself, having had to depart out of her father's house of Pitcairn, and leave it to the tender mercies of a ne'er-do-weel cousin. Hence her ire.

'Mr. Bourhill, an' Doctor Elliot,' announced Marget at the door, and the entrance of these gentlemen turned the conversation into a more general groove.

As the solemn clock hands went slowly round to the hour of two, the company in the drawing-room was increased by the arrival, one after the other, of Elphinstone of Elphinstone, Hamilton of Dryburn, Haig of Bemersyde, Kerr of Drumkerr, and many more of the county gentry, all of whom, out of respect to the family of Nesbit, came to pay their last tribute to the memory of its Laird. William Lennox, whose forbears had been in the Mains since ever there was a Nesbit in Aldersyde, represented the tenantry at the house. The rest of them were to await the funeral company outside.

When all expected were gathered together, it behoved Mr. Bourhill to read the appropriate passage of Scripture and engage in prayer, which he did with many a falter in his manly voice. When it was over, Hugh Nesbit, Sir Walter Scott, and Doctor Elliot went out to the landing, while William Lennox and three of his brother tenants went up-stairs and bore the coffin down, and out at the door. Then one by one the guests filed out of the drawing - room, till the women were left alone.

From the front window Miss Nesbit watched the solemn procession till it disappeared through the trees into the path leading to the loch; then she turned about, hiding her face in her hands, and went up to the empty room.

Oh, but it was empty! I think that not till we see our dead borne out at the door do we realize that we have lost them.

The mists had lowered over Bourhope, and in its shadow the lonely loch lay grey and still, save on the narrow shore, where it broke with a restless sobbing. Up the winding path to the chapel burying-ground, Miss Nesbit could see the line of black figures wending its way, bearing its burden at its head. With eyes sharpened to painful keenness, she saw them gather about the newly-opened grave and take the cords, and chafed to observe one in the hands of Hugh Nesbit, though as the nephew of the deceased it was his right. She saw Mr. Bourhill take off his hat, followed by all the rest of the company; she almost fancied she heard that awful, drear sound of the earth being shovelled on a coffin lid. She could not bear it any longer. She moved over to the door in a swift, sudden way, turned the key in the lock, and then laid herself down upon the floor, not to cry, as Tibbie was doing in the lower room, but to beat down the agony which had gained the mastery at last, and which she could not bear unless aided by the God of her fathers.

In the dining-room Marget was setting the table for dinner, weeping noiselessly the while, not so much for her dead master as for his orphan bairns and Aldersyde.

D

Only a few intimate friends of the family returned to hear the will read, and partake of Miss Nesbit's hospitality in Aldersyde for the last time. In grim state, with her mittened hands decorously folded on her lap, sat Miss Grizzie with red-eyed Tibbie beside her. Miss Nesbit not feeling the near presence of her kinswoman any comfort, but rather the reverse, sat by herself in the eastern window.

Without any preliminaries, Mr. Douglas stood up, and read aloud the contents of the blue document in his hand. It was very brief, merely stating that Walter Nesbit of Aldersyde and Windyknowe, being in his sound judgment, bequeathed to his daughters Janet Hay Nesbit and Isabel Anne Nesbit, all moneys pertaining to him, together with the furnishings of the house of Aldersyde, and all plate, and jewels, and napery therein, to be equally divided between them ; as also to the aforesaid Janet Hay Nesbit, the house of Windyknowe, in the parish of Aldershope, to hold for a habitation as long as she choose, but which she was at liberty to dispose of at any time without let or hinder.

The substance of the will Janet Nesbit had been acquainted with before, except the clause which made Windyknowe exclusively her own. Mr. Douglas did not deem it needful to state that the last clause had only been changed to its present reading on the day before the Laird's death.

I cannot but think that some foreboding of what the future held for his elder daughter, had impelled Walter Nesbit to secure for her the shelter of a roof-tree as long as she lived.

The contents of the will were not pleasant to Hugh Nesbit. He was standing not very far from Miss Grizzie's chair, and she saw his frown, and heard him mutter:

'The old flint made sure there would be nothing for me but the bare walls of Aldersyde.'

Whereupon she exploded :

'Ye mean, graspin', black-herted scoondrel,' she said shrilly, to the no little amazement of those assembled, 'ye hae gotten an inheritance withoot a hapny o' debt on't, an' ye're no content. Ye wad tak the verra claes aff the orphans' backs. It's an ill wish, but I pray that ye mayna flourish in Aldersyde, nor hae a meenit's pleasure o' yer inheritance.'

'Wheesht, Miss Grizzie !' fell from the pale lips of Janet Nesbit.

Hugh Nesbit showed his teeth in a smile which Miss Grizzie afterwards described as resembling the ' girn o' a rat,' and made the old lady a sweeping bow.

'Much obliged, ma'am, and am only sorry that this being certainly the last time you will sit in my house, you will not have the extreme satisfaction of observing whether your courteous desire is likely to be fulfilled.'

Then turning his eyes on the face of his cousin, he said suavely:

'Business being concluded, cousin, with your permission, we will retire to the dining - room, as these gentlemen, I am sure, stand in need of some refreshment after the protracted exercises in which they have engaged.'

Miss Nesbit bowed, and led the way to the dining-room.

The meal passed in uncomfortable constraint, none of those present feeling inclined for sociable conversation. Sir Walter Scott was indeed so heartily disgusted with the new Laird of Aldersyde, and so overflowing with fatherly sympathy for the orphans, that his joviality was quite extinguished. Miss Grizzie sat upright in her chair, only occasionally relieving the monotony of her silence by grimacing in the direction of Hugh Nesbit. In spite of apparent unconcernedness, that young man was far from being at his ease. Miss Nesbit did the honours of the table with her usual quiet grace, but while studiously attending to the wants of others, she did not break her own fast.

Whenever the meal was past, the company withdrew. At the door, Sir Walter came back to give Miss Nesbit another grip of the hand, and to whisper with a suspicious moisture in his eyes:

'Come ower tae Scottrigg, Tibbie an' you, an'

my Leddy Kate 'll mak ye as welcome as her ain.'

A wan smile flitted across the face of Miss Nesbit, and her eyes answered what her lips refused to do. Then she went away slowly up to the drawing-room, where sat Miss Grizzie and Tibbie. Before she had been many minutes in the room, Hugh Nesbit followed her, and asked pointedly for a few minutes' private conversation with her.

'Say yer say afore me, like an honest man,' quoth Miss Grizzie, to which Hugh Nesbit made answer with more energy than courtesy, 'Peace, you old hag!' and quitted the room before Miss Grizzie recovered from the shock.

Opposite the dining-room there was a little room, where the old Laird had kept his guns and fishing tackle, and where also he had transacted business with his factor, and received his tenants on rent days. Into this apartment Miss Nesbit followed her cousin, and stood near the door waiting for what he had to say.

'I'm going off to Edinburgh to-night, Cousin Janet,' he said, 'from whence I shall proceed early to-morrow morning to London. I wish to settle and wind up all my affairs at Woolwich, and will be back, I expect, at Aldersyde within the fortnight.'

Miss Nesbit bowed her head.

'Tibbie an' me will by that time be settled in

Windyknowe,' she answered quietly. 'Ye wull find yer roof-tree yer ain when ye come back.'

There was nothing offensive in her words nor in her manner, yet they angered Hugh Nesbit, and caused his sallow face to redden :

'Look here, Cousin Janet ; I want to know why you and all these county gentry look askance at me as if I had committed some atrocious crime, instead of simply coming to claim my own ? '

Miss Nesbit lifted up her head and looked him all over.

'*I* feel, an' my father's freens may feel also, Hugh Nesbit, that ye micht hae shown mair cousinly kindness tae Tibbie an' me than ye hae dune the day. No that we need it or want it,' she said with a sudden pride in her voice. 'It's no the new Laird they dinna draw tae ; it's the man.' Then Miss Nesbit went away out of the room, and left him to digest her plain-spoken words.

By six o'clock, Aldersyde was left in the possession of the women folk. Round the drawing-room hearth in the firelight sat Miss Grizzie and the two Miss Nesbits. Fain, fain would they have been alone this one night ; but since Miss Grizzie was there, it behoved them to show her the courtesy due to a guest.

'Noo, Janet Nesbit,' said she, 'we're left in peace, and I want tae ken what way Sandy Riddell didna mak his appearance the day. Was he bidden ?'

'Yes, Miss Grizzie.'

The peculiar ring in Miss Nesbit's voice might have warned the old woman that she was treading cn delicate ground.

'I misdoot ye'll no be gaun tae be the leddy o' Ravelaw efter a', Janet Nesbit,' continued she with malicious satisfaction.

This woman, soured and disappointed in her own youth, was jealous of all feminine youth, especially if it were accompanied by comeliness or beauty, which was likely to secure its possessor a good matrimonial settlement.

Miss Nesbit answered nothing, but reached out her hand and took hold of Tibbie's, prompted by that dumb instinct for human sympathy which we feel when sorely driven.

'Men are a' alike, Janet Nisbet; an' tho' Sandy Riddell jilts ye, ye needna mak a mane. Mony a better an' a bonnier lass has been thrown ower for want o' gear, or jist oot o' fickleness.'

'We'll speak o' somethin' else, Miss Grizzie, if ye like,' said Miss Nesbit steadily.

'Oo ay! It hurts yer pride, I'm thinkin', tae be telt a lad's gaun tae jilt ye. They say ye can get Mr. Bourhill if ye like; but I dinna wunner that ye wad raither bide among the godless splendour o' Ravelaw afore the plainer doon sittin' in the manse o' Aldershope.'

'I maun leave ye tae yersel', Miss Grizzie, my guest though ye be, if ye winna let that subject abe,' said Miss Nesbit, a red spot burning on either cheek.

'Ye may draw yersel' up in yer pride, my wummin,' said Miss Grizzie, whose ill-nature was getting the better of her entirely. 'But prood an bonnie though ye be, ye're no a denty eneuch bite for a Riddell o' Ravelaw.'

Miss Nesbit rose up, and, keeping hold of Tibbie's hand, bent her flashing eyes full on Miss Grizzie's spiteful face. Her slim figure was drawn to its full height, her proud head held up in womanly indignation.

'I can pit up wi' a guid deal, Miss Grizzie; but I will *not* bear sic words frae you, auld though ye be. I maun hae ye tae understand that ye canna meddle in my inmost affairs, or maybe I'll forget the hospitality o' Aldersyde, an' bid ye gang back tae Yair.'

Up rose Miss Grizzie, bristling all over, and fairly glared upon the fearless face of Janet Nesbit.

'My certy, d'ye ken wha ye're speakin' till, Janet Nesbit?' she screamed. 'Am I no yer bluid relation? It's eneuch tae mak yer faither turn i' his grave.'

'Mind what's passed the day,' pleaded Janet Nesbit; but Miss Grizzie was not to be appeased.

'Umph! I'm nae suner insultit by that limb, wha, mair's the peety, ca's himsel' Laird o' Aldersyde, than I'm ca'd upon tae staund impidence frae a lassie. Weel, I'll gang back tae Yair this verra nicht, an' my hands are washed o' the Nesbits for evermair.' Whereupon Miss Grizzie stalked out of the room, and retiring down-stairs, surprised Tammas Erskine at the kitchen fire by bidding him get the coach ready to return to Yair. She then ordered Marget up to carry down her boxes, a task which Marget immediately proceeded to perform with great willingness.

If there was a woman in the world Marget Drysdale had an aversion to, it was Miss Oliphant of Yair.

In the drawing-room the sisters sat side by side listening to the rumbling in the south room, and when they heard Miss Grizzie taking her departure down-stairs, Tibbie rose.

'I'll gang an' bid her fareweel, Janet,' she said with unusual thoughtfulness. She was not gone many minutes, and came back laughing.

'What a woman that is, Janet! She nearly snapped my head off at the door. I hope she'll keep her word and not come near us any more.' Then they drew their chairs close together again, and listened to the commotion at the hall door, and the rumbling of the yellow chariot as it drove away.

So again, as in bygone days, the Miss Nesbits sat alone by their drawing-room fire; but, oh, what a difference was in their lives! Desolation in hearts and home, an uncertain future and a new-made grave, were their portion now. What wonder that they sat very quiet, holding each other's hands, and feeling that life was very hard for them, and that no sorrow could equal theirs! Ah! it is well for us all that the future is hid within the veil!

CHAPTER IV.

IN the window of her own sitting-room, which looked out upon a wide expanse of rich pasture land, sloping gradually down to the Ettrick, sat my lady of Ravelaw. Her white and slender hands, on which sparkled many gems, were crossed upon her silken lap, and her fair face wore an expression of deep seriousness. She was young still, and very fair to be a widow and the mother of a six-foot son. She had been a wife at seventeen, and a mother before she was twenty.

Slight and fragile of form, my lady was yet a very haughty and formidable person, being descended from the old and honourable house of Arngask.

The wealth and goodly dwelling-place of rough Sandy Riddell had tempted the penniless daughter of the Napiers, grown tired of the genteel poverty of Arngask ; and with the reluctant consent of her proud kinsfolk, she had come to reign at Ravelaw.

For ten years Sandy Riddell and his wife lived stormily together, till the unhappy wedlock was ended by his death, when their heir and only child was eight years old. Since that time Mrs. Riddell had lived an easy, luxurious life ; but she was beginning to have her cares again, for Sandy had grown to manhood, and she was in daily fear of becoming the dowager Mrs. Riddell, and of beholding a young wife in her place at Ravelaw.

It was indeed this very subject which made her so serious this November morning, one week after the burying of the Laird of Aldersyde. She had heard it rumoured in her own circle even, that her son was paying unmistakeable attention to Miss Nesbit. Knowing the nature of the girl, she trembled ; and the instability of the Riddells was her only hope. Sandy Riddell did not confide all his goings out and comings in to his mother ; therefore, although she was aware that he had not attended the funeral of the Laird, how was she to be sure that he had not seen Miss Nesbit a dozen times since ? It entered into her head suddenly, that she could not do better than ask her son a plain question ;

therefore she rang the bell, and ordered the servant to request the Laird to step into her sitting-room.

He obeyed the summons with unusual promptitude, because at the moment he had no other thing engrossing his attention. He came lounging into his mother's presence, with his hands in his pockets, and inquired carelessly what she wanted of him. He was a great, powerful giant, with a ruddy, well-featured face, big blue eyes, and a mass of tawny hair. His *physique* was faultless, yet it was easy to see that nature had not endowed him with a large share of her higher gifts. He was not a man, one would think, likely to win the heart of a pure, high-souled maiden like Janet Nesbit ; yet won it he had, away from a man who would have prized it above any earthly thing, and who was undoubtedly worthy of her in all ways. It is not a good thing to sit down and dwell upon such twists in the cord of life. To our narrow comprehension, they seem needless and inscrutable; but when we reach the fuller light beyond, we shall see how what we thought jarring discord was after all deep, sweet-toned harmony.

'Have you been at Aldersyde to see Miss Nesbit since her father died ?' asked the lady of Ravelaw, fixing her piercing eyes on her son's face.

His full red lips parted in a curious smile.

'No, mother, I have not.'

She looked for the moment as if she disbelieved
him, yet she knew enough of him to be sure he
would not tell an untruth to spare her mortification.

'I am very glad to hear it,' she said heartily.
'Then there is no truth in the rumour that I would
need to welcome her as mistress of Ravelaw?'

Sandy Riddell laughed a laugh which might
mean anything.

'Were you afraid of it, mother?'

'Yes,' she answered candidly.   'Knowing you
were often at Aldersyde, and that she is not one of
these light-headed things a man might find amusement in playing with, I had made up my mind
to it.'

Mrs. Riddell did not guess that it was the very
fact of her being so unlike other girls that had caused
the pastime of making love to her to be so enjoyable
to Sandy Riddell. No woman in the world ever
thought less of lovers or marriage than Janet Nisbet,
therefore her treatment of all young men was, though
courteous, very cool and indifferent. This piqued
the Laird of Ravelaw ; it annoyed him to find one of
the daughters of Ettrick Vale quite unimpressed by
his charms. So he set himself in earnest to break
down the barriers of her indifference. It had been
a hard task. She had taken a very long time to
discover that he was making love to her ; and after
the discovery was made, her own heart had awakened

very slowly. He had succeeded well, and now she believed herself pledged to him, though there never had been any formal troth plight between them.

There are engagements which are not the outcome of a plain request to marry; also there are looks and actions, and a thousand indefinable things which constitute as perfect an understanding as any words that ever were uttered. To all these Sandy Riddell had confined himself, and to Janet Nesbit they seemed sacred and binding. It was the difference in their natures which caused them to estimate so differently.

'Janet Nesbit will never be mistress of Ravelaw,' said Sandy Riddell.

My lady breathed freely to hear the decided words, yet she desired to be at the bottom of the whole matter.

'I doubt you have led her to expect it, Sandy, if all rumours be true?' said she.

'What has Mistress Rumour not said about me, mother?' he asked in his easy, careless way. 'You may set your fears about Miss Nesbit at rest; she's not the wife for me. I'd rather have the other one, if I had to choose.' Mrs. Riddell took fresh alarm.

'If it's to be one of them, let it be Janet, Sandy; I couldn't think to see that saucy, fair-faced Isabel Nesbit mistress of Ravelaw.'

'She'd make you turn right about face, eh, mother?' asked Sandy with a mocking smile. 'Well, if you have no more questions to ask, I'll be off to the meet at Drumkerr; I promised Patrick Kerr to be over by eleven.'

'I am satisfied, my son, only remember that I want you to take a wife who will do honour to Ravelaw. I would have no objections to Patrick Kerr's sister Susan, for instance, or to Marjorie Scott of Scottrigg.'

'Marjorie Scott won't look at me, mother, and Susan Kerr is a big, rough young woman,' returned Sandy in his coarse way. 'Well, good-day; and don't make any matches for me, mother. I'll marry when the spirit moves me, and bring home whoever I take a fancy to, though she should be a peasant lass herding her ewes on the braes of Ettrick,' with which polite and consoling assurance the Laird of Ravelaw departed out of the presence of his lady mother.

For awhile she sat cogitating on what had passed; then she called her serving - woman, Rebecca Ford, and bade her order the coach to drive to Aldersyde. Then Rebecca had to attire her mistress in a very stiff silk gown, made in the newest and most expensive fashion, a sable cloak of priceless value, and a bonnet with nodding plumes. Also, Mrs. Riddell did not forget to adorn herself with sundry articles of jewellery likely to inspire awe and envy in the minds of poor young women like the Miss Nesbits.

The family coach of the Riddells was a very cumbersome affair, of a genteel claret-colour, with the Ravelaw crest, an uplifted sword in a mailed hand, painted on the panels of the doors. The inside was comfortably cushioned in drab repp, with claret-coloured buttons and braidings. It was drawn by a pair of very fine, high-stepping greys, which accomplished the distance to Aldersyde in less than an hour. It was noon when they swept through the lodge gates and up the avenue to the house. The Miss Nesbits being busily engaged with their one domestic in packing their goods prior to their removal to Windyknowe, did not observe its approach till a loud and pompous knock at the front door awoke sounding echoes in the quiet house.

Marget very hastily made her hair straight, and putting on a clean apron, went with no very good grace to answer the summons. She was rather chagrined to behold alighting from the coach the magnificently-attired lady of Ravelaw, particularly when, at that moment, the Miss Nesbits, in the plainest, homeliest garb, were performing the work of menials up-stairs. But there was nothing for it but to show my lady up to the drawing-room, and announce her arrival to Miss Nesbit.

Janet's face flushed deep red, and she retired

immediately to her own chamber to remove her white apron and wash her hands. She had to go down alone, Tibbie requiring first to attire herself in her best gown before she could appear before the lady of Ravelaw.

Mrs. Riddell rose up when Miss Nesbit entered the room, and approaching her with outstretched hands and sympathetic smile, kissed her on the brow. To Janet's mind such treatment, coming from the mother of the man she loved, could have but one meaning.

'My dear Miss Nesbit, you look wretchedly ill,' said Mrs. Riddell sweetly. 'This has been a sad and trying time for you.'

'Yes, Mrs. Riddell,' answered Miss Nesbit very low

'How is your sister?' was the next question.

'Isabel is weel ; she'll be doon by an' by. We're very busy, Mrs. Riddell, makin' ready tae flit tae Windyknowe.'

'Oh yes, I understand. Your cousin, of course, will take up his abode in Aldersyde. You will feel to leave the only home you have ever known.'

'It's tae be expectit that we couldna leave withoot feelin', Mrs. Riddell,' said Miss Nesbit somewhat sharply, the words seemed to her so needless.

A silence fell upon the two women then. A ray of sunshine stole in at the narrow window, and set ablaze the rubies clasping the cloak of my lady of Ravelaw. It also shone very tenderly on the pale face of Janet Nesbit. Looking at her, Mrs. Riddell could not but think what a sweet, lovable, thorough gentlewoman she looked, even in a gown her serving-woman would not have deigned to wear.

'You would wonder at Ravelaw's absence from the funeral?' said Mrs. Riddell abruptly.

'Mair than me wondered, Mrs. Riddell,' Miss Nesbit made answer bravely, though the red dyed her cheek.

'He was very sorry, Miss Nesbit, that a previous engagement at Kelso prevented him, and he bade me convey to you his respects and apologies.'

Mrs. Riddell had learned her lesson in polite falsehood telling very well, for her lips uttered the words glibly and unconcernedly.

Miss Nesbit sat straight up in her chair, and looked her visitor in the face with calm, scornful eyes.

'He rode to the hunt at Pappertlaw on that day Mrs. Riddell,' she said quietly.

For the moment the lady of Ravelaw was put out, but as behoved a woman of the world, she recovered her equanimity.

'You are well informed, it seems, even in this solitude,' she said smoothly. 'Well, Miss Nesbit, I believe the truth to be, that the Laird, remembering certain foolish words he may have uttered to you, as is the way of young men with maidens, would not care to intrude upon you in your sorrow, knowing he could not in any way comfort you.'

Surely Mrs. Riddell's native tact had failed her, when she could make such a blundering speech.

'Did the Laird o' Ravelaw bid ye come an' tell me that, Mrs. Riddell?' inquired Miss Nesbit in clear, cold tones.

'Well, not exactly,' said my lady with a smile. 'But we were talking of you this morning, and I asked him if there was any truth in the rumours that you were likely to become mistress of Ravelaw.'

'Weel, Mrs. Riddell?'

'The young man laughed, Miss Nesbit, and answered no. Had you not been of so proud and reticent a nature, I would have ventured to warn you against setting store by anything a Riddell may have said. You remember the old rhyme concerning them?'

Miss Nesbit felt her face grow ashen grey, as if all the blood had fled from it, to gather about her heart, and make it faint within her. But she kept her clear eyes on the smooth face of the woman before her, and said in tones which her pain made sharp and strained: 'An' what brings ye here the day, Mrs. Riddell?'

'To tell you that I, his mother, am sorry for you, Miss Nesbit; for whatever Ravelaw may have said to you, he has no intention of making you his wife. I had it from his own lips not many hours ago.

Miss Nesbit's lips parted in a bitter smile.

'Ye'll be gled that a penniless dochter of the Nesbits will never get the chance tae reign at Ravelaw, Mrs. Riddell?' said she.

The lady of Ravelaw was nettled by the young woman's half - scornful and wholly calm demeanour.

'Well, since you take it for granted that such are my feelings,' she said sharply, 'I do think that Ravelaw might bring home a bride whose dower and name would do more honour to his own.'

'Aldersyde ewes grew fat on Yarrow braes afore there was a Riddell in Ravelaw or a Napier in Arngask,' said Miss Nesbit in a slow, dry way. 'An' for honour, it wadna be ill tae match the honour o' Ravelaw in mony a lowlier biggin' than Aldersyde. I'll bid ye guid-day, Mrs. Riddell, wi' mony thanks for this kind and well-meant visit. If ye'll be pleased tae sit a meenit, I'll bid my servant show ye doon the stair.'

Mrs. Riddell, however, did not choose to wait for Marget, but rose at once and got away down to her coach, where she had time to digest the insults she had received from the penniless daughter of the Nesbits. It was many a day since the proud dame had been so humbled, and had felt so wretchedly insignificant among all her splendour.

Coming out of the drawing-room, Miss Nesbit encountered Tibbie in the corridor, dressed in her best, and looking very fair.

'Is that Mrs. Riddell away, Janet,' she exclaimed in extreme surprise, 'an' me just comin' tae speak to her?'

Answer good or bad Miss Nesbit made none, but passed by her sister, and entered the room where their father had died. She locked the door after her, and walking unsteadily over to the bed, sat down by it and buried her face in the pillow. So long did she remain there, that Tibbie and Marget began to feel alarmed as well as astonished. By and by, when it was getting near the early tea-time, Tibbie crept to the door, and knocked softly.

'Let me in, Janet,' she pleaded. Then Miss Nesbit opened the door and bade her enter.

'What is it, Janet?' cried she in affright, her sister looked so unlike herself.

'I hae been at the burial o' dead hopes, Tibbie,' she said with a wintry smile. 'Like other burials, it is sair tae thole. But it's past. I dinna need tae tell ye mair, Tibbie.'

No, for Tibbie understood, and all the hot blood of the Nesbits rushed to her face, and she clenched her slender hands together, and was only restrained from indignant speech by the look on Janet's face. She made no moan, therefore Tibbie also must be silent. Miss Nesbit's one love affair ended here, and having faced the tribulation bravely, and mastered it at the first, she was ready to take up her life and live it as became a Christian woman and a daughter of the house of Aldersyde.

CHAPTER V.

'My hame ! nae ither spot can be
Sae dear tae me on earth,
For hallowed memories entwine
About thy sacred hearth.'

THE Miss Nesbits were sitting by the study fire talking soberly over their future. Mr. Douglas the lawyer had just left Aldersyde after a long interview, during which he had intimated to them that their yearly income henceforth could not amount to more than £60. To Miss Nesbit his announcement was not a surprise ; but Tibbie, who had never troubled her head about money matters, and was quite ignorant of her father's affairs, had dreamed dreams of a goodly establishment at Windy-knowe, and a life of ease and pleasure. From these dreams Mr. Douglas had rudely awakened her, and her bonnie face wore a doleful and discontented look.

'Janet, what'll we do?' she asked for the third time.

'Live and be happy thegither, my dear,' said Miss Nesbit in a wonderfully cheerful voice. 'Mony a puir gentlewoman hasna that, wha has tae pay for a roof-tree besides.'

I believe that this new turn of affairs, which compelled Miss Nesbit to devote all her thoughts to the subject of 'living,' was the best thing which could have happened at the time. Tibbie glanced up at her sister's unruffled face, then down upon her own slim, dainty hands, and said dismally :

'We'll need to turn house and kitchen maids ourselves, Janet ; we can't keep Marget off £60.'

Then, indeed, Miss Nesbit sighed.

'Marget 'll hae tae gang, Tibbie, an' that's the hardest bit o'd.'

'We'll need to tell her, Janet.'

'It's a task I dinna like, Tibbie ; but as you say, we'll need tae daet, an' the suner the better.'

So saying, Miss Nesbit touched the bell, to summon Marget, who came very slowly, as if she guessed there was something unpleasant in store for her.

'Come in an' sit doon, Marget,' said Miss Nesbit.

But Marget did not deem it a fitting thing for her to sit down in the presence of her young ladies, and therefore stood near the door, twirling her apron round her thumbs, and waiting to hear what was to be said to her.

'Ye've been a faithfu' freen tae us, Marget, an' ye hae a perfeck richt tae ken a' oor affairs,' said Miss Nesbit. 'Mr. Douglas has been tae tell us hoo we stand wi' regaird tae money maitters.'

'Weel, mem?' queried Marget with intense interest.

'There's no muckle left,' faltered Miss Nesbit, for Marget's anxious, loving gaze broke her down.

'I'm vext for that, Miss Nesbit; but there's Windy-knowe an' the bit gairden, an' gin we could keep Crummie, I'd mak a penny aff the butter,' said Marget breathlessly.

'Oh but, Marget, wi' only £60 a year atween Tibbie an' me, hoo are we tae keep Crummie, my wummin, or you either?' said Miss Nesbit mournfully.

Marget folded her arms, while a curious expression of mingled wrath and grief and wounded pride came on her honest face.

'Ye'll be gaun tae wash yer claes, an' clean yer hoose, an' mak yer meat, no tae speak o' howin' the gairden, nae doot?' she said scornfully.

'We'll need tae try, Marget,' said Miss Nisbet with a smile and a tear.

'A bonnie like thing for the Nesbits o' Alder-syde!' quoth Marget. 'Weel, gif ye think ye'll get rid o' Marget Drysdale as easy's that, yer mista'en—

that's a'. Wha said I wanted wages? Wha said I wanted ony thing but a moothfu' o' kirn milk, an' a bite o' pease bannock for my meat? Whaever said it, or said I wad leave them that's mair than flesh an' bluid tae me, telt a lee—that's a',' with which Marget whisked out of the room, and clattered down the kitchen stair with a great din.

After that, of course, there was no more said anent Marget leaving; but Miss Nesbit had a plan of her own, whereby she would find the wherewithal to pay her labour.

The days wore on, till the fortnight of Hugh Nesbit's absence elapsed, and it came to be the Miss Nesbits' last night in Aldersyde, the last time they would sleep beneath their father's roof-tree. Ah me, but that 'last' has a dreary sound in it! It is one of the saddest words in any tongue. The house was stripped of its furnishings, which under Marget's supervision had been conveyed by degrees to Windy-knowe. All that remained on the last night was the study table and chairs, and the beds they three were to occupy.

But there was one room furnished ready for the use of the Laird of Aldersyde. Miss Nesbit had selected some articles of later date, which were not so dear and sacred in her eyes, and had set them in the south room. Also, with her own hands, she had fastened up clean curtains about the bed, and at the window—a proceeding which considerably exercised Marget's spirit, and caused her to make some observations the reverse of flattering to the individual who was to occupy it.

There was no sleep for Miss Nesbit that night. A north wind was roaring over Bourhope, with a warning of snow in its teeth. To a nervous or superstitious person, sleep in the house of Aldersyde on a windy night was a thing impossible. It might have been haunted by wraiths or warlocks, so varied and uncanny were the sounds which could be heard in it. But it was not the eerie moaning and wailing in the empty rooms and desolate corridors which banished sleep from Miss Nesbit's eyes, but heartache—bitter, regretful pain over the parting from the home of her forbears. Once in the night she rose from her slumbering sister's side, and crept across the bare floor to the uncurtained window. A wild sky, across which great inky masses of cloud were drifting southwards, frowned down upon the lone loch, and a heavy shower was beating against the panes. Oblivious of cold, she stood looking out upon the dark picture, till, suddenly from a rift in the cloud overhanging Bourhope, the moon shone out with a fierce defiant gleam, which fell straight upon the ruined chapel of St. Mary, and made so plain its neglected burying-ground that she could almost see the mound of the new-made grave. Then sobbing,

she crept back to her bed, and tossed beside unconscious Tibbie till the dawning.

All three rose early and made a pretence of eating
breakfast, before Mr. Lennox's cart came for the
remainder of the things.

Marget was to go first with it to Windyknowe, in
order to have a fire lighted before her young ladies
arrived. A little while after the departure of the
cart, the Miss Nesbits, feeling that nothing was to
be gained by remaining in the empty house, tied
on their bonnets, and stood together in the hall of
Aldersyde, two desolate women, holding each other's
hands, and with nothing in the world but each other.
Tears were raining down Tibbie's cheeks, but Miss
Nesbit was pale and tearless. It is the inward grief
which eats out the heart.

'Come, Tibbie,' she said with a kind of gasp, and
they passed out of the house, locking the door
behind them, and walked quickly till they came to
the bend in the avenue, when they both turned
about to look their last on Aldersyde.

It was a grey, rambling building, with a quaint
old tower, entered by a low arched doorway. Its
windows somewhat resembled the gratings of a
gaol, but its clustering ivy and moss-grown walls
made it lovely in its age, for it was clothed with all
the beauty which time loves to lavish on the build-
ings of the past. Giant beeches and elms sheltered

it on every side, while behind, solemn and grand, towered the peak of Bourhope, above which the grey and cloudy sky seemed mourning for the desolation of Aldersyde.

'Oh, Janet!' said Tibbie piteously, 'we could have borne our father's death if we could have stayed in Aldersyde.'

Miss Nesbit did not seem to hear. 'God keep Aldersyde,' Tibbie heard her whisper very low, then they went slowly and silently upon their way.

Miss Nesbit tapped at the door of the lodge, and handed the key to the old man, but did not seem to hear his murmured words of blessing and farewell. As they passed through the gates, a gig came rattling up the road, and the driver drew rein close to them.

'I make bold to come an' offer tae drive ye tae Windyknowe,' said the honest and sympathetic voice of William Lennox of the Mains.

'Mony thanks,' said Miss Nesbit quietly and gratefully ; 'Tibbie and me hevna muckle heart tae walk five miles this day.'

So the dwellers in Aldershope, who had been greatly exercised of late regarding the Miss Nesbits and their changed fortunes, had the satisfaction of beholding Mr. Lennox drive them through the village on the way to their new abode.

The road to Windyknowe turned round by the kirk, and passing the manse, took a steep incline

away up to the moorland.   It was a by-way not
under highway supervision, and was cut up by great
deep ruts, which caused the gig to jolt in a very
disagreeable manner.   When they reached the top
of the brae, they could see the grey walls of Windyknowe peeping out in the middle of one of the
clumps of the scraggy fir which here and there
dotted the moorland.   A thin blue line of smoke
curling upward to the sky told that Marget was
already within.   When they reached the broken
gateway, Mr. Lennox stopped his horse and assisted
the ladies to alight.   Then Miss Nesbit shook
hands with him, and though she spoke never a
word, the honest farmer understood her mute parting, and when he climbed into his gig his eyes were
wet with unwonted tears.   Slowly the Miss Nesbits
wended their way up the grass-grown avenue, till
they came face to face with the house.

It was a great barn of a place, naked and desolate looking, and crumbling to decay.   A chill struck
to the hearts of the two lonely women, the contrast
between the new home and the old was so painful.

'Let's get in as fast's we can, Tibbie,' said Miss
Nesbit, 'an' no stand breakin' oor hearts here.'

Hearing voices, Marget hurried to the door, and
stood on the threshold trying to smile.

'Ye've gotten a fire on, I see, Marget,' said Miss
Nesbit cheerfully.

'It's in the dinin'-room. This way, mem,' said Marget, and ushered them through the wide hall into a large dingy room, only made tolerable by the glow and crackle of the fire. In order to make it look as much as possible like the dining-room at Aldersyde, Marget had set the furniture in the same way, and hung the pictures in the same places. For a moment Miss Nesbit's eyes brightened, it looked so like home.

'Ye hae dune weel, Marget,' she said, and reaching out her hand, touched that of her faithful servant with a gentle appreciative touch which to Marget was sufficient reward.

'Gin ye've sutten a wee, and warmed yersels, ye'll maybe come ben tae the kitchen, an' syne up the stair, tae see if a' thing's as ye wad like it,' she said, and then withdrew.

Tibbie sat down at the fire to warm her chilled fingers, while Miss Nesbit walked over to the window, and stood there, salt tears blinding her eyes.

They were far up on the dreary moorland. Far away down in the hollow, the roof-trees of Aldershope clustered on the bank of the rushing Yarrow. Farther up the stream, the trees in the den of Aldersyde made a dark patch on the landscape, while beyond them towered the solemn peak of Bourhope.

By and by Miss Nesbit turned about, and coming over to the fire, knelt down before Tibbie, and put her arms round her waist, with the look on her face Tibbie had seen but once before.

'We hae built up oor hame, Tibbie,' she said solemnly; 'an' since there's only you an' me, my dear, let's stick close thegither, and thank God that in His mercy there are twa insted o' ane, though we hae neither father, nor mother, nor Aldersyde.'

CHAPTER VI.

PON the Sabbath day, the Miss Nesbits appeared in the parish kirk of Aldershope. The high-backed pew with the crimson linings, where they had sat so many Sabbaths in time gone past, was not theirs to-day. Many eyes turned compassionately to an obscure pew near the door, where sat two figures in deep mourning, but whose faces could not be seen through their thick crape veils. Doctor Elliot occupied his pew opposite that of Aldersyde, having on each side his wife and daughter.

Punctually at noon, Mr. Bourhill, preceded by Caleb Lyall the beadle, came out of the vestry and ascended the pulpit stair. When he stood up to pray, a late-comer entered the church, and a quick martial step echoed through the church as the new Laird of Aldersyde went down the stone passage to the crimson - lined pew. Many curious eyes were directed towards him, and it was whispered afterwards, that never once had his bold black eyes left the sweet face of Mary Elliot, the Lily of Aldershope.

At the close of the service, the Miss Nesbits made haste to get away before the rest of the congregation; but Mrs. Elliot and Mary, hurrying out also, overtook them at the churchyard gate.

'You will come and have dinner with us, Miss Nesbit,' said the doctor's wife in her motherly way. 'Nay, my dear, you must not turn from your oldest friend,' she added, for Miss Nesbit had shaken her head.

'Let's go, Janet,' pleaded Tibbie ; 'it's so dreary at Windyknowe.'

'Thank you, Mrs. Elliot ; then we'll come,' said Janet, and taking Mary's arm, was about to turn up the village street, when Doctor Elliot came out of the churchyard in company with Hugh Nesbit.

'Captain Nesbit will dine with us to-day, Mrs. Elliot,' said the doctor in his stern, pompous way, and what could the shrinking little body do but say she would be very glad to have his company.

Hugh Nesbit shook hands with all the ladies, politely thanked the doctor's wife for her kindness, and then placed himself by the side of Mary Elliot, who kept a firm hold of Miss Nesbit's arm. She had felt an unaccountable shrinking from Hugh Nesbit that day at Aldersyde, and the feeling now returned to her more strongly than ever.

'I enjoyed the service to-day immensely, Miss Elliot,' said he by way of beginning the conversation.

'Every one likes Mr. Bourhill,' she answered in her gentle way. Even to those she most disliked, the Lily of Aldershope could not be anything but gentle.

'I was not thinking of Mr. Bourhill, who, I daresay, is a very estimable person,' said Hugh Nesbit meaningly, and bent his eyes again on the sweet face beside him.

Miss Nesbit felt her friend's fingers tremble on her arm, and hastened to change the theme.

'Are ye like tae be settled in Aldersyde, Cousin Hugh?' she asked courteously.

'By and by. I expect to have an upholsterer coming from Edinburgh to make the place habitable,' he returned. 'Ahem! I was much obliged to you, Cousin Janet, for leaving me a bed to sleep in. I did not expect it, and felt quite overwhelmed, I assure you.'

'It was only common courtesy, Hugh Nesbit,' she said somewhat sharply, which speech brought them to the gate of Doctor Elliot's dwelling. It was a substantial, handsome house, standing back from the road in a garden which was the pride and admiration of Aldershope.

'Your family is considerably increased to-day, Mrs. Elliot,' said Hugh Nesbit lightly. 'I am afraid that if you once open your hospitable doors to me, I may become a weariness to you.'

'You could scarcely be that, Captain Nisbet,' said the doctor, thus saving his wife the trouble of answering.

All the ladies went away up stairs at once, Mrs. Elliot going to her own room, and Mary taking the Miss Nesbits to hers. Tibbie removed her bonnet and cloak, and smoothing her hair, said lightly she would just go down and leave them to their secrets. When she was out of the room, Mary Elliot sat down by the bed, and covered her fair face with her hands.

'What is't, Mary?' asked Miss Nesbit in anxious surprise.

'Do you believe in presentiments, Janet?' asked Mary very low.

'I canna say I dinna believe in them,' said Miss Nesbit. 'I had a warnin' an' a fear o' comin' evil baith afore my mother's death an' my father's. But what presentiment o' evil can you hae, Mary?'

'That man down-stairs, Janet,' said Mary, shivering; 'when he looks at me, I feel like to die. The old fear of him I had when I was a child and played with him at Aldersyde yon summer he lived with you, has come back to me far stronger and more real. What can it mean?'

'Ye arena weel, Mary; it's jist a fancy,' said Miss Nesbit tenderly. 'Come, my dear, let me help ye off wi' yer things. We maunna keep Mrs. Elliot waiting at the table.'

Then with a sigh, Mary Elliot rose, and taking off her bonnet and cloak, smoothed her yellow hair, and fastened her lace collar about her throat.

Doctor Elliot cast a keen glance at his daughter when she entered the dining-room, and motioned her to come and sit by his side, which also happened to be the seat next Hugh Nesbit. It was a curious and painful thing to observe how Doctor Elliot's women-folk relapsed into subdued silence in his presence, and seemed to be in a state of nervous dread and fear of him all the time. In general he either remained silent, or monopolized the conversation; but that day he seemed anxious that Mary, at least, should take part in it. She answered Hugh Nesbit's remarks only in monosyllables, till her father said half jokingly:

'Unless you find something more to say, Mary, Captain Nesbit will come to the conclusion that you are either an ignoramus or a painfully bashful country girl.'

'Whether she speaks or remains silent, Miss Elliot must always be charming,' said Hugh Nesbit gallantly.

Mary knew well that her father's seemingly playful speech was in reality a command, so with her customary submission to his will, she forced herself to carry on a conversation with the young man beside her. Sitting by Mrs. Elliot at the foot of the table, Miss Nesbit observed her dim eyes fill with tears, which she strove to hide by bending over her plate.

You will notice that the feminine relatives of coarse, unfeeling men, are generally women of refined and acute sensibilities, to whom their home life is almost always a species of martyrdom.

None present at Doctor Elliot's dinner-table that Sabbath day, save perhaps Hugh Nesbit, enjoyed the meal. When it was over the ladies retired, and the Miss Nesbits begging to be excused, as Marget would be anxious about them, went away home at once.

'What would you think if Mary Elliot became lady of Aldersyde, Janet?' asked Tibbie as they turned up the steep road to Windyknowe.

'I wadna wish tae see her the wife o' Hugh Nesbit, Tibbie.'

'See it ye will, Janet,' said Tibbie shrewdly. 'Doctor Elliot has got the plan in his heid. Did ye no see how he made Mary sit beside Hugh Nesbit, and scolded her for not speaking to him. It angers me to see how Mrs. Elliot and Mary fear Doctor Elliot : I never saw man that would fear me yet.'

'He's maybe tae come yet, Tibbie,' said Miss Nesbit with a slight smile.

'I canna bide Doctor Elliot,' said Tibbie. 'Can you ?'

'There's some I like better,' answered Miss Nesbit with characteristic caution.

'Like better!' echoed Tibbie. 'He's a mean, graspin', ill-natured man. They say he married Mrs. Elliot for her gear, an he'll try tae make Mary do the same.'

'Wheesht, Tibbie,' said Miss Nesbit gently. 'If ye canna say ony guid o' a body, dinna say ony ill.'

'Look here, Janet,' said Tibbie suddenly. 'I dinna ken what Mrs. Riddell o' Ravelaw said tae ye that day she came tae Aldersyde, but d'ye mean tae say ye bear her nae ill-will for the way she has treated us since we kenned her first.'

'Wad it better us tae keep up a spite at her, Tibbie?'

'Maybe no,' returned Tibbie impatiently. 'An' I ken the Bible bids ye forgive yer enemies. But for a' that, an' I must say'd though it anger ye, Janet, if Sandy Riddell had treated me as he has treated you, I would hate him, an' live but tae be revenged on him.'

The fiery, implacable spirit of the Nesbits was roused in Tibbie's breast. Looking at her, Janet almost trembled. For what tribulation might it not lead her into in years to come?

'Speak o' the deil, Janet,' cried Tibbie. 'Here's Sandy Riddell comin' ridin' ower the brae, on that black beast o' his—a bonnie like thing on a Sabbath afternoon.'

Miss Nesbit cast one glance at the horse and rider, and then helplessly round, as if seeking a way of escape from the inevitable meeting.

'Janet, for ony sake dinna let the man see ye care sae much,' said Tibbie sharply. 'Wait till he comes up, an' I'll gie him a word he'll no forget in a hurry.'

'Tibbie, if ye daur!' said Janet, and gripped her sister's arm with fingers that had no faltering in them, and which effectually silenced Tibbie.

The Laird of Ravelaw looked well on horseback. He rode a great, powerful black animal, which chafed under bit and bridle, but carried his master superbly. His purpose in coming that unfrequented way, was solely to see Janet Nesbit. It did not suffice him that he had treated her shamefully, he desired to see for himself how she bore it. He actually drew rein in front of the Miss Nesbits, and lifting his cap, bade them good afternoon.

Tibbie kept her head down, lest she should be tempted to forget Janet's 'daur!' But Miss Nesbit drew herself up in her proudest way, and putting back her veil, looked straight into his face. The curl in her long upper lip, the matchless contempt in her clear eyes, the haughty calm of her whole demeanour, left him in no doubt of what she thought of him. This was scarcely what he had looked for, and it made him shrink into himself, and curse himself for coming in the way of such humiliation. After that one look, which had not the shadow of recognition in it, Miss Nesbit drew down her veil and passed on. Then the Laird of Ravelaw dug his spurs into the black charger's sleek sides, causing him to rear, and afterwards to plunge forward in a mad gallop.

Faithless Riddell had got a lesson at the hands of a woman, which he would not forget for many a day. Not being a person of much discrimination, he concluded that Janet Nesbit must have received his attentions as they were offered, to wile away an idle hour.

The first Sabbath evening in their new home passed but drearily for the Miss Nesbits. They had little in common, and did not talk much together, after the manner of other sisters.

They lingered long over their early tea; then Tibbie threw herself on the sofa, and folding her fair arms above her head, built her castles in the air. Miss Nesbit sat in the window, watching with yearning eyes the night creeping over Bourhope to envelope Aldersyde in its grim shadows. Her feelings being like to get the better of her, she rang the bell and bade Marget bring in the lamp, and took up a book. At nine o'clock it behoved her to call Marget again, to listen to the lesson she must read, as their father had done every Sabbath night since they were little toddling bairnies, who could not comprehend what it was all about. It was no wonder her voice faltered; for it is a sore thing for a woman to feel that she is the head of a house, and responsible for the well-being of its inmates. But I trow not many take up the charge with so earnest a spirit as Janet Nesbit.

Thus the Sabbath closed.

Upon the Monday afternoon, when Miss Nesbit

was sitting alone in the dining-room, Tibbie having gone to Aldershope, Marget showed in Mr. Bourhill, the minister. Miss Nesbit rose from her seat, and held out her hand to him in frank welcome, but for the moment neither cared to speak. The memory of bygone days, and other greetings never more to be heard this side the grave, rose up before them, and made words difficult to come.

'I met Miss Isabel at the manse gate,' said Mr. Bourhill after a little. 'She is looking well, Miss Nesbit.'

'Yes, she is weel. I was jist sittin' when ye cam' in, Mr. Bourhill, wonderin' what I wad dae wi' Tibbie. She's a restless, thochtless lassie; I'm jist fear'd Windyknowe will be ower quiet a hame for her.'

Mr. Bourhill's heart beat quicker at this evidence of her perfect faith and confidence in him. He knew well there was no other to whom she would have spoken with such unreservedness.

'Could you not take her to Edinburgh for the winter months?' he suggested. 'The change would do you both good.'

Miss Nesbit lifted up her head and smiled slightly.

'Sixty pounds a year 'll no pay for mony changes, Mr. Bourhill.'

The minister heard her in no little surprise.

'Miss Nesbit, is it possible *that* is all your income?'

She nodded.

'I'm no ashamed o'd; why should I be? As I said tae Tibbie, mony a puir gentlewoman hasna as muckle. It's plenty for us if Tibbie'—

She paused, and a sigh escaped her.

'She has a constant cravin' after a gay life, an' a' the luxury that money can buy, Mr. Bourhill— a very natural thing in a young an' bonnie lassie.'

'Is that work not trying for your eyes, Miss Nesbit?' asked the minister in a queer, abrupt way.

Miss Nesbit laid her lace work down on her lap, a little humorous smile rippling about the corners of her mouth.

'I maun tell ye the meaning o' this, Mr. Bourhill. When Mr. Douglas tell'd us what was left, Tibbie an' me cam' tae the conclusion that we wad hae tae let Marget gang, an' I said sae till her. I wish ye had seen her, Mr. Bourhill: her honest wrath fairly took the breath frae Tibbie an' me. She just refused tae gang. So tae fill up my time, an' help tae pay Marget's wages, I mak this lace, which my mother learned me tae dae long ago, an' send it tae a shop in Edinburgh. It's atween you an' me, Mr. Bourhill; for if Marget suspeckit it, she wad tak my heid aff. I've tae stow'd away in my apron pocket whenever I hear her comin'.'

While she was speaking, the minister of Aldershope had risen and gone over to the window. He could not always force back from outward sight that which filled all his heart.

'We can see the den o' Aldersyde frae here, ye see,' said Miss Nesbit cheerfully; 'no tae speak o' Dryhope Tower, an' Bourhope. So we dinna feel a' thegither awa frae hame.'

Then Mr. Bourhill turned about, and Miss Nesbit, happening to look at him at the moment, knew what was coming. She rose up trembling, and let her work fall down to the floor.

The deepest feelings do not find their expression in a multitude of words. Mr. Bourhill held out his hands to Janet Nesbit, and said in tones which his great emotion made hoarse and tremulous:

'Janet, I love you next to God. Let *me* make your happiness my greatest earthly care!' That was all.

A lesser nature might have misjudged him, and thought his offer was the outcome of pity. But Janet Nesbit's great heart read that other like an open book, and knew, ah! none better, the priceless value of the love she could not take.

There was no coquetry about her, no shrinking from telling the truth; she answered the question as it had been put, in words grave, true, and earnest, coming from the heart.

'Mr. Bourhill, I would to God I could come, kennin' what it is ye offer, an' that there's no muckle love like yours in this weary world. But I hae nane tae gie, an' I could be wife tae nae man unless my love could match his ain.' Then she broke down and covered her face with her hands.

To a true woman it is terrible to refuse the offer of a good man's love; because, if she has loved herself, she knows what her answer must mean to him.

It was no light thing for the minister of Aldershope; for, when love comes to a man for the first time, late in life, it is no child's play, but terrible earnest.

'In time to come,' he said slowly; but Miss Nesbit held up her hand deprecatingly.

'Never, never! Mr. Bourhill. I'm a woman to whom love can come but aince. I hae gien mine already, an' though unworthily for a',' she said. 'Ye ken what I think o' ye when I bring mysel' tae tell ye this; but ye were my father's freend an' mine.'

Then Mr. Bourhill went away over to the window, and stood there for what seemed a very long time to Miss Nesbit. Yet she dared not disturb him, nor go away out of the room. These were sharp moments for the minister of Aldershope. When he turned about by and by, it seemed to Miss Nesbit that

never before had Mr. Bourhill's face so reflected the
light of his great heart and meek, unselfish soul.
He went up to her, and taking both her hands in
his firm yet gentle clasp, looked full into her
eyes.

'It was too much happiness for me, and God has
willed it otherwise. Forgive me if I have distressed
you—nay, I know I have ; but there are moments
when a man is not altogether master of himself.'

'I wasna worthy,' faltered Janet, unable to say
more.

'You will forget this, Miss Nisbet, and let the
old friendship grow deeper and stronger between
us,' he said with his true bright smile ; 'and only
remember me as the one to whom your father
ever accorded a warm welcome in happier days
at Aldersyde ?'

'I hinna that mony freens that I should care tae
lose the best o' them,' Miss Nesbit made answer
with brimming eyes. 'God bless ye, Mr.
Bourhill.'

The minister bent low over the clasped hands, and
touched them with reverent lips: 'God bless *you*,
my friend !'

CHAPTER VII.

AFTER meeting the Miss Nesbits on the Sabbath afternoon, Sandy Riddell rode home to Ravelaw in a great rage. At the dinner-table he was so rude and sulky, like some schoolboy who had been whipped for transgression, that his mother found it necessary to remonstrate with him, and ask him what had happened to ruffle his temper. Whereupon her gentlemanly and respectful son swore at her, and Mrs. Riddell retired to her chamber in hysterics.

In the lifetime of Sandy Riddell the elder, such scenes had been of so frequent occurrence that the domestics thought nothing of them. Since the young

Laird had grown to manhood he had given large
evidence of having inherited his father's coarse, rough
nature, rather than the courtesy which had ever been
characteristic of his mother's family. This was the
price my lady had had to pay for the wealth and stately
home she had won. She did not appear down-
stairs again that evening, which mattered little to
her son, he being in the stables smoking and talking
familiarly with the groom.

On Monday morning Mrs. Riddell did not feel
herself equal to the exertion of rising at the
usual hour, but rang for her waiting - woman
to bring her a cup of strong tea, and thereafter
remain in the next room till she was again required.
At eleven, Mrs. Riddell pulled her bell-rope again,
and Rebecca, who had been down-stairs gossiping
with the maids, came running up in breathless haste.

'You've been down - stairs, Rebecca,' said her
mistress peevishly. 'I might have fainted or died
while you were gone.'

'I had the toothache, ma'am,' said Rebecca,
telling her lie as glibly as her mistress could have
done, 'and just ran down for a mouthful of whisky
to deaden it.'

Mrs. Riddell did not believe her serving-woman's
statement. There are no greater suspecters of the
veracity of others than those who have little regard
for the truth themselves.

'Dress me, then, Rebecca,' she said languidly, 'and then go down for some vinegar and water to bathe my head; it aches intolerably, the result of the wretched night I have had.'

Rebecca had passed the night on a couch in her mistress's bedroom, and knew she had slept soundly till the dawning. But being only a poor waiting-woman, it did not behove her to have any opinions of her own. There was a bit of news burning her tongue; but she dared not breathe it, lest she should betray that even in the agonies of toothache she had been able to gossip down-stairs. Having got her mistress into her clothes, she went away for the vinegar and water, with which she bathed her lady's head, she lying back in her easy chair the while.

'When did the Laird breakfast, Rebecca?' asked my lady.

'At six o'clock, ma'am,' answered Rebecca; 'and away driving to Galashiels to catch the coach for London.'

Mrs. Riddell gave a faint scream.

'You are talking sheer nonsense, Rebecca,' said she sharply.

'I beg pardon, ma'am; I had it from Gibson's own lips when I was down just now,' said Rebecca smoothly.

'Go and send Gibson to me directly; I cannot

comprehend what you tell me, Rebecca,' exclaimed her mistress with considerable energy.

Rebecca departed at once, and returned shortly with the housekeeper, a stately personage in stiff black silk, with a bunch of keys jingling at her side.

'What is this Rebecca tells me about the Laird, Gibson?' asked Mrs. Riddell.

'I don't know what Rebecca may have told you, ma'am,' said Gibson sullenly, who still resented being ordered up-stairs by my lady's maid.

'Don't exasperate me, Gibson. Has the Laird gone to London, or has he not?'

'I gave him his breakfast myself at six o'clock, ma'am, and packed his bag while he ate it; and I saw him drive away at half-past six. Duncan has just returned from Galashiels.'

Mrs. Riddell bit her lip.

'He must have taken a sudden whim in his head,' said she. 'Did he make any allusion to his return?'

'As he was going out of the door, ma'am, he turned about and said to me, "Gibson, tell my mother I'm off for a holiday, and she may expect me when I come."'

Again Mrs. Riddell bit her lip. To leave such a message for her with a servant; it was intolerable!

'He only took one change of linen, ma'am,' went

on Gibson, 'and said he would get what he needed in London.'

'You may go,' said Mrs. Riddell haughtily, and Gibson withdrew, secretly delighting over her mistress's humiliation.

No dependant ever became attached to the house of Ravelaw, being made to feel that they *were* dependants, and as such must keep their place.

Being left alone, Mrs. Riddell began to think over this extraordinary proceeding of Sandy's. She made her head ache in earnest, trying to fathom his motive for this sudden journey, but was obliged in the end to give it up in despair.

A trying week dragged itself away, during which Mrs. Riddell fretted night and day, and almost resolved to journey to London herself, in search of her truant boy.

But first she bethought herself of making a visit to Arngask, to seek advice in her extremity from her bachelor brother Philip Napier, and her maiden sister Jean, who dwelt together in lonely poverty in the house of their fathers. But they just laughed at her, and asked her what else she could expect from a Riddell of Ravelaw.

'I heard he was after Nesbit's daughter of Aldersyde—a fine young woman, Lady Kate Scott of Scottrigg tells me, Harriet,' said Miss Jean. 'Has she turned against him, that he has grown tired of

Ravelaw? That's the way men take disappointments
in love, they say.'

This was the last drop in the cup of the lady
of Ravelaw.

'Forsaken by Janet Nesbit indeed, Jean!' she
exclaimed scornfully. 'It was the very opposite
way: she would have taken him gladly. But Sandy
was only playing with her, as so many young men
play with silly girls. And I set my face against
it from the first.'

'Little cause ye had to do that, Harriet,' said
Philip Napier grimly. 'Janet Nesbit's worth six of
your big rough son. Take you care that such sinful
pride doesn't get its just reward. Ye'll maybe get
a daughter - in - law ye'll have more cause to be
ashamed of than Janet Nesbit. She would have
been the making of Sandy.'

Mrs. Riddell quitted the house in disgust. All
the world was turning against her, surely. Stop a
little, my lady ; the worst has not come yet !

Other seven days passed, and still no word came
from or of the Laird of Ravelaw. Then his mother
took alarm lest some evil thing had befallen her one
son, and on the Monday morning sent for Mr. Douglas
the lawyer from Melrose, and deputed him to journey
to London immediately after the missing Laird.

Mr. Douglas not being able to spare the time
for such a journey, tried to allay her fears by

assuring her that he would be enjoying the novelty of London so much that he would not have time to write or send word, and would doubtless be home, safe and sound, before many days. But Mrs. Riddell was not to be assured. Then Mr. Douglas respectfully informed her that the claims of business would keep him in Melrose till Thursday of that week, but that on Friday morning he would be ready to depart on her mission of investigation. With that she was obliged to be content, and Mr. Douglas departed from Ravelaw fervently hoping the scapegrace would turn up before Friday, and thus save him a task for which he had neither time nor inclination.

On the Wednesday evening, after having partaken of her solitary dinner, Mrs. Riddell was sitting by the fire in her spacious drawing-room, turning her rings round and round on her slender fingers, and thinking of her absent son. Her face wore a restless, worried expression, and she did not seem in the best of health or spirits. Nevertheless she was attired with her customary care, having on a gown of stiff mauve silk, and a cap of the same material trimmed with rich lace.

The house was drearily silent. In spite of all its magnificence, Ravelaw had never been a *home.* If Harriet Riddell had been put to the test, after twenty-eight years' experience of it, she would have infinitely preferred the poverty of Arngask to the loveless splendour of her husband's dwelling-place; because, with her own kith and kin, she would not have had to endure the rough ways and coarse speech which had been her daily bread since her marriage.

In the middle of these ruminations the mistress of Ravelaw was disturbed by the rumbling of carriage wheels on the gravel, followed by a loud knock at the hall door. She rose up, her heart fluttering, and listened breathlessly. In a moment she heard Sandy's voice, then another, that of a woman! What wonder that as she listened to the approaching footsteps on the stair, she should require to lean against the oaken mantel for support!

While she stood thus, the door was flung open wide, and the Laird of Ravelaw appeared on the threshold, having upon his arm a lady of tall and commanding presence, dressed in furs, beside which my lady's would have shrunk into insignificance. They came forward into the room, and Sandy, in no way disconcerted, led the lady up to his mother.

'Permit me, mother, to introduce to you my wife, the mistress of Ravelaw.'

Mrs. Riddell's soul failed within her, and for the moment her eyes drooped from sheer inability to meet either of the pairs fixed upon her.

'Come, mother, give us a welcome after our long journey,' repeated Sandy in his rough, impatient way. 'Shake hands with my wife, and say you are glad to see her.'

Then having somewhat recovered herself, Mrs. Riddell the elder lifted up her keen eyes, and looked the new wife over from head to foot. She was marvellously beautiful, with a subtle Eastern loveliness, unlike any Mrs. Riddell had ever seen in Scotland. Her hair and eyes were as black as the raven's wing, her face exquisitely featured and of a warm brown hue, as if it had been tanned by southern suns. She was smiling, and showing two rows of teeth like pearls; and had also ungloved one dainty hand, and was offering it to the lady of Ravelaw. But Mrs. Riddell drew haughtily back, and keeping her hands clasped before her, said icily:

'When I know who Mrs. Sandy Riddell is, I may touch her hand, *perhaps*.'

'Take care, mother,' said Sandy meaningly, but the warning did not take effect.

Mrs. Riddell's passion was at white heat, her eyes shone like stars, and her bosom heaved, only her face preserved its dead haughty calm.

'Ah! I do not understand your Scotch ways,' said Mrs. Sandy with a shrug of her shoulders and a grimace. 'Madame your mother seems vexed, Sandy ; why does she look as if she were made of stone ?'

She spoke good English, though with a strong French accent, and her voice was musical indeed.

'Will you be good enough, Alexander,' said Mrs. Riddell the elder, fixing her blazing eyes on her son's face, 'to tell me who this woman is, whom you have forced upon me in the privacy of my own drawing - room at this unseemly hour ?'

'Such talk will serve you no end, mother,' Sandy made answer. 'This *lady* is Honorè Riddell, my lawful wife, and, I repeat, mistress of Ravelaw.'

His mother waved her hand in scorn of his words.

'I desire to know who she was, what she was *before* she became Mrs. Alexander Riddell of Ravelaw.'

'With that you have nothing to do,' said the Laird of Ravelaw, fast losing his temper. 'Sufficient for you that she is my wife. Bid her welcome, or there is but one alternative.'

Then Mrs. Sandy laughed merrily, as if heartily enjoying the *tableau*.

'Do not be so vexed with me, madame, although I have stolen a march upon you,' she said, flashing her black eyes on Mrs. Riddell's face. 'You will find me the most amiable of women, when I am not crossed. I have no desire to make you feel not at home here with me; though, as Sandy so often puts it, *I* am the mistress of Ravelaw. You shall have your own apartments, your own servants, if you will, provided they do not quarrel with mine, and we shall set an example to all mothers-in-law and daughters - in - law, by being the best of friends!'

Again Sandy's wife offered her hand to Sandy's mother; but my lady darted back as if she had been stung, and looked magnificent in her scorn and wrath. She turned her back upon her son's wife, and looked at him. Any man but Sandy Riddell would have quailed beneath that look.

'To that woman I have nothing to say,' she said slowly, 'and only one word to you before I quit this cursed house for ever. It is simply this, that from this day I disclaim any connection with you, my son though ye be. You have disgraced your father's name and mine, and permitted a stranger to insult me upon my own hearthstone. For such awful sins Heaven reserves punishment heavy enough, therefore I forbear to leave my curse with you.'

Then she swept from the room, and, calling her waiting-woman, commanded her to order a coach, then to come and help her to dress, and get her own goods together for a journey to Arngask.

The white set face and gleaming eyes of her mistress feared Rebecca, and she dared not open her mouth. She did not need to be told what had passed in the drawing-room, having had her ear to the keyhole all the time.

'Get yourself ready also, Rebecca,' said Mrs. Riddell; 'you will come with me.'

But Rebecca had other plans.

'Pardon, ma'am, but I engaged to serve the lady of Ravelaw, *at* Ravelaw, so I shall stay,' she said respectfully but firmly.

Mrs. Riddell did not look surprised or angry. This was a fitting termination to the night's tribulation. Not many minutes later, the coach came round to the door, and Mrs. Riddell went downstairs, her face growing dark as she passed the drawing-room door, for she could hear within Sandy's voice, and the mocking, sweet tones of the woman who had supplanted her. So in the darkness of the night, alone and unattended, the lady of Ravelaw crossed for the last time the threshold of the home where she had never known a day's happiness. During her solitary drive she had time for reflection. She had scorned and flaunted that true gentlewoman Janet Nesbit, only to be turned out of Ravelaw by an impudent, mocking Frenchwoman, who, not having any name or family pride of her own, had no respect for that of others.

Oh but these were sharp moments, and the proud head was bent low in the very depths of humiliation and pain.

In the middle of the night, the slumbering inmates of Arngask were aroused by a thundering knock at the door, and when cautious Philip Napier, pistol in hand, inquired from within who desired admittance, what was his amazement to hear the voice of his sister, Mrs. Riddell of Ravelaw! Thinking some grievous thing must have befallen his scapegoat nephew, he made haste to undo the bolts and let her in. She staggered forward into the hall, white and haggard, and immediately fell into a deathlike swoon. Then Arngask ran for his sister, who aroused the women of the house, and among them they managed to get her to bed and restored to consciousness. Then she told them of the evil that had befallen the house of Ravelaw, and that henceforth her home must be with them at Arngask.

All three remembered the warning words uttered in careless unthinkingness by Philip Napier, and which to-day had bitterly come to pass:

'Ye'll maybe get a daughter-in-law ye'll have more cause to be ashamed of than Janet Nesbit!'

CHAPTER VIII.

PON the afternoon of the day before Christmas, the Miss Nesbits were sitting in their dining-room, Miss Nesbit at her lace, and Tibbie altering a gown for herself. Tibbie's work was always for herself. The first snowstorm had swept over Ettrick vale. Minchmoor, Broadlaw, and Bourhope wore their weird white caps, and the headstones in the lonely chapel-yard of St. Mary had all their rude letterings hidden by frosted snow. To gay folk this was a season of festivity and rejoicing, but to the two women abiding in loneliness at Windyknowe it made no difference, save in the contrast it presented to happier Christmas times gone by.

H

'Janet Nesbit,' said Tibbie in a very wearied voice, 'I'm sick, sick to death of my life!'

'Many a one's been sick, and had to grow well again, Tibbie,' answered Miss Nesbit quietly, though her heart sank. At times it grew very heavy about her young sister.

'We rise up in the morning, and go through the same round of weariness,' Tibbie continued. 'There is not a thing to brighten our days. What have we done, Janet, that we should be shut out from what other women enjoy? It's not right.'

'Wheesht, Tibbie!' said Miss Nesbit gently. 'We micht be waur.'

'No much, I'm thinkin' I wish Sandy Riddell's wife would take us up. Whatever she may be, she can make gay doings in Ravelaw.'

Miss Nesbit's long upper lip curled slightly.

'I dinna think ye weigh your words, Tibbie,' she said slowly.

Tibbie yawned and shrugged her shoulders, then casting her half-finished gown upon the floor, she sauntered over to the window, and looked out on the whitened landscape with discontented eyes.

'I see a coach comin' up the brae,' she exclaimed. 'O Janet, if it would but come here! Ay, even if Grizzie Oliphant was in it, I'd dance a reel.'

Miss Nesbit laughed, and pausing in her work, looked with tenderest eyes on her fair young sister. Oh, but she was fair, with hair like summer sunshine, eyes like the forget - me - not, and bloom like the rose and lily combined!

'O Janet, Janet! It's comin', and it's the bay horses from Scottrigg. I know them,' she cried in ecstasy, and without more ado danced out of the room, and up-stairs, to adorn herself in her best.

Miss Nesbit looked well pleased. Not only for Tibbie's sake was she glad, but also relieved to find that the hard things she had been thinking of the Scotts, for their long neglect, were without foundation. Very well pleased also was Marget Drysdale to behold the splendid equipage of Scottrigg at the door of Windyknowe, and to show in, with many curtsies, Sir Walter with his lady and their sweet daughter Marjorie.

Lady Kate Scott had been Mrs. Nesbit's friend in girlhood, and had almost a mother's love for her orphan girls. She took Miss Nesbit in her arms without ado, and whispered a few words of tenderness in her ears. Then somewhat to Miss Nesbit's discomfiture, Sir Walter followed suit, laughing heartily at his own audacity. Then it was Marjorie's turn to clasp Miss Nesbit's hand, and say, from her loving heart, '*Dear* Janet!'

She was a fair, winsome maiden, just what her mother had been thirty years ago when she was bonnie Katie Graeme of Mosslee.

Presently Tibbie came down, and was warmly greeted also, although Janet was the favourite at Scottrigg.

'Before we say anything, my dears,' said Lady Scott, 'I must explain that I would have been at Windyknowe long ago, but I have had one of my troublesome illnesses, and Marjorie had to nurse me. But I'm come as soon as I'm able to carry you both away to Scottrigg for Christmas. You will come, Janet?'

'Mony thanks, dear Leddy Scott,' returned Miss Nesbit, lifting grateful, pathetic eyes to the motherly face. 'Tibbie 'll gang wi' ye the day, and I'll come when she comes hame. I couldna leave Marget alane, ye ken, at Windyknowe.'

'Bring her tae,' suggested Sir Walter.

But Miss Nesbit shook her head.

'Let it be as I say, dear freens. I'm mair than gled tae let Tibbie gang; and I gie ye my faithfu' promise tae come when she wins hame.'

'Knowing of yore that you are as immoveable as Minchmoor, Janet,' laughed Lady Kate, 'we must be content. Well, now that's settled, how have you been all this time? and how do you like your new home?'

'We strive to be content, Leddy Scott,' answered Miss Nesbit, and seeing her lips quiver, Lady Kate knew all that the words implied.

'Well, what do you think of the marriage of the Laird of Ravelaw?' she asked. 'Have any of you seen the new wife?'

If Lady Scott had guessed what a tender spot she was touching, she would never have asked the question; but though she had heard many rumours coupling the names of Sandy Riddell and Janet Nesbit, she had thought the thing to be all of Riddell's seeking, not considering him a likely person to win Janet Nesbit's regard.

'We saw her in the kirk one Sabbath day,' answered Miss Nesbit quietly. 'She is a very beautiful woman.'

'Yes; but hardly a fit mate for one of our oldest families,' said her ladyship slightingly.

'Who is she, Lady Scott?' asked Tibbie. 'Did the Laird of Ravelaw only meet her after he went to London.'

'No; they say he met her the last time he was in London, two summers ago. She belongs to a respectable enough French family, I understand, but wretchedly poor. Her brothers and she are mere adventurers, on the look-out to take advantage of foolish folk like the Laird of Ravelaw.'

'Have you called on her, Lady Scott?' asked Tibbie.

Her ladyship smiled.

'My dear, you ask an absurd question. I had the very slightest acquaintance with Mrs. Riddell the elder, when she was Harriet Napier; but even if she had been my most intimate friend, I should hardly have called on her new daughter-in-law. Marjorie and I met a riding party from Ravelaw on the Yair road yesterday. Mrs. Sandy looked superb on horseback; her brother was by her side, a dark, heavily-moustached man. They rode up to Arngask, they tell me, to be received with some coolness, I assure you. I'm sorry for the young man's mother. This has been a sore blow to her pride.'

'Which gangs afore a fa',' put in Sir Walter.

'Where is Mrs. Riddell the elder?' asked Miss Nesbit.

'At Arngask, which she makes very unpeaceable for Mr. Philip Napier and Miss Jean.'

'She's like a hen on a het girdle,' said Sir Walter in his broad way.

'If she hasna ae thing tae girn aboot, she'll mak anither. I hae nae patience wi' yon woman.'

'Hush, Walter!' said his wife gently. 'Let the poor lady alone. Tibbie, my dear, run and get your things together,' she added to Tibbie.

‘We must be going, as we expect some friends to dinner this evening.’

‘I’ll get Mary Elliot frae Aldershope tae bide wi’ me while Tibbie’s awa,’ said Miss Nesbit when her sister left the room. ‘Ye ken Mary Elliot, Lady Scott?’

‘Yes, a very sweet girl. I remember her at Aldersyde. I heard an absurd rumour from your kinswoman, Grizel Oliphant, at Yair yesterday, that your cousin Hugh Nesbit is courting Doctor Elliot’s daughter.’

‘Whaur does Miss Grizzie get a’ the news?’ asked Miss Nesbit with a smile.

‘You may well ask,’ laughed Lady Scott.

‘She has naethin’ else adae,’ put in Sir Walter drily, ‘but nurse her cat, an’ thraw wi’ yon servin’-wummin, an’ gether up the news.’

Presently Tibbie, having made good use of her time, returned to the room dressed, ready for her journey, and the visitors rose.

Marget had carried out her young lady’s bag to the coach, exchanged a civil good-day with the stately individual in bottle-green livery on the box, and stood ready to show the company out.

But Miss Nesbit herself came to the door, and bade them all a hearty farewell. When she returned to her deserted hearth, she wondered why her heart should be so heavy, when it ought to have been lightened by the loving kindness of these true friends.

Early on the morrow she went away down to Aldershope, to see about getting Mary Elliot up to Windyknowe. At the manse gate she met Mr. Bourhill, and told him her errand. In spite of what had been between them, there never was any constraint in their manner toward each other. Having buried the past, they were indeed *friends.* I am aware that some scout the idea of such a friendship—Platonic, as it is called—in these days; but I, who have seen it in life, hold that it is the most beautiful and perfect of any friendship.

Mrs. Elliot's maid showed Miss Nesbit up to the drawing-room, and went for her mistress. But it was Mary who returned to greet the visitor, and upon her entrance Miss Nesbit was struck by her exceeding paleness.

'Mother is not well. You will come up and see her, Janet?' said Mary in her gentle way.

'Ay; hae ye been up a' the nicht tae, lassie? Ye dinna look very brisk.'

'When the heart's sore it's not easy to look well, Janet. But come away up to mother: she will be impatient,' said Mary, and without further talk they proceeded up-stairs.

Mrs. Elliot was sitting in her dressing-gown by

her chamber fire, looking very worn and ill ; yet she stretched out her thin hand to Miss Nesbit with the old smile of welcome.

'I'm vext tae see ye lookin' sae ill, Mrs. Elliot,' said Miss Nesbit. 'Mair especially as I cam thinkin' tae get Mary back tae Windyknowe wi' me, Tibbie bein' awa tae Scottrigg for Christmas.'

'My dear, you will certainly get Mary. I'm not that ill but what I can do without her. I'll need to learn to want her,' said Mrs. Elliot with a heavy sigh. 'Mary, my dear, go and get your things together ; I would speak a little with Janet.'

'Yes, mother,' said Mary in a very willing voice, and whenever the door closed upon her, Mrs. Elliot stretched out her hand to Miss Nesbit as if seeking her help, and burst into tears.

'Oh, Miss Nesbit, my poor Mary !'

'What ill has happened, or is gaun tae happen, tae Mary, dear Mrs. Elliot ?'

'The worst thing that can happen tae a woman,' she answered mournfully ; 'being forced to give her hand without her heart. In plain words, Mary is to marry your cousin, Hugh Nesbit of Aldersyde, whom I believe she dislikes above mortal man.'

'Oh, wha's gaun tae force her intae such an unholy marriage, without affection or respect, Mrs. Elliot ?' asked Miss Nesbit sharply.

'Her father,'

No more would the loyal wife say. Whatever were her thoughts of him, they would not be uttered, even to Janet Nesbit.

'Hugh Nesbit an' your Mary are no weel matched, Mrs. Elliot.'

'It will be her death, poor, timid, sensitive thing as she is. But I can't make her father see it. He thinks only of the honour it will be to have his daughter lady of Aldersyde. It is a sad thing, Miss Nesbit, when a man values the pomp of the world above the happiness and well-being of his child.'

'Is Mary submittin' tae this sacrifice o' herself withoot a murmur?' asked Miss Nesbit.

'You know her gentle nature, Janet; and she has been brought up to obey her father in all things. Besides, what would the protestations of two frail women avail against such a will as Dr. Elliot's?'

Miss Nisbet had nothing to say; such an argument was unanswerable.

'What may be Hugh Nesbit's aim in this, Mrs. Elliot?' she asked by and by. 'I thocht he wad hae marriet for gear.'

'He loves her, Janet, as such men love, with a fierce, wild passion which cannot last. Her gentle beauty has been her dool, as they say here. But Mary will not be a tocherless bride. Her father will give her five thousand pounds on her wedding-day, and she inherits my fortune at her death.'

'Was Hugh Nesbit aware o' this afore he socht Mary ?' asked Miss Nesbit drily.

Mary's entrance at the moment interrupted the conversation. Miss Nesbit turned round to look at her, and to feel a great rush of pitying tenderness go out to her, such a feeling almost as a strong man might have for a little child. Hers was the fairness of the lily, which lasts but till the wind comes and breaks it on the stalk ; so was there not a mournful fitness in the name they had given her, the Lily of Aldershope? Janet Nesbit loved her well ; and if Hugh Nesbit had been worthy of her, what a joy it would have been to see them living together in Aldersyde, with toddling bairnies growing up about their knees.

'I'm ready, Janet,' she said. 'Mother, I'll leave the bag, and Peter or one of the girls can bring it up to Windyknowe in the evening.'

'Very well, my dear. Good-bye ; I know you will take care of her, Janet,' said Mrs. Elliot. 'God bless you both.'

At Windyknowe, secure with her friend, Mary Elliot abode in peace. The subject of the marriage was never mentioned between them, until one night when they had been about a week together. They were sitting by the fire in the gloaming, when a shadow fell athwart the window, and there came a knock at the door. Then, to the surprise of both, they heard the voice of Hugh Nesbit in the hall. Mary started to her feet and clung to Janet, lifting beseeching eyes to her face.

'Janet, Janet! don't let him come in,' she whispered brokenly.

'Keep quiet, my dear ; ye needna fear here wi' me. Hugh Nesbit canna come in tae my rooms if I want tae keep him oot. Bide here an' I'll speak tae him,' said Miss Nesbit, and setting Mary down, left the room, locking the door after her.

In the hall Hugh Nesbit was taking off his over-coat, and Marget eyeing him suspiciously from the kitchen door. He turned round quite unconcernedly at sight of his cousin, and offered his hand.

'Ah, Cousin Janet, how do you do?' he said smoothly. 'I have been long in coming to pay my respects to you in your new home.'

'Ay, ye hinna been in a hurry,' she answered drily, and led the way into the study, at the same time desiring Marget to bring a candle. When it was brought, she desired Hugh Nesbit to be seated, and he looked round the room in a displeased way. His welcome was cold enough.

' Hae ye gotten settled in Aldersyde, Cousin Hugh?' asked Miss Nesbit politely.

'Yes, but it's dreary enough. I can't think how

you supported existence in such a place. It will be changed when the mistress comes home. You will have heard, I suppose, that I am to be honoured with the hand of the young lady who is at present your guest.'

'Ay, I hae heard ye are tae get Mary Elliot's *hand*,' she said with direct emphasis on the last word.

He knew well enough what it implied, but deemed it wise to ignore it.

'Have you no congratulations to offer, Cousin Janet?'

'If the winnin' o' an unwillin' bride be matter for congratulation, ye hae mine,' she said quietly.

'Who says she is unwilling?' asked Hugh Nesbit angrily.

'Had I no kenned afore, her look when she heard yer voice the noo wad hae telt me.'

'Well, to be plain, Cousin Janet, I came to see her to-night. Since you are so plain with me, I need not mince my words to you,' said Hugh Nesbit sullenly. 'Be good enough either to take me to her presence, or ask her to come to mine.'

'I can dae neither,' answered Miss Nesbit without hesitation. 'Mary Elliot is my guest, and I maun respect her wishes. She desired me tae keep ye frae her; and if ye be a man ava', ye'll gang awa withoot insistin' on't.'

'I do insist upon it. I claim a right to see my promised wife, no matter where she may be.'

'Against her will, tae, I suppose,' said Miss Nesbit with a dry smile.

'It is mere imagination on your part, and that of her silly mother, to think she is unwilling to become lady of Aldersyde. Any woman would jump at the offer.'

'An' you tae the bargain, I dinna doot,' said Miss Nesbit sarcastically. Then it entered her head to try and appeal to her cousin's better nature to release Mary from a bond so irksome to her.

'Ye ken brawly, Hugh, that Mary disna care for ye,' she said with gentleness. 'Be manly enough tae refuse a wife wha has naething tae bring tae ye but her haund wi' its tocher.'

'I don't care a rush for her tocher, as you call it,' said Hugh Nesbit passionately. 'It is her I want, and her I mean to have. Once for all, will you let me see her?'

'No, I winna,' returned Miss Nesbit quietly. Whereupon Hugh Nesbit with an oath made haste from her presence, and lifting his coat and hat from the hall, took an indignant departure from Windyknowe.

'My certy, ye hae made quick wark o' the Laird the nicht,' said Marget in well-pleased tones.

Miss Nesbit smiled somewhat sadly, and went back to Mary.

'He's awa, my dear,' she said, taking the poor fluttering thing in her brave arms, and soothing her as a mother might have done. 'Ay, greet, my bairn; it'll ease yer heart, for I ken there's a sair load upon it. But mind through a', that amang many sorrows there's aye a God wha can help ye tae bear, as well as tae avenge them!'

CHAPTER IX.

THREE weeks did Mary Elliot abide at Windyknowe, for all that time was Tibbie absent at Scottrigg. Mary never knew what her mother suffered at home, between Doctor Elliot and Hugh Nesbit, to let her have unmolested this time of peace. But it ended at last. The coach from Scottrigg brought Tibbie home, and Mary went back to Aldershope to make her preparations for her bridal.

'An' what hae ye been daein', Tibbie, a' this time at Scottrigg?' asked Janet when they sat alone again by their hearth.

'Oh, I've had a grand time, Janet! I never enjoyed anything half so much. So many people

I

come and go at Scottrigg, one never has time to weary.   Yon's the life I would like.'

'Ye may get it yet, Tibbie,' said Miss Nesbit slily, 'if ye let young Walter Scott speak his mind.'

Tibbie tossed her head.

'He's a very soft young man, Walter Scott, an' just sits like a calf in a lady's presence.'

'Did ye see onything o' Miss Grizzie?' inquired Janet, hastening to change the subject.

Tibbie coloured slightly.

'She came up to Scottrigg one day an' lectured me on the pomps and vanities, and bade me not think too much of what I saw at Scottrigg, as it would make me discontented at hame.'

'She micht no be very faur wrang, Tibbie,' said Miss Nesbit with a sigh.

'Sandy Riddell an' his wife were three times at Scottrigg when I was there, Janet.'

Miss Nesbit looked much surprised.

'Bonnie wild Lady Scott was, I can tell ye, Janet. What a handsome woman Mrs. Riddell is, and how grandly dressed!'

'I hardly thocht Sandy Riddell wad hae taen his wife tae Scottrigg,' said Miss Nesbit musingly.

'She made him come, I think.   She'll rule him if ever woman rules man.   Lady Scott was very distant and scornful, but Mrs. Riddell didna care.

She'll mak a place for herself, yon woman,
Janet.'

' Are a' the strangers awa frae Ravelaw ? ' asked
Miss Nesbit.

'A' but her brother, Mr. Louis Reynaud, Janet,'
answered Tibbie, and turned her face away, though
at the time Miss Nesbit did not take any notice of
it.

' So Mary Elliot *is* to be lady of Aldersyde, after
all,' said Tibbie. 'Are ye no gled, Janet? We'll
can go often to Aldersyde when she's there.'

'It's no o' Mary's seekin', Tibbie. Hers 'll be a
dreary bridal.'

' It needna be, then. She's getting a fine man, an'
a bonnie hame. I think ye are too hard on Cousin
Hugh, Janet. He came once to Scottrigg when I
was there, and I liked him very well. He's a very
gentlemanly young man.'

' Ay, he's a' that ; but he'll no make oor Mary
happy,' said Miss Nesbit sadly.

' Marjorie Scott's comin' for ye on Monday afternoon, Janet ; and they'll give you a warm welcome
to Scottrigg, and make a great fuss over you : I
found it very pleasant.'

Tibbie got up and wandered restlessly up and
down the room, looking discontentedly on its plain,
old-fashioned furnishings. Evidently she was sigh-
ing after the flesh-pots of Egypt.

Again the old fear of something, she could not tell what, stole into Janet's heart as she looked on her fair young sister.

Next afternoon, when the Miss Nesbits were getting themselves dressed to go to Aldershope, they were disturbed by a great clattering of hoofs on the avenue, and two horses were reined up at the door. Tibbie flew to the window and then turned round, a wave of crimson sweeping over her face.

'It's Mrs. Riddell of Ravelaw and her brother,' she said confusedly. 'She said at Scottrigg she would maybe call on me at Windyknowe.'

Miss Nesbit shut her lips together, and a red spot began to burn on either cheek. This was not the behaviour she had been taught to think fitting in a newly-married gentlewoman. But as it behoved them to get away down-stairs at once, she made no remark.

No sooner had they got into the dining-room than Marget announced 'Mrs. Riddell an' a strange gentleman.'

The lady came first, attired in an exquisitely fitting riding - habit, and a coquettish hat with nodding plumes. She approached Tibbie with a great show of affection, and, to the horror of Miss Nesbit, kissed her on both cheeks. Then she turned to Miss Nesbit, and said prettily:

'You are Miss Nesbit. Forgive the liberty I take, but your charming sister won my heart at Scottrigg; so I made bold to come and see her, though they tell me it is not the fashion in Scotland for a stranger to call first. Ah! one might wait for ever; so I have broken through the custom.'

Miss Nesbit bowed coldly, not offering to touch the outstretched hand.

'Permit me to introduce to you my brother, Louis Reynaud, Miss Nesbit,' said the lady of Ravelaw, looking towards the gentleman who had followed her into the room.

He immediately stepped forward, and placing his hand on his heart, almost bowed himself to the earth.

Miss Nesbit looked him over from head to foot, and acknowledged him by a distant bow. His resemblance to his sister was very marked, and he was undeniably a handsome man. But his was not the face of a good man, nor one likely to inspire trust in man or woman. To the no little dismay of Miss Nesbit, he greeted Tibbie after the manner of an old friend, and then retired with her to the farthest window. Never had Tibbie looked so beautiful, so full of vivacity and life. Then the new lady of Ravelaw, without being invited, sat down near Miss Nesbit, and commenced to talk to her.

'You are so cool, so unlovable, in this bleak Scotland,' she said in her most winning tone. 'If

you see one kiss a friend, as I did your sister just
now, you look all so horrified as if you thought it
some great sin. I do not know what you are made
of. In my dear country, if we love we show it;
here it seems the right thing to hide it out of
sight.'

'It is the way of Scotch folk, Mrs. Riddell,' answered Miss Nesbit stiffly, her eyes watching the
pair in the window.

The Frenchman was sitting much closer to Tibbie
than Janet's idea of propriety approved, and his handsome head was bent down on a level with hers.

'I came to your home to-day to see if you and
your sister would honour us on Friday at Ravelaw.
We have a little dance—only a few in honour of my
brother, who leaves us next week; then indeed I
shall be quite alone to make my home in Scotland.'

'I am obliged to you, Mrs. Riddell; but the
mourning Tibbie and I wear forbid us takin' part
in ony gaiety,' said Miss Nesbit coldly.

'Pardon; I had thought it was three months
since your dear parent died. In our country a quiet
party is permitted at the end of that time.'

Miss Nesbit made no answer.

'You refuse, then? How cruel! Well, you will
at least come and spend a quiet evening with us?'
said Mrs. Riddell.

'I thank ye for yer offered kindness, Mrs. Riddell,' said Miss Nesbit, rising ; 'but neither Tibbie nor me can accept it, now or at any other time.'

A curious gleam shot through Mrs. Riddell's dark eyes, but she preserved her smiling exterior.

'Ah! well, you are inexorable. I am sorry, because I think your sister would be my friend, if you would let her,' said she, gathering her skirts in her hand. 'Come, Louis, we are dismissed. Your Scotch way may be very good, Miss Nesbit, but I do not appreciate it.'

Very deliberately Louis Reynaud bent over Tibbie, and whispered something in her ear, then bowing himself again to Miss Nesbit, preceded his sister out of the room. She kissed Tibbie, and Janet saw that her sister not only permitted the caress, but returned it. When the door closed upon the intruders, Janet looked toward Tibbie, her face flushed with indignant anger.

'Tibbie!' she said almost roughly ; 'hae ye forgottin' what is befittin' a young gentlewoman, that ye permit sic liberties in strangers ?'

'You are too strait-laced!' said Tibbie sullenly. 'Mrs. Riddell is a very nice lady. She knows how to enjoy life, at any rate, which is more than you do.'

'What richt has that ill man tae sit as near tae ye, an' whisper in yer ear ?' demanded Miss Nesbit. 'Hae ye seen him afore ?'

'At Scottrigg, three times, I telled ye, Janet.'

'Ye telt me Sandy Riddell an' his wife cam tae Scottrigg, but ye made nae mention o' the brither,' said Miss Nesbit slowly.

'Ye needna scold me, Janet Nesbit,' said Tibbie, firing up. 'I'm old enough to take care o' mysel' I winna brook tae be called to account for every word an' action as if I was a bairn.'

Miss Nesbit turned about, and went away up-stairs, dazed, bewildered, and half afraid to think what a terrible responsibility Tibbie was. For the first time in her life she realized that there might be things worse than death.

'Father, father!' she whispered, bowing her burdened head on her patient hands, 'ye didna ken hoo heavy a chairge ye left me when ye said, "Tak care o' Tibbie."'

With this terrible new anxiety concerning Tibbie, she could not go away to Scottrigg, unless she could be assured that Louis Reynaud had gone clean away from Ravelaw.

She never spoke a word on the subject to Tibbie, but many an earnest talk she had with Marget. On the Saturday, when Marget had been to Aldershope for her weekly errands, she returned with the news that Louis Reynaud had left Ravelaw for London in the morning. So there seemed to be no just impediment in the way of Miss Nesbit's visit to Scottrigg.

'I wonder ye would go away, Janet,' said Tibbie saucily when she observed her sister making preparations; 'I would have thought I couldna be left my lane at Windyknowe?'

Janet made no answer. Tibbie had spoken in the same bitter manner since the Riddells had called, and seemed bent on wounding Janet in every possible way.

On the Monday afternoon, Marjorie Scott came in the coach to Windyknowe in great glee to carry off Miss Nesbit. She was aye full of nonsense and fun, and while Janet went to get on her bonnet, began to tease Tibbie about the Frenchman's attention to her at Scottrigg. Tibbie took the teasing in good part till she heard Janet's foot in the passage, when she held up a warning finger to let Marjorie know the subject must not be mentioned in her presence.

Listening to Marjorie's blithe chatter as they drove to Scottrigg, Janet forgot her worries, and began almost to feel light of heart. Louis Reynaud being gone from Ravelaw, she need have no fear concerning Tibbie. As for Mrs. Riddell, it was not likely that she would come to Windyknowe after the way her first call had been received. So it was a very bright and peaceful-faced Janet Nesbit who thanked Lady Kate for her motherly welcome, and at the dinner-table she answered Sir Walter's jokes in a mirthful way which no little delighted him. These true friends took Janet Nesbit home to their hearts, and made very much of her in their quiet way—a new experience for her, having been rather accustomed to take care of others than be taken care of herself. The days passed pleasantly, and Marjorie declared at the end of the week that their guest looked years younger for the rest and change. She had thought to be home on Saturday afternoon, but was persuaded to remain over the Sabbath at Scottrigg. They walked to Yarrow Kirk on Sabbath morning, the road being frozen hard, and very pleasant to the feet. Miss Nesbit beheld Grizel Oliphant sitting in grim state opposite to them, and observed her face grow red when, at the beginning of the discourse, Sir Walter very deliberately composed himself for a nap in the corner.

After the service, Miss Grizzie stalked out of the church in haste, and waited in the churchyard for the party from Scottrigg. Marjorie Scott, aye ready for fun, was so amused by the old lady's appearance that she kept in behind Janet, to hide the ripple of laughter on her face; but Miss Grizzie saw it for all that.

'Weel, Miss Grizzie, hoo's the warld usin ye?' asked Sir Walter heartily.

'Middlin',' answered Miss Grizzie sourly. 'I thocht it my duty tae wait here an' reprimand ye, Walter Scott, for sleepin' in the hoose o' God. It's no seemly for a Laird, the heid o' a family, an' an elder in the Kirk.'

'I thocht I saw ye winkin' i' the kirk yersel' the day, Miss Grizzie,' said Sir Walter with a twinkle in his eye.

'That's but ill-timed mirth, Scottrigg,' said Miss Grizzie with increased sourness. 'Weel, Janet Nesbit, ye look brawly; but I misdoot ye'll no get what godly inclinations ye may have strengthened amang sic mockers as the Scotts o' Scottrigg.'

'Canny, ca' canny, Miss Grizzie,' laughed Sir Walter.

'I find my abode at Scottrigg very pleasant, Miss Grizzie—sae pleasant, indeed, that I'll be wae tae leave the morn,' said Janet.

'The morn! Then I'm thinkin' ye wasna ettlin' tae come tae my humble biggin' afore ye gaed hame?' said Miss Grizzie in a highly-offended voice.

'I didna think ye wantit me tae come, Miss Grizzie,' said Janet truthfully.

'Wha said I did? No me, I'm sure. Weel, weel, the day may come when you an' yer saucy sister 'll be glad o' auld Grizel Oliphant's shelter.'

'Isabel called for you when she was at Scottrigg, Miss Grizzie,' said Marjorie Scott.

'Oh, indeed! I'm vext. I never set een on her.'

'You must forget, Miss Grizzie,' said Marjorie. 'She had tea with you, and told us you were quite well when she came back.'

'Then she telt a lee, the biggest ane she ever telt, for I've no set een on her since Janet Nesbit there put me oot o' Aldersyde at nine o'clock at nicht,' said Miss Grizzie triumphantly.

'Come awa, lassies!' cried Sir Walter. 'Miss Grizzie, ye maun come up tae Scottrigg an' end yer crack ; it's ower cauld tae staund thrawin' here, on the Sabbath day tae.'

Miss Grizzie turned her back on Scottrigg in righteous ire.

'I'll mask tea for you an' Marjorie Scott the morn's afternune, Janet Nesbit,' she called out ; 'an' if ye dinna come an' drink it, it'll be the waur for ye—that's a'.'

So Miss Nesbit was in a manner obliged to remain another day at Scottrigg ; and on the Monday afternoon, Marjorie and she got themselves ready to go and drink tea with Miss Grizzie. She dwelt in a little cottage, standing in a well-tilled garden, by the side of the beautiful and picturesque road to Yair. There was a stable and coach-house at the back, which Miss Grizzie had caused to be built immediately on her departure from Pitcairn, for the reception of the lean brown mare and the yellow chariot, which had been specially bequeathed to her in her father's will. The furnishings of the house had been mostly removed from Pitcairn also, and were of a handsome and massive description, apt to look cumbersome in the little apartments of the cottage.

On her tea-table there was a goodly array of fine china and silver, which Miss Grizzie regarded with no small amount of affectionate pride, and which, she was wont to say, were a thorn in the flesh of her cousin's flighty wife at Pitcairn, who doubtless expected they would be hers some day, but was much mistaken.

She was dressed in her best that day to receive the young ladies from Scottrigg, and though she made use of no superfluous phrases, they felt that they were made welcome.

Marjorie had much ado to restrain her mirth sometimes ; but the time passed pleasantly till six o'clock, when they were amazed by the arrival of Walter in the coach, to bid them come home immediately, Miss Nesbit's servant having arrived from Windyknowe, desiring to see her mistress.

A terrible dread rushed into the heart of Janet Nesbit, and her fingers trembled so, she could hardly fasten her bonnet strings.

Miss Grizzie, who was devoured with curiosity regarding Marget's mission, stood by the dressing-table making all sorts of absurd surmises.

'I wadna wunner, nae, if yon limmer, Tibbie, has fa'en intae Yarrow, or broken her neck at the stair - fute, Janet Nesbit. It was a great risk leavin' her at hame hersel'; I wunner ye had the conscience tae daet. If onything happens tae her, ye'll hae remorse a' yer days.'

Grey, grey grew the face of Janet Nesbit, seeing which Marjorie's ire flew up.

'Miss Grizzie, you frightful old woman, if you don't hold your tongue, I'll make you! Never mind her silly talk, Janet. Nothing will have happened to Tibbie, only they would be very anxious about you not returning on Saturday, and Marget would come to see that you were all right.'

For the life of her, Janet Nesbit could not have spoken a word, neither did she hear Miss Grizzie bidding her good-bye, and stating her intention of coming over to Windyknowe to see what was the matter.

The Scotts having more consideration than Miss Grizzie, did not offer to speak to her during the drive home; and when they reached Scottrigg, she almost flew into the house. The servant who admitted them took her direct to the housekeeper's room, where Marget sat, with her bonnet and shawl on, the picture of impatience.

'Come awa hame, Miss Nesbit,' she said, getting up at once.

'What's happened tae Tibbie?'

'Naething yet,' returned Marget grimly. 'But Mrs. Riddell's brither's back at Ravelaw, an' there's bonnie ongauns at Windyknowe, I can tell ye.'

Miss Nesbit sat down upon a chair and covered her face with her hands. Her worst fears were realized, and the danger was thickening round Tibbie's path.

'Tell me first, Marget, an' syne we'll gang awa hame.'

'Weel, Miss Nesbit,' began Marget with a curious mixture of grief, and sympathy, and indignant shame in her voice, 'nae suner were ye awa on the Monday night than ower comes Mrs. Riddell in her coach, an' wants Miss Tibbie awa tae Ravelaw. God forgie me for settin' up tae my betters, but I daured her tae gang, an' set the leddy to the door.'

'God bless ye, Marget,' said Miss Nesbit fervently.

'The bairn was in an unco rage, but I wasna mindin' for that,' continued Marget. 'I went about my wark singin' neist mornin' thinkin' *that* was putten an' end till, when lo, in the afternune, up comes my leddy again, an' that ill man, her brither, wi' her. An' they cam in, in spite o' me ; an' Tibbie ordered me tae the kitchen, an' bade me keep my place. They bade a lang time. A' next day Tibbie was up at Ravelaw frae mornin' till nicht, an' the Frenchman brocht her hame. An' I dinna ken hoo mony mair times they hae been thegither, an' me poorless tae help. So I jist cam awa for ye, Miss Nesbit, tae come an' pit a stop tae sic ongauns, which hae been waesome tae me tae see, an' her a Nesbit o' Aldersyde !'

Miss Nesbit rose up, very white, and stern, and sharp-looking.

'I'll get my bag, Marget, an' spier if Sir Walter will gie us his coach. Can onything be happenin' tae Tibbie while we're awa ?'

'Na, na ; for I gaed down by Aldershope as I walked the day, an' telt Miss Elliot a' about it, an' askit her tae gang up tae Windyknowe till we cam back ; an' there she is the noo, for I saw her awa up i' the gig wi' my ain een.'

'God bless you, Marget,' repeated Miss Nesbit, then she went to seek Lady Scott in her own chamber, and kneeling down by her couch, told the dear motherly woman all her trouble, and begged that they might have a coach at once to take them back to Windyknowe.

'My dear, of course. This is terrible !' said her

ladyship in much concern. 'I may tell you now, that that day Tibbie went from us, saying she was going to Yair to see Miss Oliphant, she met a strange gentleman and walked with him up past Lochside. Mrs. Gray herself told me she saw them from her window. I said nothing about it to any one, but I make no doubt it was Mrs. Riddell's brother.'

'Tibbie has fa'en frae her name as a Nesbit when she stooped tae sic deceit,' said Janet almost in a wail. 'Oh, Leddy Scott, there are things waur, faur waur than death!'

Before many minutes Miss Nesbit and Marget had quitted the hospitable roof-tree of Scottrigg, and were being whirled as fast as Sir Walter's fleet thorough-breds could carry them over the long miles to Windyknowe.

CHAPTER X.

INSTEAD of looking pleased to see Mary Elliot that morning, Isabel Nesbit did not even show her the commonest courtesy. A very disagreeable person could Tibbie be when she liked ; she possessed the very knack of making those about her uncomfortable. She felt that she was being watched, and resented it ; besides, she was not easy in her mind at the prospect of seeing Janet.

Mary, feeling instinctively that she was helping her dear absent friend, did not mind Tibbie's sour looks, but sat quite coolly at her sewing in the dining-room, thereby compelling Tibbie to remain in the house. But it was dreary work sitting opposite a sulky face, and listening to the ticking of the clock, and the soughing of the winds in the firs. Nine o'clock struck before the sound of wheels broke on

her listening ear. She got up at once, and ran out
to open the door, and welcome Janet home.

Very white and haggard looked Miss Nesbit's face
in the flickering candle light, and she did not seem
to be able to utter a word, but pressing Mary's
hand, hurried past her to the dining-room. Tibbie
looked up quite unconcernedly, but her eyes did not
meet her sister's gaze.

'Tibbie!' said Janet.

Never in her life has Isabel Nesbit heard Janet
speak in such a voice.

'Well, Marget's got ye hame,' she said carelessly.

Then, to her amazement, Janet came over to her
in a swift, sudden way, and took her in her arms
with that terribly close grip with which she had
held her on the night her father died.

'Tibbie, my bairn, I hae come hame tae save ye.
Nay, dinna shrink frae me. We are twa orphan
lassies, but I'm the elder, an' ye were left in my
care,' said Janet, and holding up Tibbie's face, she
looked at it with passionate, yearning eyes. 'Tibbie,
it's no true,' she said hoarsely.

'What? Let me be; ye hurt me,' said Tibbie
pettishly. 'Whaur's Mary Elliot, wha ye set tae
watch me?'

'Bide there, see, till ye tell me,' said Miss Nesbit,
her manner changing from tender entreaty to stern
command. 'What is there between you an' that ill

man at Ravelaw?   It canna be that ye are gaun tae leave me for him, Tibbie?'

'Marget has been filling your head with nonsense, Janet,' said Tibbie defiantly. 'Mrs. Riddell called here with her brother once or twice, an' I was up at Ravelaw—that's a'. I had to do something to keep myself living when you were away.'

'Had I thocht he was still at Ravelaw, I wad never hae gane to Scottrigg,' said Miss Nesbit passionately.

'Marget should hae been surer o' her news,' said Tibbie maliciously. 'He only gaed tae Carlisle an' cam back on Monday mornin' As ye are the mistress, Janet, I hope ye'll speak sharply tae Marget for her outrageous treatment o' Mrs. Riddell. She actually told her to go away.'

A wan smile flitted across Janet's face.

'As I wad hae dune, had I been at hame,' she said drily. 'It was weel Marget was here tae uphaud the respeck o' the hoose. Ye are a puir dochter o' Aldersyde, Tibbie.'

She could not keep back the half-pitiful, half-scornful remark, she was so sorely driven. But beyond curling her red lip and tossing her head, Tibbie took no notice of it.

Seeing her young sister was only defiant and sullen, Janet went away in search of Mary, whom she found chatting with Marget at the kitchen fire. They went away up-stairs together, and talked long over the matter, and Mary's gentle sympathy did Janet's tired heart good.

'Yer bridal is comin' very near noo, my Mary,' said she tenderly. 'Is't aye a heavy thocht tae ye yet?'

'It's my weird, I think, Janet,' said Mary listlessly. 'I've ceased to fret about it. I'll make a good wife to Hugh Nesbit, and try to be a worthy mistress of your dear Aldersyde. Oh, Janet, you'll come and see me often?'

'Surely, Mary.'

Then their hands met, in seal of their friendship, and they went down-stairs again to Tibbie's sulky presence.

Early next morning Peter came up with the gig for Mary, and she bade her last good-bye to Windyknowe. Only one week, and the Lily of Aldershope must go to bloom for Hugh Nesbit in Aldersyde. She had indeed resigned herself to the inevitable, and if she was not a glad-hearted bride, she was at least a passive and uncomplaining one.

Her mother's health was failing every day. As for Doctor Elliot, having the height of his ambition to see his Mary a lady of high degree within his reach, he was to outward semblance a happy man.

Hugh Nesbit was impatient for the day when he could claim his wife. He loved her with all the love of which his selfish heart was capable. But it was not that steady, all-careful tenderness which makes a woman's heart enduringly happy, but a fierce lava tide of passion which would never last a lifetime.

The preparations moved on apace, for Doctor Elliot insisted on Mary getting a marvellous quantity of gear; and she was distracted between milliners and mantlemakers, when she would fain have spent her last days in peace at home.

The Miss Nesbits were asked to the quiet wedding. In Mrs. Elliot's state of health it did not behove them to make a great fuss or grand display; so, excepting the Miss Nesbits, there were no strangers to be at Mary's bridal.

During the week intervening between Miss Nesbit's homecoming and the wedding, Janet watched Tibbie night and day. The fear that was in her heart would not give her a moment's peace. Louis Reynaud was still at Ravelaw, but neither he nor his sister ever came near Windyknowe; and as Tibbie was never beyond the garden, surely there was nothing to fear.

On the Saturday before the wedding, Miss Nesbit being very busy, she sent Tibbie in Marget's charge down to Aldershope, with a wedding keepsake to Mary, in the shape of a pair of massive silver candlesticks, which had stood on each end of the mantelpiece in the drawing-room at Aldersyde. They came home to tea at six, Tibbie looking particularly defiant and unconcerned, and Marget worried and anxious. Instinctively Miss Nesbit went into the kitchen after Marget, while Tibbie ran up-stairs.

' I took Miss Tibbie to the door o' the doctor's, as ye bade me, ma'am,' said Marget without preface, 'an' syne gaed doon the toon for my errands. I micht be aboot half an hour, I think, an' was comin' slow up, ettlin' tae gie her time for a crack wi' Miss Mary, when tae my horror I sees her staunin' speakin' tae the Frenchman at the heid o' the toon, jist fornent Robbie Harden's door. I jist flew up to her, and grippin' her airm, says, " Come awa hame." Syne the Frenchman maks his bows till her, an' gangs awa; an' bonnie gled I was tae see his back, but hoo lang they micht be staunin' I dinna ken.'

Miss Nesbit sighed, and a sorely troubled look came upon her face. She had been trying to lull her fears to rest during the past few days ; but so long as Louis Reynaud remained at Ravelaw, there was abundant cause for apprehension.

' Oh, by the bye, Janet,' said Tibbie blithely when they sat down to tea, ' has Marget been making another long story to you? I met Mrs. Riddell's brother as I came out of Mary's, and he stopped to say good-bye, as he's going back to France in the beginning of the week, called back to fight. He would have called to make his adieu, but was afraid of Marget and you.'

'I can verra weel dispense wi' his adieu, Tibbie,' said Miss Nesbit drily.

'Janet, I believe ye thocht I would have married him,' said Tibbie with a smile of artless amusement, which made Janet involuntarily give a sigh of relief.

After that, how could she mistrust Tibbie; for if ever face expressed innocent amusement, hers did at that moment.

'I didna ken verra weel what tae think, Tibbie,' she said, and the subject was never mentioned between them again.

On the morning of the wedding-day, Tibbie complained of not feeling well, and indeed lay down on the sofa after breakfast.

'I'm afraid I can't go to the wedding, Janet,' she said dolefully; 'I can't keep my head up. I'll need to go to my bed, and let you go yourself.'

This Miss Nesbit was very loth to do, and proceeded to doctor Tibbie to the best of her ability. But when the hour came, Tibbie was looking so white, and said so positively she was unable to go, that Miss Nesbit was obliged to make ready to go herself. When she was dressed, she came down again to Tibbie, who lifted up her languid head, and looked at her sister in genuine admiration.

'Oh, Janet, how nice you look!'

Ay! she looked well in her neat mourning silk, with its delicate lace ruffles at her wrists, and about her graceful neck. Her soft hair was braided smoothly into its coil behind, and rippled in sunny ringlets on her brow. She was a sweeter woman by far than Tibbie, and one to be held in reverence.

'Come here, Janet!' said Tibbie in a queer, hurried way. 'Kneel down by me, never mind your gown, and put your arms round me like you did the first night we came here, till I whisper something to you.'

In sore amazement Janet obeyed.

'I have been a wicked, ungrateful sister to you, Janet,' sobbed Tibbie. 'I'll never be able to repay all your love and care. Can you forgive me for all the way I have done to you?'

'Ay, my bairn,' whispered Janet very low.

'In all your life, Janet, you'll never remember me as a wicked, ungrateful girl, but only as I am to-night, penitent, and very weary at heart? Promise me, Janet. Oh, I do love you, though I am such a heartbreak to you.'

'My bairn, my bairn, I promise.'

Very close did Miss Nesbit hold her young sister, and the whispered words were almost a benediction. Tibbie felt hot tears on her clasped hands, and, putting her arms about Janet's neck, kissed her for the first time for years. Such endearments had never been frequent between them.

'Now run away an' see Mary made the lady of Aldersyde, an' kiss her for me, an' wish her joy. An' be sure an' bring me the bit bridecake wi' the ring in it, so that I may dream of Walter Scott.'

Miss Nesbit rose up and departed into the kitchen, to give certain charges to Marget concerning Tibbie. Then, it being four o'clock, it behoved her to get away down to Aldershope, as the wedding was to be at half-past five.

When she reached the house, she found that all the invited guests, chiefly relatives of the Elliots, had already arrived.

The bride being in the hands of two aunts, who were assisting her to get her gown on, Miss Nesbit could not expect a private word with her. But before she had got herself seated in the drawing-room, one of the aunts, a grim spinster from Kelso, came down-stairs and requested Miss Nesbit to come with her, as the bride desired to see her.

She followed the lady up-stairs to the room where Mary stood, a lily indeed in her bridal robes, which were no whiter than her face. She shook hands with Janet, then looked toward the aunts, as if desiring them to withdraw. They, however, did not take the hint, whereupon Mary took Janet's arm, and leading her into the adjoining room, shut the door.

'Mary, will ye be able tae get through it?' asked Janet anxiously.

'Oh yes; I'm not one of the fainting maidens,' said Mary with a wan smile. 'I am a fair bride, they say,' she added, pointing to her finery. 'Is it not a mockery to deck me in these garments? Oh, Janet! better like I had been nursing my dying mother, than decking me for my bridal.'

'Wheesht, my lamb; yer dear mither will be spared tae ye for mony a year yet, please God,' said Janet tenderly.

Mary shook her head. Then an impatient knock at the door warned them that time was passing.

'Bless me, Janet!' faltered Mary. 'Speak some true, strong words to me. I am so weak and frail; you are so brave and stedfast. Oh! Janet, if I have you for a friend, and Aldersyde to live for, I may be happier than I trow to-night.'

'In years tae come, my dear,' said Janet, 'ither ties will rise up tae mak ye strong, an' gled o' heart, an' bairnies' hands will gie ye the sunshine for the cloud.'

Then she laid her hand on the trembling girl's

shoulder, and looked straight into her mournful eyes, her own shining stedfastly.

'The Lord bless ye, my freend, an' gie ye peace in yer new life; an' if there be tribulation, help ye tae bear it; an' syne in His guid time, tak ye tae His rest.'

The solemn service was over, and Hugh Nesbit and Mary Elliot stood side by side, husband and wife. She looked as if she were in a dream, and when Hugh touched her arm and bade her sign the register, she started and did not seem to comprehend him.

Being sore afraid lest their niece should mar the harmony of the proceedings by any display of feeling, the grim aunts hurried her away, reminding her she must change her gown to travel to Carlisle.

Miss Nesbit saw her no more till she came down-stairs to get into her husband's coach.

Then having a word to say to Hugh Nesbit, Janet slipped out of the open door, and touched his arm.

'Ye hae gotten a dear young wife the day, Hugh Nesbit; be gentle wi' her,' she said almost prayerfully.

No man is wholly bad. What better feelings slumbered in Hugh Nesbit's heart were roused then, and shone in his face, in the moment's emotion.

'I'll try,' he whispered back in tones as earnest as her own.

'Ye hae ta'en a heavy vow upon yersel',' she added solemnly. 'The Lord deal wi' you as you deal wi' Mary, Hugh Nesbit. Fare ye weel.'

Then she had but time to clasp Mary's hand, and bid her a broken God - speed, for already the coachman was on the box, and the restive horses impatient to be gone.

'What is often a pleasant duty, did not come so pleasantly to me to-day,' said Mr. Bourhill to Miss Nesbit as they returned up-stairs.

She looked at him questioningly, and saw that he divined the nature of the marriage.

'I pray it may turn out better than we anticipate, Mr. Bourhill,' she made answer, and she heard him say under his breath, 'Amen!'

Miss Nesbit remained behind the other guests to comfort awhile the ailing and desolate mother. In his study alone sat the doctor, not greatly caring to seek his wife.

About eight o'clock Miss Nesbit rose to go away home, promising that if Tibbie were no worse, she would come down to Aldershope early in the morning, and spend part of the day with Mrs. Elliot.

Peter had the gig ready at the door, and while he went for another wrap, Doctor Elliot, who was standing by the horse's head, turned round to Miss Nesbit and said almost roughly:

'Are you one of those, Miss Nesbit, who think and say that my daughter has been forced into a marriage entirely against her wish or inclination.'

'I hae said naething, though I hae my ain thochts,' answered Miss Nesbit quietly. 'But noo since ye ask me, I'm no sweer tae say that had Mary got her way, she wadna hae been Hugh Nesbit's wife the day; an' brawly ye ken that, Doctor Elliot.'

Peter returned at this moment, and the doctor without answering, helped her into the gig, and bade her good night.

It was a grand night. In a cloudless sky many stars were shining, and above solemn Bourhope a young moon was coming up shyly. A weird and lovely light enveloped Aldersyde. No sound broke the stillness, and the very air was redolent of tranquillity and peace.

In Miss Nesbit's quiet heart there was no prevision of sorrow, no foreshadowing of the cloud which had already fallen upon her hearth.

Whenever Marget heard the sound of wheels approaching Windyknowe, she ran to open the door.

'Guid nicht, Peter,' said Miss Nesbit as she alighted. 'Weel, Marget, hoo's Tibbie?'

'I hinna been up this while, ma'am. I gae her her gruel as ye bade me, an' carried up a spunk o' fire, an' left her sittin' beside it. She said she wad sit up till ye cam hame; so I jist gaed awa intae the back kitchen tae my ironin', an' I never heard a cheep sin' syne. If she had wantit onything, she wad hae rung.'

Strange that to-night, also, Marget Drysdale should be ironing, even as she had been the day the Laird of Aldersyde died.

Without a thought of evil, Miss Nesbit ran lightly up-stairs, and entered Tibbie's room. The fire had burned low in the grate, but there was light sufficient to see that the place was empty. A strange chill fear crept into Janet's heart, though she told herself Tibbie might be in the dining-room. She was about to go in search of her, when her eye fell on a scrap of paper lying on the little table by Tibbie's chair on the hearth. She reached out a trembling hand for it, and bent over the firelight to decipher what was written on it.

'I am away,' it said. 'Oh, Janet, try and think kindly of poor wayward Tibbie!'

'Gude Lord, whaur's the bairn?' asked Marget's voice in absolute dumfoundered amazement.

Then a cry ran through the quiet house, the like

of which Marget Drysdale never heard before or after, and Miss Nisbet turned round her ashen face, and pressing her hands to her head, said in a low, bewildered way:

'She's awa, Marget. I hinna ta'en care o' Tibbie; I hinna ta'en care o' Tibbie!'

END OF BOOK I.

BOOK II.
THE BAIRNS.

CHAPTER I.

REBECCA FORD had been quarrelling with her mistress, and had received her dismissal from Ravelaw. It was not the first time that Mrs. Riddell, in a fit of passion, had given her presuming attendant warning ; therefore, thinking it likely that her mistress would once more repent when her temper cooled, Rebecca discreetly quitted her presence, and wrapping a shawl about her, went out for a breath of the morning air.

It was nine o'clock, the servants' breakfast hour at Ravelaw, but Rebecca did not sit down at their table. The Laird had already breakfasted alone, dinner being the only meal at which he might expect the company of his wife.

Just as Rebecca stepped out of the hall door, she

beheld, greatly to her astonishment, the figure of a lady coming swiftly up the avenue towards the house. Very composedly she stood leaning against the lintel waiting for the visitor, and her astonishment was considerably increased when she recognised Miss Nesbit of Aldersyde.

'Can I see Mr. Riddell?' asked Miss Nesbit, putting back her veil from her colourless face.

'He's not in, ma'am,' answered our Rebecca with a very respectful curtsey. 'Will the mistress do?'

'Yes; be good enough to tell Mrs. Riddell that Miss Nesbit of Windyknowe desires to speak with her for a minute,' said Miss Nesbit, and being invited to enter the house, followed Rebecca across the handsome hall and into the library.

Magnificent without and within was the home of the Riddells; but though Miss Nisbet had never before set foot upon its threshold, the errand upon which she had come diverted her thoughts from what might have been interesting to her at another time.

Greatly exercised regarding Miss Nesbit's visit to Ravelaw at so untimely an hour, Rebecca shut the library door and went up-stairs to her mistress's chamber, where that lady sat in an elegant morning gown of pink cashmere, sipping her chocolate, and gazing absently into the fire.

'Is that you, Rebecca?' she asked in clear, sharp tones. 'I thought I told you not to come into my presence any more, you presuming creature.'

'Miss Nesbit from Windyknowe is in the library, ma'am, and would speak with you,' said Rebecca. 'I met her at the door, and was obliged to announce her, the rest of the servants being at breakfast.'

Mrs. Riddell changed colour, and then hastily rose.

'Get me a cap, Rebecca, sharply, and come and brush my hair,' she said ; and Rebecca, perceiving that her mistress would likely again retract her dismissal words, flew to obey.

A very fair picture made the lady of Ravelaw when she swept into the presence of Miss Nesbit. The bright rich colour of her gown became her dark beauty well, and its ample train gave to her figure the grace and dignity of a queen. She was, indeed, a strong contrast to Miss Nesbit's slight, insignificant, plainly-robed figure, standing expectantly by the table.

But instinctively Sandy Riddell's brilliant wife shrank into herself, for there was something in the resolute face of Janet Nesbit which made her feel uncomfortably nervous. Nevertheless, she went forward, and would have embraced her, had

not Miss Nesbit very pointedly taken a step back-
ward.

'What! Not a greeting, when we are by this
time sisters - in - law?' she said with a pretty
grimace of surprise.

'Then, it *is* true, Mrs. Riddell,' said Miss Nesbit
in clear, sharp, forced tones; 'and I have come
tae the richt person tae seek my puir misguided
sister?'

'You express yourselves so oddly here in Scotland,' said Mrs. Riddell, shrugging her shoulders,
'I don't quite understand what you say. Let
me tell you the charming little story correctly.
Louis loved your pretty sister to distraction,
she returned his passion, but we all knew you
would never consent to a union; so we laid
our heads together, and decided to make your
sister happy without your leave. Was it not a
charitable'—

'I'll dispense wi' sic questions, Mrs. Riddell,'
said Janet Nesbit in a strange stifled way. 'Proceed, and be as brief as ye can.'

'There is no need to look so agonized, to
speak in that absurd way, Miss Nesbit. Your
sister has got a good husband, who loves her
tenderly, and their marriage is a charming romance.
They left Windyknowe last night in a coach
and pair from here, and were to change horses

at Tushielaw Inn; and all going well, they hoped to be married this morning at that most convenient place for runaway lovers — Gretna, is it? There, then, that is all,' said Mrs. Riddell with a gleam of triumph in her black eyes.

'I thank you for the truth, Mrs. Riddell,' said Miss Nesbit in a low voice, and began to move toward the door.

'Stay,' said the lady of Ravelaw. 'Breakfast is laid in the morning-room. You have had a long walk; rest awhile, and break bread at our table.'

Miss Nesbit could almost have smiled. Break bread beneath the roof-tree of the faithless Riddells, and on this day of all days!

'I thank ye for yer offered kindness, Mrs. Riddell,' she made answer; 'it may be weel meant, but it is wasted on me. Permit me tae wish ye guid-day.'

So saying, she very quietly passed the lady of Ravelaw, and went away out of the house. Quietly, did I say? The wildest storm which had ever swept over Bourhope was nothing to the tempest in Janet Nesbit's breast. But the old indomitable spirit, the resolute will which had been handed down to her from an iron-souled ancestry, enabled her to show a front outwardly calm. She had not gone many yards along the avenue, and Mrs. Riddell was still watching her from the window of the morning-room, when out from among the trees came the Laird of Ravelaw. He looked haggard and ill at ease, but he stood in the middle of the way, evidently for the purpose of meeting Miss Nesbit, and she was obliged to stand.

'I saw you go into the house, Janet,' he said in a strange, low, humble voice, as if he expected some punishment at her hands.

Then a change swept across the face of Janet Nesbit, like the first wave of a great storm.

'Sandy Riddell!' she cried in a hoarse, bitter wail. 'Was't no enough that ye made me desolate in the simmer o' my days? Could ye no leave me my sister, a' I had upon the earth?'

Down dropped Sandy Riddell's eyes beneath the scathing rebuke.

'As I live, Janet, I had no hand in this, and would have helped it if I could,' he said in tones she could not doubt.

Only one question more she would fain ask before she passed on, one which she had been too proud to put to the lady of Ravelaw.

'I believe ye are speakin' truth, Sandy Riddell. Weel, will ye tell me noo, if that man has the wherewithal tae keep Tibbie; or has she gaen tae beggary as weel's misery?'

'He is able to keep her in comfort if he likes, Janet—that's all I can tell you.'

'If he likes!' echoed Miss Nesbit in her heart. Sandy Riddell knew the man well, and the words implied much.

'I hae but anither thing tae ask at yer haunds, Sandy Riddell,' she said with dreary calmness. 'If ye ever see Tibbie mair, maybe ye'll tell her that I forgie her, an' that as lang as I live, she'll find a hame ony day, an' a' days, at Windy-knowe?'

Then she bowed her head, and would have passed on; but the Laird of Ravelaw touched her arm, and bent yearning, passionate eyes on her face.

'I would to God, Janet, that ye had been my wife this day, instead of yon black-browed woman who has brought only trouble on Ravelaw. I have sinned, but I have suffered, and the hardest of my punishment is the thought of what might have been.'

Ah, that mournful refrain, the saddest in any tongue; it has been echoed in desolate hearts since the world began, and will till the world is done.

'Life is fu' o' care,' returned Miss Nesbit in a

low, gentle way; 'an' a'body maun bear their ain. But let us mak the best o' the guid we hae, an' keep oor minds set on the sure hope which is tae come. God be wi' ye, Sandy Riddell, an' mak ye mair mindfu' o' Him in time tae come than ye hae been in time past.'

Then she went on her way, scarcely seeing where she was going, only longing to place miles between herself and Ravelaw. Despair had made her feet swift and untiring for her early walk from Windyknowe; but now that suspense was ended, physical strength failed, till her limbs could scarcely sustain her tottering weight.

It was almost mid-day when Marget Drysdale's anxious vigil at the gate of Windyknowe was ended, and her strained eyes caught sight of her beloved mistress toiling up the brae. Heedless of the deserted house, and of the door left open to all intruders, Marget flew down the road to offer the support of her strong arm. She could endure much, but the suspense of the last few hours had been almost more than she could bear.

'My certy, yer legs 'll be braw tired noo,' she said abruptly and sharply. 'Weel, hae ye gotten ony-thing for yer trail to Ravelaw?'

'I hae gotten mair than I bargained for, Marget,' returned Miss Nesbit, taking the offered arm, and leaning very heavily upon it. 'Tibbie's a marriet wife noo ; so we'll jist hae tae settle doon thegither at Windyknowe, you an' me, and leave the bairn wi' a mercifu' God. I doot she'll hae sair need of His help yet.'

'She's made her bed, an' she can lie on't, noo, I suppose,' said Marget snappishly, but turned her face away, poor soul, to hide the tears raining down her cheeks.

To think that Tibbie, 'her braw bairn,' whom she had hoped to see reigning at Scottrigg, should have chosen such a thorny path of life, so different in all ways from that befitting a daughter of Aldersyde, was more than she could bear. She was glad to run away into the back kitchen, and take her 'greet,' while Miss Nesbit shut herself into her own chamber. When Marget heard the key turned in the lock, she knew that for a time even she dare not intrude, and rocking herself to and fro on her stool, she cried between her sobs :

'Lord! Lord! hae ye forgotten godly Walter Nesbit's bairns a' thegither ? '

In a little while she rose, and stirring up the smouldering fire, set on the kettle to make tea for Miss Nesbit, whose fast had not been broken since she partook of Mary Elliot's bridal feast. When it was ready and set out on a little table drawn close up to the hearth, Marget slipped softly up-stairs and tapped at the locked door.

'I hae made a cup o' tea, Miss Nesbit. For guidsake, come doon an' tak a mouthful, or I'll hae ye ill on my hands,' she whispered through the keyhole.

'By and by, Marget,' Miss Nesbit made answer, and with that Marget was forced to be content.

Nearly another hour slipped away, then the first visitor came up to the door of Windyknowe. It was Mr. Bourhill on his sturdy cob, which was flaked with foam, as if it had ridden many miles that day.

'I'll just leave Chestnut here, Marget; he will stand like a lamb,' said Mr. Bourhill. 'Can I see Miss Nesbit?'

'Come in, sir, an' I'll speer,' said Marget, and ushering him into the dining-room, went up once more to her mistress's door.

'Here's the minister, mem. I hae put him i' the ben end, an' ye *maun* come doon,' she said desperately.

Miss Nesbit opened the door at once, and Marget saw that though her face was haggard and worn, she had shed no tears.

'Eh, mem, this is a waefu' day! I never thocht I wad hae leeved tae see sic a day for the Nesbits!' she said, and putting out her hand, touched her mistress's slender fingers with great gentleness.

Then Miss Nesbit took the rough red hand in her

own, and laid her cheek against it a moment, saying in a dry, weary voice, 'Oh! Marget, Marget!'

Then she went away down very quietly to Mr. Bourhill in the dining-room. They shook hands in silence, and Miss Nesbit with difficulty motioned him to a chair.

'Did you wonder why I delayed my coming so long?' he asked, striving to speak calmly.

'No; I hae thocht o' but ae thing the day, Mr. Bourhill, an' it has been ower muckle for me,' she answered. 'I needna ask hae ye heard?'

'Doctor Elliot told me this morning in Aldershope before seven o'clock,' returned the minister, 'and I set off at once.'

Miss Nesbit visibly started.

'Where tae Mr. Bourhill?'

'To follow them, and bring back news good or bad for you.'

'Weel?'

'I had no difficulty in learning all I wanted to know. They were married this morning at Gretna about nine o'clock, and immediately afterwards continued their journey to London,' said Mr. Bourhill, and turned away towards the window, not caring at that moment to look upon the face of Miss Nesbit.

When he turned to her again, he saw that

she was weeping. God alone knew what it was to him to see her thus, and be denied the privilege of trying to comfort her as he longed to do.

'God comfort you,' he said, using the words which had fallen like balm on her heart that dreary November morning, when her father lay dead in the west bedroom at Aldersyde. Then he went away out of the house.

By and by Marget slipped in, and to her delight was desired to light the dining-room fire, and bring in the tea-tray. 'For oor wark an' oor life maun gang on,' said Miss Nesbit, 'though we hae nae heart tae pit in't.'

When Miss Nesbit was sitting at her solitary meal, she was disturbed by a great rattling and rumbling of wheels coming nearer the house, and shortly she beheld the yellow chariot from Yair draw up at the door.

Before she had time to recover from her surprise, Miss Grizzie stalked into the room, having on her usual satin gown and towering head-gear, and positively trembling from head to foot with curiosity and excitement. Miss Nesbit rose up, and certainly the look on her face was hardly one of welcome. Little cared Grizel Oliphant for that. She had come to hear the details of Tibbie's flight, and had no intention of departing without them.

'So that glaiket sister o' yours has gien ye the slip at last, Janet Nesbit,' she exclaimed shrilly. 'A bonnie doonfa' tae yer pride, this 'll be. I heard it this forenune in Yair, from Doctor Elliot, an' cam awa owre as sune I got a bite o' denner. When did she gang? Whaur is she? An' is she mairret, think ye?'

'Tibbie was mairret tae Louis Reynaud at Gretna this morning, Miss Grizzie,' said Miss Nesbit, forcing herself as of yore to answer her kinswoman's questions calmly; 'an' she's awa tae Lunnon—that's a' there is tae tell.'

'A' ye *wull* tell, ye mean,' said Miss Grizzie savagely. 'I'm yer bluid relation, an' though I got nae muckle courtesy frae yer mother Isabel Shepherd o' Staunin-stane in her lifetime, for yer faither's sake I hae an' interest in ye, an' maun hae the oots an' ins o' this. I heard ye were up at Ravelaw. What passed there, micht I spier?'

'Ye may spier, but that 'll be a' the length ye'll get, Miss Grizzie,' said Miss Nesbit with reddening cheek and kindling eye. 'I kenna what brings ye tae me aye in the middle o' my tribulations, tae mak them waur tae thole.'

'It wad seem that a' yer tribulations canna humble that thrawn speerit o' yours, Janet

M

Nesbit,' said Grizel Oliphant sourly. 'Weel, I dinna envy ye yer conscience, when ye think o' the puir strayed bairn. Ye had nae richt stravagin' aboot Scottrigg, an' her at hame hersel''

'Oh, Miss Grizzie, wheesht!' cried Miss Nesbit, her voice sharp with pain.

To have such a stab given to her was more than she could bear. Delighted was Miss Grizzie to find that she had struck home.

'An' what for should I wheesht?' she queried shrilly. 'It's nae mair than a'body 'll say, an' nae mair than ye deserve.'

Miss Nesbit turned away a moment, and gathered all her much tried patience to enable her to present an outward appearance of calmness at least to her unfeeling kinswoman.

'Tak aff yer bannet, Miss Grizzie,' she said at length, 'an' bid Tammas tak oot the beast. Marget will mask anither cup o' tea for ye.'

'Na, na! Muckle obleeged, I'm sure, Miss Nesbit; but I hae a roof-tree o' my ain, thank the Lord, and need tae be behauden tae naebody, let alane you. I only cam tae express my neeborly sympathy; but happen tae ye what likes, ye'll see my face nae mair this side o' Yair Brig,' with which Grizel Oliphant, having for the second time washed her hands of the Nesbits, took her wrathful departure from Windyknowe. As her coach drove past the kitchen window, Marget very deliberately shook her fist at its irate occupant, which very nearly sent Miss Grizzie into hysterics.

CHAPTER II.

'A dreary home-coming, and a desolate hearth.'

WHEN Hugh Nesbit brought his young wife home to Aldersyde one evening early in March, she found spring already there to welcome her. Every tree and hedgerow was delicately, freshly green, birds twittered and sang on every budding bough, the early flowerets nodded their heads cheerily in the gentle air.

She had seen the bloom of many spring times in that lovely spot, and in her childish days had helped Janet Nesbit to find the first violet and primrose, and later the red-rowan and purple bramble, in the den of Aldersyde. How little either of them recked in these days of this home-coming.

They drove in a close carriage; but when they neared the house, she pulled down one of the windows, and looked out with dim yearning eyes upon her home.

'We will try to be worthy of Aldersyde, Hugh,' she said, turning to her husband, and speaking almost wistfully.

He laughed, and answered back that the first thing was to make it worth possessing, as in its poverty-stricken state it hardly repaid the trouble it was to a man.

He spoke almost rudely, for already Hugh Nesbit was tiring of his six weeks' bride. He was not a man who could love unselfishly. It galled him to see that, though gentleness itself, his wife never assumed the love she did not feel. She showed him plainly, indeed, that she would only give him wifely duty, not wifely love.

A throng of new servants waited in the hall of Aldersyde for their master and mistress. Young Mrs. Nesbit glanced timidly round the faces, which were all strange to her, then passed on with a slight bow. At the door of the dining-room Doctor Elliot met her, and held out his hand in greeting; but Mary looked beyond him, and interrupted his words of welcome by the question:

'Is mother here?'

'No; she has not been so well lately, and was unable to come to Aldersyde to-day. She will expect you to-morrow.'

'Is she *much* worse, father?'

'She is very weak,' he was obliged to answer, and turned to welcome profusely his son-in-law, the Laird of Aldersyde.

Then one of the servants, an elderly person with a pleasant face and kindly eyes, came forward, curtseying respectfully.

'I am Susan Gordon, the housekeeper, ma'am; may I show you to your rooms? They have been made ready for you.'

Mrs. Nesbit made a gentle assent, and followed her up the familiar staircase to the west bedroom with the two windows, one looking up the Yarrow, and the other on the Loch of the Lowes.

'This is the room where the old Laird died, I believe, Mrs. Nesbit,' said the housekeeper. 'If you do not like it'—

'Every room in Aldersyde is alike familiar to me, Susan,' said her mistress with a faint smile. 'This one will do very well. Just leave me for a little; I shall ring if I want anything.'

'Can I not help you with your dressing, ma'am?' asked Susan, drawn to the gentle young creature in a marvellous fashion.

'No, thanks; I shall not change my gown to-night. I am much fatigued, and will retire early. Let dinner be taken in at once,' returned Mrs. Nesbit, and began to unfasten her bonnet strings.

The servant respectfully withdrew, and her mistress made haste with her dressing, not daring to pause a moment to think. Countless memories thronged about her heart, and countless fears of the future.

The gentlemen were glad of her entrance into the dining-room, for their conversation was constrained. Neither liked the other, though at all times their behaviour was studiously courteous.

Very quietly did Mary take her place, for the first time, at the head of her husband's table, without any show of that glad pride which might have been looked for in the mistress of lovely Aldersyde. While the servant was in the room, they talked chiefly about London and other places they had visited; but to her father's questions Mary returned but indifferent answers, her heart being in her mother's sick-room at Aldershope. But when dessert was placed on the table, the conversation turned immediately upon the secret marriage of Isabel Nesbit.

' How does Janet bear it ? ' Mary asked.

The doctor shrugged his shoulders.

' Did anybody ever see Janet Nesbit's innermost self ? I believe she is a woman devoid of feeling of any kind. I shall never forget her unnatural indifference at the time of her father's death '—

Mary could have smiled. So the world judged
or rather misjudged Janet Nesbit. She was a
woman known to the few, not to the many.

'I saw Isabel in London,' she said by and by.

Hugh Nesbit looked up from the apple he was
paring, and looked suspiciously at his wife.

'You did not think it worth your while to
mention the fact to me,' he said with a slight
sneer.

'You guess correctly, Hugh,' she answered
serenely. 'It was in Regent's Park one day,
father, while Hugh went to speak to a gentleman, and left me alone a few minutes. I saw
her pass in a coach.'

'Did she see you?' asked Hugh Nesbit.

'Yes; I spoke to her.'

'What did she say?' asked Doctor Elliot in
the old commanding way.

'She only gave me a message for her sister,
which is not mine to repeat; but she looked
well and happy,' returned Mary. 'Hugh, if you
are quite ready, I shall retire, and leave father
and you to your wine.'

Hugh Nesbit rose and opened the door for
his wife. She bowed slightly in acknowledgment,
just as she would have done to the merest
stranger. Hugh Nesbit bit his lip, and an ugly
light crept into his eyes. His father-in-law looked

at his scowling face when he resumed his seat, and smiled in a pleasant way, as if he enjoyed it.

'I am afraid you find your wife just a little indifferent, shall I call it, Hugh?' he said, poising a piece of apple neatly on his knife.

Whereupon the Laird of Aldersyde very deliberately swore at his father-in-law, and bade him mind his own concerns if he desired to keep his seat at the table. Not thinking it desirable to quarrel openly with his daughter's husband, Doctor Elliot took the hint, and discreetly changed the subject. They did not sit very long over their wine, for presently the doctor rose, and said he would bid his daughter good-night and go home, as in all likelihood he would be in request at some sick-bed.

Both went up-stairs to the drawing-room, to find Mary sitting alone in the front window, the long shadows of the twilight falling all about her. She rose and bade her father a brief good-night; then returned to her musing watching of the night creeping over Bourhope. By and by she became aware that she was not alone, and started to see her husband standing close beside her. He was quick to note how her face changed, and how she seemed to shrink involuntarily from him.

'Well, Mary, we are likely to have a lively life if

you are always to be as cheerful as you have been to-night,' he said grimly.

'I am tired, Hugh,' she pleaded, and as she said the words there rushed into her heart a wild yearning to be able in all sincerity to turn to her husband and find her best resting-place on his breast. But love cannot be forced, so she sat perfectly still, trying to conquer the impulse to flee from his presence.

Oh, but theirs was a mockery of marriage, a dreary home-coming, and a desolate, loveless hearth. God pity and help them ! I believe both felt it at that moment.

'I think I must go up-stairs, Hugh,' she faltered, feeling that she could not keep her composure much longer. 'To-morrow, perhaps, I shall be better able to look at all you have done to make Alder-syde comfortable for me.'

So passed their first evening at home.

Early next forenoon, while the Laird of Alder-syde was riding round his estate, his wife went away alone in the coach to Aldershope. She dismissed it at her father's gate, and without knocking, entered the house, and ran lightly up to her mother's room. To her surprise she found her in bed, apparently asleep. The weeks of Mary's absence had wrought such a woful change in the dear face, that for the moment the daughter, who loved her, was well-nigh overwhelmed. She knelt down by the bed, and hiding her face in the coverlet, gave way to the pent-up grief of her heart. Thus Mrs. Elliot found her on her awakening. For a moment there was nothing said, but the long, close, lingering clasp was enough.

'I have prayed, Mary, that I might be spared till you come home,' said Mrs. Elliot feebly.

'Mother! mother! it is not so near as that?' whispered Mary brokenly.

'You can see for yourself, my darling; and save for leaving you, I am content. Where is your husband?'

'At home,' answered Mary with a sudden hardness in her voice.

'Mary!' Feebly the weak hands pressed the firm white fingers of the child she loved. 'Are you nearer to your husband in heart than you were on your wedding-day, or have you drifted farther apart?'

'We need not discuss my marriage; whatever it may be, neither of us can remedy it. Let us speak of you. I came to see you, to be with you, to comfort you, as I used to do,' said Mary in the same hard dry way, and rising up, laid aside her bonnet and shawl. At that moment a servant entered the room, saying that Miss Nesbit was in the drawing-room.

'She's a faithful friend, Janet Nesbit, Mary,'

said Mrs. Elliot; 'hardly a day has passed without bringing her to see me.'

A tear trembled on Mary's eyelid. None knew better than she how faithful a heart beat in Janet Nesbit's bosom.

'I'll go down and speak a moment with her, mother,' said she, and went away to the drawing-room, slipping in so softly that Janet was unaware of her presence till she felt a gentle arm steal about her neck and a cheek pressed to hers.

'Mary,' she said, the word breaking from her lips almost in a sob; then she clasped her close in her arms and added tremulously, 'Welcome hame, Mary, thrice welcome tae Aldersyde. Ye look weel, my dear; I wad fain believe ye happier than ye thocht tae be.'

'Oh, I am quite well,' returned Mary, averting her eyes for a moment. 'Janet, this trouble has left its mark on you. You look twenty years older, and there are grey threads among your hair which I never saw before.'

'Ay, the storm will leave its mark even efter it be past, Mary,' returned Miss Nesbit in a low voice.

'It *is* past, then?' said Mary inquiringly.

'I hae learned tae cast my care on God, Mary, an' leave my bairn wi' Him. He can uphaud through mony tribulations.'

There was a moment's silence. Looking upon

the brave, stedfast face of Janet Nesbit, Mary honoured and loved her at that moment above anything on earth.

'I saw her in London, Janet,' she said by and by.

A gleam of intense eagerness flashed into Janet's eyes, and Mary answered the mute question at once.

'She bid me tell you, Janet, that she was well and happy, and but for you, did not regret leaving Windyknowe.'

'The man, Mary; was he wi' her?' asked Miss Nesbit after a time.

'Yes, sitting beside her in the coach. I do not like his face, Janet.'

'I wish his face be na the best o' him,' said Janet shortly. 'She lookit weel an' happy, ye say?'

'Yes, and so gaily attired that I would not have known her but for the bonnie face under the nodding feathers. I have seen none so bonnie as Tibbie in all my travels, Janet.'

Miss Nesbit sighed.

'A bonnie face 'll no dae muckle for a body without the grace o' God. Gaily attired, was she? Has she laid aside her mourning already?'

'Yes.'

'Well, truly, a mourning gown would ill befit a new married wife,' said Janet with a dry smile.

'I judge a body by my ain sombre feelin's, which are faur enough frae gay attire. How's Mrs. Elliot the day?'

'Very weak. Ah, Janet, you and me have no had much joyfulness in our lives! We are not likely to forget that man is born to trouble, as the Book says.'

A faint smile flitted across the face of Miss Nesbit.

Ay; but greater will be the reward, Mary. Weel, I'll be awa again, an' no' disturb Mrs. Elliot the day. Tell her I'm awa tae Scottrigg for a bit, tae get the coddlin' she's aye tellin' me I need. Oh, Mary! Marjorie Scott's a blythe bairn, perfect sunshine in a hoose.'

'Bring her back with you, and all come up to me at Aldersyde, then,' said Mary. 'It has sore need of sunshine, though the spring is bonnie all about it. Now run away, and don't stay too long: we in Aldershope cannot spare you, Janet.' Then with a warm hand clasp, the friends parted once more.

At sundown the coach from Aldersyde drew up at Doctor Elliot's gate, and the man said he had been sent for Mrs. Nesbit. She went down herself, and bade him tell the Laird, that Mrs. Elliot was so ill she would remain all night with her —a message which he seemed loth to take.

'What carriage was that, Mary?' asked her mother when she returned to the room.

'Hugh sent it for me, mother,' answered Mary gently; 'but I returned a message, saying I could not leave you.'

'You should not have done that, my child. Your husband claims your first attention.'

'I do not know how other women feel, but to me, in comparison with my mother, my husband is as nothing. So here I stay in the meantime. Do not let us talk of it, mother, if you please.'

But Mrs. Elliot could not rest.

'If he sends again, promise me you will go, Mary,' she said uneasily. 'You must try and live at peace with Hugh Nesbit: you are his wife, and owe him wifely duty.'

'It is not my nature to live at enmity, dear mother,' answered Mary.

'I know it; but there is a quiet warfare carried on without words, which has more bitter issues than open quarrelling. Avoid it, and '—

Doctor Elliot's entrance at that moment interrupted their talk. His brow darkened, and he cast a look of displeased surprise on his daughter.

'Did you send your husband's carriage home?' he asked harshly.

'I did,' was all she answered, and busied herself about her mother's pillows.

'He will be angry—justly so,' he continued sternly. 'Your place is at Aldersyde.'

'Father!' Mary drew herself to her full height, and looked at him as the Mary of old had never dared to do. 'My mother is dying, and my place is by her side. The time is gone for you to tell me what my duty is.'

Strange words to fall from the lips of the Lily of Aldershope! Little wonder that her father turned away unable to answer, for she had struck straight home.

Before ten o'clock next morning down came the coach from Aldersyde again, and the servant brought the message to Mrs. Nesbit, that she must return to Aldersyde immediately, such being the Laird's express desire.

For a moment she rebelled, but the dumb entreaty in her mother's eyes conquered, and she went to make herself ready without a word. Then she knelt down by her mother's bed, and bade her a solemn farewell, both feeling it was the last. In the bitterness of her pain, she could not re-echo her mother's assurance that sundered hearts would be re-united in another and happier world.

Strange thoughts chased each other through her aching brain, during her lonely drive to her home. She was only beginning to realize that

she was bound to Hugh Nesbit, tied down by
the letter of her marriage vow to obey him
in all things. Therefore, whatever he might
require of her,—ay, to the very leaving of her
mother in her dying hour,—it behoved her to
submit. Galling were the fetters, but they must
be borne ; and as she drove up through the
budding trees to Aldersyde, she resolved to take
up anew the yoke of her unblessed wifehood,
and bear it with all meekness and patience. For
her it was the better way. With that thought
uppermost in her mind, she crossed the threshold
of her husband's home, and sought him in the
study.

He was sitting moodily by the table, evidently
nursing his wrath for a war of words.

'I have come home, Hugh, as you desired,'
she said simply, and bent her great sad eyes
on his face. 'I am sorry if I vexed you by
staying in Aldershope last night.'

'You ought to have come when the carriage
was sent,' he said sullenly.

'My mother is dying, Hugh,' she answered
with a break in her voice; 'is it a wonder that
I had no thought for anything but her?'

He noted the deep, sad undertone of tenderness
in her voice, and the unspeakable yearning in
her eyes, and hated her for the love which

prompted it. She was his wife, but he had no place in her heart. It needed no words to tell him that, the commonest perception could not have failed to read it in her face when he was by. The brief passion of a day, kindled by her gentle beauty, had long since burned out, and her unconcealed dislike of him raised the devil within him.

'You hate me, I know,' he said slowly; 'but you are my wife—mine, do you hear?—and I can compel you to obey me. I forbid you to go to Aldershope again, and you must make ready for a journey to Edinburgh to-morrow. I am sick to death of this dreary hole.'

Ashen pale grew the face of Mary Nesbit, but she bowed her head meekly, and made answer in a low, quiet voice:

'I shall be ready, as you wish, to-morrow.' Then she turned about, and went away out of the room, the burden of her yoke pressing very heavily on her heart. How would it end?

On the morrow, when a messenger came in hot haste to Aldersyde, to summon Mrs. Nesbit to her mother's death-bed, he was told that the Laird and his lady had gone off in the early morning to Edinburgh, leaving no message behind, or any word concerning their return.

When they told Mrs. Elliot, she turned and

said to her husband, who stood stern and un-
moved by her bed :

'I pray, Robert, that you may never have
bitter cause to rue the day you forced your
daughter into unwilling wedlock.'

These were her last words.

When they bent over her by and by, wondering
why she lay so still, they found her gone.

CHAPTER III.

T Scottrigg, Miss Nesbit abode till March, which, having come in like a lamb, went out like a lion.

A night's keen frost and a wild blast of north wind stripped trees and hedgerows of their tender bloom, and blighted the early blossoms which the New Year's spring had brought into life before their time.

When she returned to Windyknowe in the first week of April, she found Marget mourning over the desolate garden, which was her special care and pride. She had washed her hands of it; but when she saw Miss Nesbit get her hoe and her garden gloves the very afternoon of her return, she followed her, and set to work, grumbling all the time.

You needed to know Marget Drysdale well

before you could appreciate her. She was like
the chestnut, all burs outside, but sweet and
true and wholesome at heart. No sooner had
they got set to work, than up comes a carriage
with Aldersyde coachman on the box, bearing
a note for Miss Nesbit.

It was from Mary, saying they had returned
from Edinburgh, and begging her, if she was
home, to return with the carriage.

Marget tossed her head when the contents
of the note were made known to her and she
saw her mistress lay down her hoe and take
off her gloves.

'My certy, folk has a guid stock o' impidence,
I'm thinkin' It wad seem ye canna get sittin'
doon in peace at yer ain hearth-stane, noo-
a-days, for this ane an' the neist ane seekin'
ye.'

Miss Nesbit laughed, and went away up-stairs,
leaving Marget to grow cool again.

Janet had never been within the gate of
Aldersyde since that dreary morning Tibbie and
she had bidden good-bye to the only home they
had ever known. She had been often to the
burying-ground of St. Mary, but it could be
reached without entering the policies of Aldersyde. Her heart was full when the coach swept
through the gates, and a sudden rush of bitter

tears blinded her eyes when she saw that Hugh Nesbit had fulfilled his threat and felled some of the stateliest trees in the park. Also, when she approached the house, she observed that it was stripped of its graceful foliage of ivy and honeysuckle. But though sadly changed without and within, it was Aldersyde still; and oh, how she loved it! She could have kissed the very doorstep as she stepped upon it, remembering the dear feet that had crossed it in other days.

The servant who admitted her ushered her up-stairs at once, saying her mistress was impatient for her coming.

She paused but a moment on the threshold of the best bedroom, for memories, like to overwhelm her, thronged about her heart. Then very gently she opened the door, and went over to the sofa on which Mary lay, and kneeling down by her, drew the motherless head to her breast.

'Now, Janet, I am no more lonely when I feel and know you are here,' said Mary by and by. 'Take off your bonnet, and come and sit down by me, as if you meant to stay a long while.'

Miss Nesbit laid her bonnet and cloak on the bed, and then coming back to the sofa, looked with grieved eyes on the face of her friend. Truly she was a lily now, for her face was as white as the lace about her throat. There were great shadows under her eyes, and about the sweet mouth, which made Janet's heart sink.

If these things spoke truly, Hugh Nesbit's young wife would not long live in sadness and loneliness at Aldersyde.

'How things change!' said Mary by and by. 'Here am I, who used to be a kindly welcomed guest at Aldersyde, its mistress, and you the guest. That's not as it should be, Janet.'

'What makes you think it's no as it should be?' asked Miss Nesbit.

'Oh! I can hardly tell; but in my mind, Janet, you are inseparable from Aldersyde, and Aldersyde from you. I never feel as if Hugh and I had any right to be reigning here.'

At the very mention of her husband's name, a shadow fell on Mary's face.

'Where is Hugh?' asked Janet abruptly.

'I have not seen him since breakfast, Janet. There are two gentlemen, friends of Hugh's, staying in the house, and he is always out with them. I don't see much of him; perhaps just as well,' returned Mary, a little bitter smile curling her lip.

'How did you like Edinburgh?' asked Miss Nesbit, hastening to change the subject.

'It is very beautiful,' answered Mary listlessly; 'far surpassing any of the cities I have ever seen.

I used to sit by the window of our hotel in Princes Street, and look out for hours at the Castle Rock. Its rugged strength had a fascination for me. I would rather look at it than the fairest smiling landscape in all the world.'

'Ay, it's a braw rock the Castle Rock,' answered Miss Nesbit with honest pride; then for a little there was nothing said.

'Janet, I fear Aldersyde will not be much the better of Hugh,' said Mary by and by.

'We'll hope for the best, Mary,' returned Miss Nesbit.

'Ay; but hoping will not save us, either for time or for eternity,' said Mary in a strange abrupt way. 'Janet, I suppose you know my husband is not a man of blameless habits. He squanders his money recklessly, in gambling, betting, and other wicked ways.'

'I'm wae tae hear that,' said Miss Nesbit mournfully. 'Hae ye nae influence ower him ava, Mary?'

Mary laughed, and the sound grated on Miss Nesbit's ear.

'You've seen a tree branch carried down the Yarrow, Janet. Well, I have about as much influence with Hugh as it has against the current of the stream.'

No answer made Miss Nesbit.

'Do you remember long ago, Janet,' said Mary, leaning forward and laying her thin hand on that of her friend, 'when Hugh Nesbit came to see you at Aldersyde, when we were all children, and how cruel he was to Tibbie because she was terrified for him?'

Ay, Janet remembered well.

'An' how he used to torture all helpless things. Janet? Well, Hugh Nesbit has not changed since then ; but instead of a baby cousin, he has a poor, shrinking, delicate wife to torture—that's all the difference,' said Mary bitterly, and covered her face with her hands.

'Oh, Mary! Mary!' said Miss Nesbit in low, distressed tones.

'He used to be afraid of you, Janet,' continued Mary by and by, ' and was always a better boy, you'll mind, when you were by. If he had married a woman like you, he would have been a better man. But, you see, I am only a poor, weak, shrinking body, whose very heart fails within her before his anger. You could rise above your own misery, and find something to live for, but I only succumb. Do you despise me, Janet?'

Despise her! Miss Nesbit's whole soul was filled with compassion unutterable for the poor unhappy wife of her cousin.

'Surely them that's dune this thing will hae tae answer for it,' she said solemnly.

'I've told you all there is to tell now, I think,' said Mary, not seeming to hear what she said. 'Just ring the bell, and we'll have tea here ; then I'll wrap up, and we'll go together up to the chapel yard.'

'Na, na, Mary. Sic a walk's no for you the day,' returned Miss Nesbit as she rose to touch the bell.

'Well, perhaps not, but I *am* going, Janet. Have you looked at all my grand furniture yet? It might turn any young woman's head ; but to my thinking the Aldersyde of old was a sweeter, dearer place than it is now.'

'To my thinking also,' re-echoed Janet Nesbit.

Presently the maid entered with the tea tray. It pleased Miss Nesbit to observe her care and thoughtfulness for the comfort of her mistress.

It was a service of love, indeed ; for there was not one in Aldersyde, save its master, who would not have died to serve the fair and gentle mistress.

The two friends partook of their slender meal almost in silence; then seeing Mary seemed set upon going to the burying-ground, Miss Nesbit forbore to object further, and helped her on with her wraps.

Great was the astonishment of the domestics to behold their mistress venturing out into the evening air, which was as bleak and chill as January's dreariest moods.

Out on the gravel in front of the house, Mary paused and looked mournfully at her friend.

'This is not the Aldersyde of old, either,' she said, pointing to the dismantled walls. 'It made my heart sore to see that when I came home, and to see the great gaps in the park. I '—

'Dinna speak o'd, Mary,' interrupted Janet in a choking voice. 'Come, ye mauna stand here in the bitter air.'

So they turned about and took their way through the park to the wicket, which opened out to the side of the loch. From thence a steep path sloped up the hill to the chapel of St. Mary. They had to pause often on the brae, for Mary's breath came quick and fast with the slightest exertion. But at length they reached the ruin, and entered the gate into the lonely God's acre where slept their best and dearest.

The graves did not lie far apart. Within the Aldersyde enclosure the turf was green and fresh, with here and there a pink-lipped daisy and sturdy snowdrop, to tell that loving hands aye tended it. Miss Nesbit stooped down, and gathering one or two of the bonnie blossoms, strewed them gently on Mrs. Elliot's neglected grave.

'Thank you, Janet,' said Mary with a faint smile; 'you'll do as much for me when I am sleeping here too.'

'Ay, gin ye gang afore me,' answered Miss Nesbit huskily.

'Before the year is out, I shall be at rest,' said Mary dreamily. 'In case I may not be able to come here again with you, Janet, promise me what I am about to ask.'

Miss Nesbit bowed, unable to speak.

'You will see that I am laid here beside my mother, no matter what they may say or wish. I shall give you sufficient to erect a stone here, on which you will cause to be written : " To the memory of Margaret Elliot, and her daughter Mary." When I am laid beside my mother, I am her daughter, and belong to no one else. One last request and I am done, Janet. It is that you will come to me in the last days, and stay with me to the end. I could die easier, I think, if I had a grip of your faithful hand.'

'Mary, Mary, I fear sic fancies o' an' early death may hasten it on. Ye're no that ill, my dear.'

'Not yet; but it is coming, and is no fancy. You have not promised, Janet.'

'A' that ye may require o' me is yours at ony time, an' a' times, ye ken brawly,' said Miss Nesbit huskily.

'God bless you, Janet,' said Mary, and their hands met in a long, close pressure.

'Now we'll go home; I feel chilly. Oh, Janet, look at the sunset on the loch. It minds one of the sea of glass in the Bible.'

The stillness and solemn beauty of that sunset hour seemed to cast a spell over them, and they descended the hill in silence. At the waterside they parted, Miss Nesbit desiring to return home before the dusk had fallen.

Not many minutes after she left Mary, Janet espied the Laird of Aldersyde and his two friends coming round from the other side of the loch. She would fain have avoided them, but they were close upon her before she turned into the upland path. Hugh Nesbit stood still in front of her, but the other two immediately passed on.

'How do you do, Cousin Janet?' he said politely.

'I am weel,' returned Miss Nesbit. 'I needna ask for your health. Ye look brawly, an' ye hae been seekin' sport, I see.'

'Seeking it, indeed; but we haven't found any. The fish won't bite to-day. Have you been up at the house?'

'Yes; I hae been seein' Mary.'

'And left before I came home; your first visit, too—that was cousinly courtesy, Cousin Janet.'

'I hae a lang road tae gang, an' the darkenin' fa's quick in April,' she answered quietly.

'Um, Mary is in the blues! I suppose she's been giving you my character?' said Hugh Nesbit sarcastically.

'I dinna need onybody tae gie me your character, Hugh Nesbit,' said Janet drily. 'I hae kenned ye sin' ye were a laddie.'

'Is there anything wrong with Mary?' asked he abruptly. 'Women always croak, you know, when things don't agree with them. I suppose you know we don't live like turtle-doves, Janet.'

'Wha's blame's that !'

'Hers! She hates me, and lets me see it in her quiet way. Your quiet women are the worst to live with. I'd rather have a thrashing from your honest tongue than her everlasting tears. Ugh, I am sick of them !'

'Ye'll maybe mind what I said tae ye that nicht ye cam seekin' Mary, when she was bidin' wi' me at Windyknowe ?'

'No ; what was it ?'

'Fine ye ken what it was. Weel, I said ye wad hae nae pleasure or happiness wi' an unwillin' bride.'

'How was I to know she was unwilling ? Women always act no when they mean yes.'

Miss Nesbit lifted her eyes to his face, and beneath their honest scorn his fell.

'Mary 'll no live lang tae trouble ye wi' tears or ony ither thing, Hugh. Already her shadow is lengthenin' tae a grave in St. Mary's. Oh, be gentle wi' her, I pray ye again, as I prayed on yer wedding day. It'll maybe spare ye a remorse which wad follow ye tae the grave,' said Miss Nesbit passionately. Then without another word, she passed the Laird, and took her lonely way up past the chapel of St. Mary.

CHAPTER IV

NATURE never intended Hugh Nesbit for the role of a country gentleman. It bored him to talk to his factor, or listen to complaints from his tenants anent the damage done to crops by game. Even the sport furnished by the moors and lochs could not reconcile him to life at Aldersyde. He missed the gay companionship, pleasant excitement, and stirring activity of his old life in camp and barracks; and save that it exempted him from the drawbacks of empty pockets, he could have regretted the chance which had made him Laird of Aldersyde. Disappointed in his marriage, tired of his wife, sick of the dreary routine of his life, he cast his eyes about for a means of release from the chain which bound him. The army was open to him still, where he could enjoy life with double zest, because the revenues of Aldersyde would provide the wherewithal. What though the world commented on his desertion of his wife! She would feel nothing but relief, and they would be better apart than living unhappily together. So he reasoned, and made his arrangements without consulting anybody.

The latter days of April made the world beautiful once more, and the first month of summer time came in with balmy breath and sunshine which whitened all the hedgerows, and surprised into bloom honeysuckle and sweetbriar in the den of Aldersyde. Before it was half gone, Hugh Nesbit announced to his wife his intention of returning to his regiment without delay, as it was being reorganized for early despatch to the Peninsula. She heard his decision with calmness, but did not appear so happily relieved as he had anticipated. She was simply indifferent whether he went or stayed.

'You will return home sometimes, I suppose?' she said listlessly.

'The chances are I shall never see Aldersyde again,' he said.

'Why rejoin the army if such risks are imminent?' she asked faintly.

'Because I'm sick to death of this place,' he answered rudely ; 'anything would be preferable to it.'

There was nothing more said, and upon the morrow they parted as strangers might have parted, without a regret on either side. Ay, truly their marriage was the grand mistake of their lives.

Great was the astonishment in Aldershope and the neighbourhood when it transpired that Hugh Nesbit was off to the wars. His intention had been kept a close secret, and even Doctor Elliot only learned of his departure one evening upon coming to Aldersyde to see his daughter. His indignation knew no bounds.

'What right has he to leave you in this great house alone, to be pointed at as a deserted wife, of whom her husband tired before the honeymoon was well past?'

'The world is very bitter in its judgment, but generally correct, father,' said Mary quietly; 'and you of all people have the least cause to marvel at any phase of my domestic affairs.'

It was a direct reproach, and silenced him at once.

'You had better dismiss the servants, and come home to Aldershope, then,' he said by and by.

'I prefer to remain here,' she answered. 'I expect Miss Nesbit to be with me a good deal; and the domestics are not mine to dismiss.'

Doctor Elliot found himself set aside at every

point, and did not relish it. During his ride home his thoughts dwelt upon his daughter's fragile appearance. Unless his professional eye strangely deceived him, she was already in a decline. Taking it all in all, the glory of being able to say, 'My daughter, Mrs. Nesbit of Aldersyde,' had its drawbacks. Ay, without doubt the wind was bending the lily, and the blast would break it on the stalk.

Miss Nesbit was much at Aldersyde—so much, indeed, that Marget began to wax indignant; for what was Windyknowe without her mistress?

The summer waned, but no word came from the Laird. One day, having occasion to be in Melrose on some business for her cousin's wife, Miss Nesbit called at the office of Mr. Douglas the lawyer, to ask if he knew anything of his client. He looked surprised at the question.

'I had a letter yesterday, Miss Nesbit, concerning the lease of the Mains, which expires at Martinmas. He is on the eve of his departure with his regiment for Gibraltar.'

'I thocht he wad hae been awa afore this, seein' we hae gotten nae word,' said Miss Nesbit.

'Has he not written to Mrs. Nesbit since he left Aldersyde?' asked the lawyer bluntly.

'No. Ye wull hae guessed, I dinna doot, that their marriage has proved a mistake, Mr. Douglas.'

'I have surmised as much,' returned the lawyer. 'It is a wise arrangement for Mrs. Nesbit to have control of her own income.'

'There should be plenty for baith, aff Aldersyde,' said Miss Nesbit.

'Do you remember Miss Oliphant of Yair's speech about the new Laird of Aldersyde making ducks and drakes of his inheritance before another year went by?'

'Ay, I mind,' answered Miss Nesbit with a sinking heart.

'I regret to say that her prediction is likely to be fulfilled. To my certain knowledge Captain Nesbit has borrowed already to an extent which the Martinmas rents will not do much more than cover.'

'That's ill news, Mr. Douglas.'

'To you it must be, remembering your mother's life-work,' said the lawyer with true regret and sympathy. 'By the bye, the rent of the Mains is to be raised a hundred pounds, and if Lennox is unwilling to pay, the place is to be advertised.'

'I hae heard enough for ae day, Mr. Douglas,' said Miss Nesbit, rising. 'As weel a'most micht Aldersyde be withoot a Nesbit as the Mains withoot a Lennox.'

'I have seen many painful changes in families, Miss Nesbit, but none which affected me as the mournful change in Aldersyde,' said the lawyer as they shook hands. 'Good-bye. Give my respects to Mrs. Nesbit.'

Bitter were Janet Nesbit's thoughts during her drive to Aldersyde. It was hard to think that her nearest and dearest had denied themselves ceaselessly in life, in order to redeem Aldersyde, only to provide for a spendthrift kinsman who cared no more for Aldersyde than the merest stranger could have done. If the expected heir should live, what a poor inheritance his father would bequeath to him! She had it in her heart almost to pray that Mary's child might never open its eyes on Aldersyde.

The days wore on, till the month was August; and while grain was whitening to harvest in bonnie Ettrick vale, all England rejoiced over her heroes' triumphal entry into Madrid; for it gave birth to the hope that the long, wearing, disastrous Peninsular war was nearing a close.

Little news of the doings in the great busy world penetrated to quiet Aldersyde. Sometimes Dr. Elliot would bring up a rare copy of a London newspaper containing brief intelligence of the war; but though it might at any time contain the news of her husband's wounding or death, it could not rouse the lady of Aldersyde from her dreary listlessness. She was fast drifting beyond all earthly interests, and the cool, golden days of September found her confined entirely to the west bedroom, where she would lie for hours looking out upon her mother's grave.

The world had many harsh things to say of Hugh Nesbit, and nothing but pity for the sweet young wife fading away alone in Aldersyde. They would have it that she was breaking her heart over his desertion, a report for which Miss Oliphant of Yair was mainly responsible. For after calling for the lady of Aldersyde one day, she went home denouncing Hugh Nesbit in righteous wrath, and praising the gentle wife without stint.

So amid peace and quietness, ministered unto by as abiding a friend as ever woman had, Mary's life drew to its close. Miss Nesbit would try to speak hopefully at times of brighter and stronger days to come, when she would have her bairn to comfort her ; but Mary always shook her head, and would say sometimes, 'Your charge will not end with me, Janet ; you will need to care for him as you have cared for his mother all her days.'

In the first week of November, Captain Nesbit was reported wounded. The newspaper list gave no particulars ; but the army surgeon wrote, as requested by the disabled soldier, to say the wound was not dangerous, and that he hoped to be sufficiently recovered to take advantage of leave at New Year.

'I should like him to come before I died,' said

Mary absently. 'If baby lives, I have a charge to leave with him.'

But what the charge was, Janet Nesbit did not hear then, nor at any other time.

December swept in with a wild snowstorm; and upon a terrible afternoon, when the world seemed a whirling mass of drifting snow, a son and heir was born to the house of Aldersyde. The poor young mother, whose life was fast ebbing, asked by and by in a whisper that the child might be brought to her. Miss Nesbit motioned the nurse from the room, and herself laid the little one in the feeble arms which could scarcely bear even so light a burden. Then she laid her arms about them both, with the firm protecting tenderness characteristic of the whole woman.

'There is no word of Hugh, yet, I suppose?' said Mary.

'No yet; but he is on his way, an' may be here the nicht, Mary.'

'He will be too late, I doubt. Well, Janet, this is the heir of Aldersyde,' said Mary with a faint, tremulous smile.

'Ay, Mary.'

'He is to be christened Walter Elliot, Janet. Tell Hugh I desired that to be his name.'

'Take him now, Janet; his poor mother is tired already, and would fain lie down,'

Tenderly Miss Nesbit laid her back on her pillows, and took the bairn in her arms.

'That's where I leave him, Janet, in your arms. You will be a mother to him, and bring him up to be a good man, so that he may bless Aldersyde when he enters it.'

Only a moment Janet Nesbit paused ere she took so great a charge upon her. Then she answered solemnly, great tears standing in her faithful eyes:

'My Mary, I will.'

'Speak to him sometimes about his mother, Janet; keep my memory green in his heart— that is all. Now give him back to Susan, and come here: I shall need the grip in a little while.'

Miss Nesbit carried the child into the next room, signed to Doctor Elliot, and they returned together.

He saw at a glance that the end was at hand, and moving over to the bed, would have raised his daughter in his arms; but she motioned him off, and looked toward the one who had befriended her through all.

Miss Nesbit leaned over her, gripping the cold hands in her strong, warm clasp.

'The Lord can uphaud in the Jordan, my Mary,' she whispered bravely.

Mary smiled and closed her eyes.

Doctor Elliot strode away over to the window, with the iron entering into his soul. His one child turned from him in her last extremity, and clung to a stranger. Ay! it was a bitter retribution.

Just then there came a great knocking at the hall door, and they heard the voice of Hugh Nesbit asking for his wife. Too late! for even as his foot was upon the threshold of the door, the wind rose, and bending the lily, broke it on the stalk.

Once more Miss Nesbit performed the last offices for the dead in the west bedroom at Aldersyde. When it was over, and Mary lay with her white hands folded on her quiet breast, her faithful friend bent over the bed, and bade her a last farewell. Then she went into the adjoining room, took the child from the nurse's lap, and, wrapping a shawl about him, carried him down to the dining-room.

Some refreshment for the Laird had been hastily set on the table; but he sat with folded arms by the fire, and the repast remained untouched.

'This is yer first-born son, Hugh,' said Miss Nesbit, and laying aside the wrap, held him out.

Awkwardly enough Hugh Nesbit took the bairn in his arms, and looked down upon him a moment in silence.

'I had no idea she had been ailing so long as the housekeeper tells me,' he said in a low voice. 'You might have written, Cousin Janet.'

'Where tae?' she asked drily.

'Well, she's rid of her wretched marriage tie now,' he continued in a reckless way. 'But what on earth am I to do with the child? It seems a pity, seeing what 'manner of father he has, that he should have lived.'

'Wheesht, Hugh Nesbit,' said his cousin sternly.

'Well, the servants are trustworthy, I suppose; so they must look after him,' he said. 'I rejoin my regiment immediately.'

'Mary desired me to care for the bairn, Hugh. If ye like, I'll tak him hame tae Windyknowe, an' see tae his upbringin' till ye come hame.'

Hugh Nesbit looked at his cousin in perfect wonderment. He had been compelled to respect her aye, but this was an unselfishness of heart he could hardly understand.

'Do you mean to say you would undertake the entire care of a child like this, from now to an indefinite period?'

Miss Nesbit bowed her head.

'I lo'ed his mither weel, an' I lo'e the name he bears,' she said huskily.

'Well, there he is,' said Hugh Nesbit, replacing the child in her arms. 'You have relieved me of a considerable anxiety, cousin. I shall provide the wherewithal to feed and clothe him, of course; but do you what you like with him, train him in any creed you please, and he will grow up a better man than his father, I don't doubt. So you will have the future of Aldersyde in your own hands, cousin.'

'I hardly think ye need fear for the bairn wi' me, Hugh Nesbit; but before God I pledge ye my word tae mak him my first earthly care,' she said solemnly, and went away out of the room holding the child very close to her heart.

She had accepted a great responsibility, but she was not afraid. The heir of Aldersyde left in her sole care, to be trained, she prayed and hoped, in the path of uprightness, sobriety, and godliness! Oh! but it was a sweet and solemn thought.

In the evening Marget Drysdale came up to Aldersyde to inquire regarding the condition of Mrs. Nesbit. She heard the sad tidings from the lodge keeper, but went on to the house to see the heir and have a word with Miss Nesbit. The maid took her up to the room where Miss

Nesbit sat by the fire with the bairn on her knee. There was no light save that given by the fire; but it was sufficient to show the traces of tears on her face. Now that everything was done, she had time to dwell upon her grief.

'So Miss Mary's at peace at last,' said Marget softly; 'an' this is the wee heir o' Aldersyde?'

'Ay, Marget,' said Miss Nesbit tremulously, and put back with gentle hand the shawl from the tiny head.

'Puir mitherless lamb!' whispered Marget tenderly.

'This is oor bairn, Marget—yours an' mine,' said Miss Nesbit.

'Ay, mem; I'm thinking ye'll be mair than ever at Aldersyde noo?'

'Na, Marget; the Laird's gaun aff tae the wars again, an' I hae gotten the bairn tae keep. As sune's the funeral's ower, I'll bring him hame tae Windyknowe.'

''Od save us a', that'll be an unco handfu' for twa single weemin that never was marriet, an' ken neist tae naething aboot bairns,' said Marget doubtfully.

'We'll hae tae learn, Marget,' returned Miss Nesbit.

Marget stood quite still, looking reflectively into the fire. From the expression of her face, Miss

Nesbit guessed she was not well pleased, but left her alone, knowing she would come round by and by.

'I was mindin' on the fecht I've seen my guidsister an' ither folk hae. D'ye think ye could be fashed wi' a bairn girnin' in yer lug mornin', nune, and nicht?' asked Marget grimly.

Again Miss Nesbit put back the shawl from the bairn's sleeping head, and touched Marget's gown to look at him.

'He's his mither's bairn, Marget, an' was left tae me. Wull ye gar me leave him among frem folk?'

'Wha said I wantit ye tae leave him among frem folk, mem? I was only makin' bold tae think that the wullint beast aye gets the load tae draw,' said Marget; then, wheeling round suddenly, she laid her rough hand on the bairn's head, her honest eyes brimming with tears. 'Let him come; he'll be an ill bairn if we dinna get him warstled through some way. God bless him, an' mak him a blessin' an' a joy tae Aldersyde!'

So did Marget Drysdale bind herself to the service of Miss Mary's bairn.

It was a great speaking in the country side when it transpired that Miss Nesbit had undertaken the charge of Hugh Nesbit's motherless son. Sundry wise and officious matrons bemoaned his fate, left to the mercies of a woman ignorant of the ways and needs of childhood ; but the majority of the busybodies prophesied that he would find a comfortable home at Windyknowe.

Doctor Elliot was sternly displeased. He had signified to his son-in-law his willingness to take the child into his own house, and see that he was well cared for, but his offer had been declined with scant courtesy. After Mary's death there was not even the semblance of friendship between them.

So what joy or satisfaction, think you, had Doctor Elliot in having the heir of Aldersyde for a grandson? Already had he rued — ay, twice over—forcing his daughter into unwilling wedlock.

After the burying of the young lady of Aldersyde, Miss Nesbit departed to Windyknowe with the bairn and all his belongings.

The Laird abode the best part of a month at Aldersyde, and considerably exercised his tenants by meddling with their concerns, and finding fault with them on all hands. Mr. Lennox had paid the desired increase of rent rather than quit the dwelling-place of his forbears, but he felt very sore against the Laird for his unjust greed.

All were relieved when he went off to the wars again, and not a single regret followed him. He came up to Windyknowe the night before his departure, and informed his cousin that Mr. Douglas would supply her with money at stated intervals for the maintenance of the child. Then he bade her good-bye, took his last careless look at his son, and went his way.

So the inmates of the muirland dwelling settled down in peace, and as the days went by, found, because of the bairn, a new interest in life, a brighter shining in the sunbeams, and a sweeter note in the singing of the blackbird on the thorn.

CHAPTER V.

'At Waterloo.'

OUR years brought about many changes in Ettrick Vale. Two children were born to the house of Ravelaw, but failed to make any link between the ill-matched pair. Their unhappy life was the talk of the country side. So also was the second marriage of Mrs. Riddell the elder, to a London banker, and her removal to the metropolis.

About the same time Scottrigg lost its bonnie flower, sweet Marjorie, who became a great lady, the Countess of Dryburgh. Her brother, true-hearted young Walter, had loved Isabel Nesbit too dearly to seek another bride, and was therefore likely to abide and comfort his father and mother for the loss of Marjorie.

In tranquil happiness at Windyknowe abode Miss Nesbit, Marget Drysdale, and the bairn. He was the very sunshine of the house, 'Auntie's pet' and Marget's 'ain, ain bairn.' He grew so like his mother that many a time Miss Nesbit's eyes filled with tears, thinking, if she had but lived, what a gladness her boy would have infused into her heart.

His soldier father was still fighting in a foreign land, for there seemed to be no end to the wars and rumours of wars. But the decisive blow which restored peace to blood - stained and exhausted Europe was struck at last.

On a fair June evening, when the air was heavy with scent of hawthorn and sweetbriar, and a great slumberous calm brooded over the earth, Mr. Douglas the lawyer came in haste to Windy-knowe. By the open dining-room window sat Miss Nesbit at her sewing, with the bairn chattering at his play by her side. It was her thirty-second birthday, and she looked her age to the full. The lovely hair was plentifully streaked with grey, and though her face was sweet and tranquil as of yore, there was a wistful drooping of the grave, womanly mouth, and a continual yearning shadow in the eyes, which told of the heart-sickness of hope deferred. I do not believe Tibbie was ever out of her heart for a moment at a time, and she still looked forward to a day coming when she should once more see her face to face. She rose when the lawyer entered the room, and welcomed him with a cordial smile. They were friends of long standing, and each knew the other's worth. Then the little Walter ran to him, clamouring for the customary toss in the air which Mr. Douglas had taught him to expect. After a minute's gay banter with him, he turned to Miss Nesbit and asked her to send him from the room for a little.

'Rin tae Marget, my pet ; Auntie 'll send for ye by and by,' she said ; and the bairn, accustomed to implicitly obey, ran off at once.

'Poor child, he is a very tiny Laird of Aldersyde,' said the lawyer ; and Miss Nesbit rose up with a deepening shadow in her eyes.

'Has onything happened tae Captain Nesbit, Mr. Douglas ?'

'There was a great battle fought near Brussels on Sunday, Miss Nesbit, and the Captain fell fighting at the head of his regiment.'

Miss Nesbit grew very pale. She could not pretend to any great grief; yet such a sudden death was a shock, though she had daily expected it for months back.

'Near Brussels on Sunday, did ye say?' she said falteringly.

'Yes ; at Waterloo. Napoleon is utterly beaten, but at awful cost. There'll be mourning in many a home to-day, Miss Nesbit.'

'So my mitherless bairn's an orphan bairn noo!' said Miss Nesbit with mournful tenderness. 'Puir wee Walter!'

'You will have an additional care on your shoulders now, Miss Nesbit,' said the lawyer, beginning to pace up and down the floor—'the keeping of Aldersyde in trust for its unconscious heir.'

'Ay.'

Very low, almost inaudible, was the monosyllable, because at the moment she was renewing in her heart the vow she had made to Mary in her dying hour.

'How does Aldersyde stand at present, Mr. Douglas?' she asked by and by.

'I regret to say that the affairs of Aldersyde have relapsed into the state in which your father found them. The estate is heavily mortgaged again,' returned the lawyer with some hesitation.

'In sae short a time!' echoed Miss Nesbit in dismay. 'Whaur did Hugh Nesbit pit its revenues?'

'He was a man of extravagant habits, and denied himself nothing,' answered Mr. Douglas. 'He could have spent double his income, and yet been in debt.'

'God helping me, Mr. Douglas, Walter shall enter on an unburdened heritage, as his faither did afore him; but I pray an' hope he'll mak a better use o't,' said Miss Nesbit solemnly. 'Ye'll look efter the interests o' Aldersyde as ye hae dune sae faithfully in the past, an' lay by all the rents tae pay aff the mortgages. I can keep the bairn brawly aff my ain.'

'Not many orphan children have such unselfish devotion bestowed on them and their interests,' said the lawyer with a smile. 'Well, I'll bid you good day : we can have a talk over matters another time.'

Miss Nesbit scarcely heard. She was looking away over in the direction of the chapel of St. Mary.

'The Laird 'll readily be buried where he fell,' she said musingly.

'Yes ; he and many thousands more have found a grave on Waterloo,' returned Mr. Douglas.

An unbidden tear trembled in Miss Nesbit's eye at the thought that the two brief lives which had been so closely linked, and had drifted so far apart, were united again by the great Leveller. She showed the lawyer out herself, and then went to the kitchen, where Marget was baking, assisted by the bairn. It was marvellous to see how she let him hinder her work, and tease her life out. Miss Nesbit lifted him from his stool, and held him close to her heart, while a dry sob broke from her lips.

'Auntie's pet, Auntie's orphan bairn,' she whispered ; and though the child could not understand her, Marget was not slow to catch the meaning of her words.

'What's an orphan bairn, Auntie?' asked the child wonderingly.

'It means that ye hae naebody in the world noo, my pet, but me and Marget,' said Miss Nesbit, and the child nestled his head on her shoulder, saying contentedly that he wanted no more in the world.

By and by when the bairn was left alone again with Marget, she wiped her floury hands, and gathered him closely in her arms. In the ben end, Miss Nesbit could hear the pitying tender words she said over and over to him : 'Marget's ain, ain bairn ; Marget's bonnie wee man: there's haunds and hearts that'll work and lo'e ye mair than them that's awa, my ain, ain bairn !'

So the little Laird of Aldersyde was not likely ever to know the innermost desolation of the word ' orphan.'

Next day, having some business in Melrose, Miss Nesbit went down to Aldershope to catch the morning coach. While she stood waiting at the inn door, she beheld the Laird of Ravelaw coming down the village on his black horse. She was ready to acknowledge him by a bow ; but he alighted at the inn door, threw his reins to an ostler, and came towards her.

They shook hands in silence ; then Miss Nesbit said inquiringly :

' Ye'll hae heard the news, I dinna doot ? '

' Yes ; Douglas told me,' returned Ravelaw.

' Did you know that my brother-in-law, Louis Reynaud, fell also ? '

Miss Nesbit paled to the lips.

' I didna ken he was a sodger,' she said with difficulty.

' Every Frenchman is a soldier,' answered Ravelaw briefly, and then stood looking at her in silence as if waiting for another question. It came at last —two faltering, eager words wrung from the very agony of her heart.

' Whaur's Tibbie ? '

' In Paris ; at least, she was there with Reynaud and their little daughter not many months ago. I have many a time been on the point of speaking to you about your sister, but you always avoided me in a very pointed way,' said Ravelaw with a slight bitterness in his deep voice.

' She could hardly come hame hersel' frae France?' said Miss Nesbit more to herself than to him.

' Not alone in the present troubled state of the country,' he made answer.

Then Janet Nesbit turned away from him, for there was something in her heart like to overwhelm her.

Oh, why was life so hard ? The longing to flee to her one sister, left widowed and friendless in a strange land, swept over her; and yet she had not in all the world as much money as the journey would cost. By and by she turned to the Laird of Ravelaw again, and forced herself to change the subject.

'Is Mrs. Riddell weel, an' the bairns ?' she asked.

'Yes, pretty well ; but my wife is never strong, you know,' said Sandy Riddell discontentedly.

'Your little Laird will be growing a big fellow now, Janet ?'

'Ay; Walter thrives brawly, an' a dear bairn he is,' returned Miss Nesbit from the fulness of her heart. 'The coach is unco late frae Rowantree the day, surely ?'

'Five minutes behind,' said Ravelaw, glancing at his watch. 'Well, good-bye, Janet. Wish me luck in my French journey : I go to-morrow.'

Miss Nesbit's startled eyes looked straight into his, but she spake never a word.

'My wife desires me to learn some particulars about her brother's death and his affairs ; and besides, some one must see to Isabel,' he continued, avoiding her keen glance.

Instinctively she guessed that Isabel was the chief object of his journey.

'Sandy Riddell, I thank ye,' she said simply and

frankly. 'Ye hae lifted a heavy load aff my heart wi' these words.'

'If she is alive and able, Janet, I shall bring her back to you,' said Sandy Riddell, his voice slightly tremulous. 'I need no thanks. God knows, anything I can do is little enough to atone for my indirect hand in your sister's unhappy marriage.'

'Nevertheless, I do thank ye, as only a sister can,' repeated Miss Nesbit gently.

Looking upon the sweet, true womanly face, and the tender, pathetic eyes uplifted to his, a great agony of regret swept across the heart of the Laird of Ravelaw ; and not knowing what thing he might be tempted to say, it behoved him to get away out of Janet Nesbit's presence as fast as possible.

'Well, I'm off!' he said with apparent carelessness. 'In about a month from now, all being well, you may expect Isabel at Windyknowe with another charge for you. The house will be lively enough, surely, with two little ones in it ?'

A tender smile crept about Miss Nesbit's lips. Tibbie's bairn ! Oh, what a treasure it would be to her heart !—nearer, dearer even than the heir of Aldersyde.

'God prosper yer journey, Sandy Riddell, an' bring ye safely hame; an' if He permits me tae look upon my sister's face again, maybe He'll help me tae thank ye better nor I can the day,' she said in her earnest way.

Then they parted, as they had not parted for many years, and she went on her way, light of heart, to Melrose.

The day seemed very long; for she was eager to be at home to tell Marget the glad news, and to speak to Walter about the little playmate he would have by and by.

The afternoon was well past when the coach again set her down in Aldershope; and what was her amazement to behold Marget and the bairn standing hand in hand at the inn, waiting for the coach !

Whenever she alighted, the bairn ran to her, and hid his face in the folds of her gown. Never in his life had 'Auntie's pet' been so long parted from the being he loved most on earth, and his little heart was full.

'Bless the bairn,' said Marget with a smile and a tear. 'I hae haen a bonnie life o't the day. Next time ye gang awa, ye'll tak him wi' ye, I mak sure. For peace' sake, I was obleeged tae bring him tae meet ye.'

Miss Nesbit lifted him in her arms, thanking God for the clinging of the little hands about her neck. Only He knew how rich she felt herself in the love of the bairn.

'The day's been a lang day tae me as weel, Marget,' said Miss Nesbit as they turned their steps towards Windyknowe. 'I hae great news tae tell. Tibbie's man was killed in the great battle, an' she'll be comin' hame tae me by an' by.'

Marget looked dumfoundered and incredulous.

'The Lord be thankit!' she ejaculated at length. 'Whaur is she?'

'Faur awa in France, Marget,' said Miss Nesbit with a sigh. 'Left alane wi' her little bairn in a strange land in the time o' war.'

'Has she a bairn?' asked Marget in an awe-struck voice.

'Ay, a wee lassie. It'll be grand, Marget, tae see Walter and her play thegither!'

'I canna think o' Tibbie wi' a bairn o' her ain. She was but a bairn hersel' in my een,' said Marget.

'I am thirty-twa past, and Tibbie's twenty-seven. No sic a bairn after a'!' Miss Nesbit reminded her.

'Mercy me, hoo time flees! Was't Mr. Dooglas telt ye a' this the day?'

'No, Marget; I met the Laird o' Ravelaw this mornin' in Aldershope, an' he's gaun awa the morn tae bring Tibbie hame.'

'That's very weel dune o' the Laird o' Ravelaw,' said Marget.

'Ay, it's weel dune. If he hadna offered, I wad hae been obleeged tae find ways an' means tae gang mysel',' said Miss Nesbit.

Marget lifted up her hands in horror and surprise.

'My certy, ye're no feared. Gang awa amang Hottentots in a foreign kintry, whaur there's naething but wars an wholesale murders, an' that awfu' Bonapairt! That *wad* be a gowk's jaunt for a lane wummin!'

Miss Nesbit laughed in the lightness of her heart, and turned to talk to the bairn at her side about the little stranger from over the sea who was coming by and by to share their home.

From that very day she began to make preparations for Tibbie and her child. The erring one would find a warm welcome waiting her, and would see what loving hands had worked for her, and what loving hearts had looked and longed for her return.

There was no bitterness in her thought of the sister who had so ill repaid her unselfish love and care, only a great unspeakable thankfulness that in God's mercy she would be permitted to shelter once more her own kin beneath her own roof-tree.

Oh, but the days were long!—not only to her, but to Marget and the bairn as well. It was an amusing and touching thing to see him lay aside certain of his playthings for the expected stranger, and to hear his constant earnest talk of her.

Slowly for them July drew to its close. Again the song of the reapers echoed over hill and dale, and again a harvest moon shone on Ettrick's silver stream, and on the rushing Yarrow. Then they began to count hours instead of days, and the bairn would sit half the time on the gate watching for the coach which was so long in coming.

One evening, when August was half gone, Miss Nesbit was sitting by the fire in the gloaming, with Walter on her knee, when there came a great rumbling of wheels on the avenue. Marget flew to the door, like a being possessed. Miss Nesbit set down the child, and rose, feeling for the moment as if strength and consciousness would leave her in the sickness of her suspense. She could not move, even when the steps came towards the room. She looked up when the door opened ; then her eyes fell again, and she pressed her hand to her heart, for the Laird of Ravelaw entered alone. He came towards her, carrying something wrapped in shawls in his arms, and spoke a few brief, hurried words.

'I was obliged to leave her, Janet. Here's the child.'

'Deid or livin', did ye leave her?' fell in a whisper from Miss Nesbit's bloodless lips.

'She died two days after I reached her. I stayed but to bury her in the English corner of Pere la Chaise, then came home with her poor little child.'

There was a moment's intense silence.

'God's will be dune!' said Miss Nesbit, then, in a strange broken voice, and stretched out her arms to take home another orphan bairn.

CHAPTER VI.

THE child was asleep. With trembling fingers Miss Nesbit put back the shawl from its head, and looked upon its face. It was perfectly featured, but dark in hue, and strongly resembling the face Miss Nesbit remembered well—that of Louis Reynaud. Long dark lashes swept the exquisitely rounded cheeks, and dark hair curled about the brow in a wild disorder of ringlets.

There was nothing about the little one which could recall the fair young mother to the mind of the sister who had loved her so well; yet she bent low over it and laid her quivering lips to its brow, Walter looking on wonderingly the while. Then she rose, motioned to him, and went away to the kitchen, where Marget was having her quiet greet to herself.

' Here, Marget ; there's the bairns. Keep them by

ye till I speak tae the Laird o' Ravelaw,' said Miss Nesbit, and placing her sleeping burden in Marget's arms, went back to the dining-room.

'Sit down, Janet,' said Sandy Riddell, offering her a chair.

'Tak it yersel',' she said wearily; 'I maun stand while I hear what ye hae tae tell.'

'Well, I can be brief,' he said. 'I reached Paris safely, and without much interruption considering the state of the country. I had Isabel's address, and found her at once.'

He paused a moment there, as if not liking his task.

'I found her very ill,—dying, in fact,—but in the care of a good, kind-hearted woman, who looked after her and the children as if they had been her own.'

'Children!' echoed Miss Nesbit.

'There were two. One had only been born a few hours when I arrived; but he did not survive the night. The doctor said I might see Madame Reynaud at once if I liked, for she could not live many hours. She was perfectly conscious, and knew me at once. Her first question was, had I brought you, Janet. I would have given a world to have been able to say yes. She asked me eagerly how you were, and if you had forgotten or forgiven her. Poor Isabel! she wept sore when I said you were making ready for her at Windyknowe.'

'What did she look like?' asked Miss Nesbit.

'A trifle older and thinner, perhaps, but just as fair as she was when she was the Flower of Yarrow,' returned the Laird, using a name which had been Tibbie's when they were boys and girls together. 'I stayed with her as much as I was permitted: she seemed happier when I was by. I never was a great friend, Janet; only mine was the "kent face in the strange land." I promised her faithfully to bring the child home to you. She had got this nurse person to promise to journey to Scotland with the child when she died; but it was more satisfaction "to her, of course, to leave her charge with me." '

'She died twa days later, ye say?'

'Yes; quietly and painlessly,' said the Laird with a gentleness and sympathy marvellous to see in him. 'She said you would find all her last messages, everything you wanted to know, in this packet, which she wrote before she became ill in case of a fatal issue. The nurse was to bring it also, to explain her presence and convince you of the identity of the child.'

Miss Nesbit took the packet from his hands, and there was a moment's silence.

'Ye wad remunerate the kind Christian soul, of course?' she said then.

'I did.'

Q

'Tae what extent, micht I spier? an' what ither expenses did ye incur on Isabel's account?' asked Miss Nesbit quietly.

'Janet, will you deny me *that* mournful satisfaction?' asked Sandy Riddell reproachfully.

She understood him at once, and coloured slightly, for her pride was strong within her.

'The little one yonder,' said the Laird of Ravelaw, motioning in the direction of the kitchen, 'will find ways and means to use your superfluous bawbees. What I did for Isabel was very little. Cannot you let it pass, Janet?'

Then Janet answered back simply and gracefully, 'Let it be as ye will,' and added, 'Is that a'?'

'Yes; only I would like to say that from what I could gather from Isabel, I do not think Reynaud and she lived very unhappily together,' said Ravelaw. 'And she seemed to be in comfortable quarters. They had been living in a chateau near Versailles, till he was drafted into a regiment; then he brought her to Paris, thinking she would be safer. She seemed to feel his death; but I have no doubt the packet will explain everything. Well, Janet, I will go now.' Another day, perhaps, you will admit me to Windyknowe to see the little one : she has learned to call me Uncle already. You'll not grudge me that, surely?'

'Surely no,' returned Miss Nesbit with a faint

smile. 'I thank ye aince mair, Sandy Riddell, an' though my words are few, I am nane the less gratefu'. What ye hae dune for me an' mine, I can never hope to repay.'

'Hush, Janet! I *wish* I could have brought her back to you,' said the Laird of Ravelaw passionately.

'It wasna the Lord's will, ye see,' she returned in a low voice. Then their hands met in a fervent grip.

The Laird went away home to his peevish, ill-tempered wife and ill-guided home ; and Miss Nesbit betook herself to the kitchen to see what her bairns were about. When she went in at the door, she could almost have smiled at the picture presented on the wide hearth. The little stranger was awake, and having permitted Marget to remove all her wraps, now stood on the floor, finger in mouth, eyeing Walter, who was looking at her with mingled love and awe on his face.

'Weel, Marget ? ' said Miss Nesbit.

Very downcast indeed was the face of Marget Drysdale at that moment.

'I'm jist wunnerin', mem, whaur the Lord's gane, that ye should hae sae mony heartbreaks ? ' she said sharply. He should ken weel ye had nae need o' anither ane.'

'Wheesht, Marget ; I can say His will be dune,

said Miss Nesbit gently. 'He kenned what a grateful heart I wad hae uplifted to Him, had He seen fit tae let me look on her face again. But His way's the best, an' we hae the bairn, an' mauna grumble.' '

While Miss Nesbit was speaking, the little stranger had been eyeing her intently, and now, as if drawn by some magnet, came to her, clinging to the folds of her gown, and lifting pleading eyes to her sweet face.

Miss Nesbit gave a great start, for the eyes were Tibbie's—the very blue depths which had been as changeful in their loveliness as the summer sea. With a great sob she lifted the child to her heart, feeling almost as she used to feel long ago, when Tibbie had been a timid, toddling thing, aye looking for protecting care from her motherly elder sister.

Then Walter, with shadowing eyes, crept over to her, and touching her gown, said in a frightened, pleading voice, as if he dreaded he was no longer 'Auntie's pet:'

'Auntie!'

Then with her other arm Miss Nesbit drew him to her side, feeling in the deepest depths of her heart what a thing it was to have these two young lives dependent on her, turning to her, and looking up to her for guidance in all things. A mother, and yet no mother! Surely never had woman been so strangely placed before. In that moment, the shadows seemed to roll away from what had been to her an inscrutable past, and the 'wherefore' of many things was made plain to her. Well might she say in her heart, God help me! She would need all His help.

'Weel, Marget,' she said cheerfully, 'we micht as weel hae been mairret, you an' me, when oor family's growin' sae fast. My certy, we'll be keepit lively noo.'

'I wunner wha's bairn'll come next?' said Marget, who had not yet got the better of her disappointment.

'We dinna ken that, Marget; but we'll open the door tae them, kennin' the Lord 'll no send ony mair without providin' for them. Come, get on the kettle, my wummin, an' get Tibbie's bairn something tae eat. 'Are ye no hungry, my pet?' Miss Nesbit added, longing to hear the little one speak.

'No, no; I want Uncle,' lisped the bairn, to Miss Nesbit's great joy speaking good English, though the foreign accent was marked.

'He'll come another day, my pet. Come, Walter, an' speak tae her. I dinna ken what her name is yet,' said Miss Nesbit, and set the little one down, whereupon she stamped her feet, and screamed in a perfect passion.

'Lord hae mercy on us! She's surely French,' said Marget. 'A Scotch bairn never yelled like that.'

'I doot she'll no be as easy tae bring up as Walter was,' said Miss Nesbit, trying to quiet her. 'But she'll be tired, likely. We'll better ken what mainner o' a bairn she'll be the morn.'

By and by, the supper past, and both the little ones in bed,—Walter in his crib, and the stranger in Miss Nesbit's bed,—she sat down by them in the dim lamplight and opened out the packet she was longing and yet afraid to read. It was written carefully and clearly, though blotted here and there, as if Isabel's tears had been falling while she wrote. Thus it ran :—

'RUE ALBOIS, PARIS, *June* 1815.

'MY SISTER,—For the first time since I scrawled the few words I left behind at Windyknowe, I lift my pen to write to you. Before I begin, let me pray you to forgive my long neglect. It was not willing on my part, for my heart has daily broken for you since I left you. I can hardly hope—and yet I do hope, knowing what you are—that you still love the wayward, erring being who so ill repaid all your love, and deceived you as I did up to the very hour of my flight; but for that and other sins I have borne my punishment. To begin at the beginning, Janet. All my days I had a longing after a life very different from ours at Aldersyde. I aye loved fine dresses, and jewels, and all the things money can buy, and used to be so sick of our poverty that I could hardly live. When we went to Windyknowe, it was worse; and I used to be afraid, I felt so desperate and wicked sometimes. So when Mrs. Riddell and her brother made my acquaintance, I was quite ready to be made of by them; for I never had your high-souled pride, Janet: as you said once, I was aye a poor Nesbit. From the first, Louis Reynaud had a power over me, he was so different from any man I had ever seen. He was so handsome, and his talk was so fascinating, that when he began to make love to me my head seemed to be dazed. But I knew well enough that the feeling I had for him was not a right one—not the love which makes the happiness of married life.

'Both of them did their best to feed my wicked discontent; but it was Mrs. Riddell first who whispered to me, when I was at Ravelaw, that I had a way of escape from your tyranny and the dreariness of Windyknowe. I had only to say the word, and Louis would take me away and make me an adored wife, the mistress of a splendid establishment, and give me my heart's desire—plenty of luxury and gaiety and pleasure.

'Ay, Janet, they called your dear, faithful love tyranny ; and I believed them, and turned traitor to you. I can't think what they wanted me for, for I had no tocher ; but since, I have been convinced that it was revenge on Mrs. Riddell's part for your treatment of her, and the coolness of her reception by other folk in the country side. She knew it would be a blow to many besides you when I ran away.

'Well, they arranged all the plans, and I agreed, even with sore misgivings in my heart. I suppose you would hear that I was married at Gretna, for I know you would sift it to the bottom. I have often pictured to myself your look when you came home from Mary's bridal that night and found me away. Oh, Janet, though I have tried to shut it out, your face will rise up before me—never in anger, but white, and drawn, and troubled as I have seen you look before. Let me hurry on, for I am like to break down.

'We stayed in London awhile ; and I saw Mary there, as she would tell you. Then Louis was called home, and we went away to France. Instead of the magnificent castle they had promised me, I found my home a ruined old chateau at Versailles ; instead of the retinue of servants, one deaf old Frenchwoman who did not know a word of English. My husband had no money, except what was made at gaming-tables; and there were days, Janet, when I knew what it was to be hungry, and not have a bite to eat.

'I had to work, too—oh, if Marget could but see my hands now! I was proud of them once, but never mind. Louis had expected some money with me, and was constantly desiring me to write and tell you to send my half of the income. But if he had killed me, I would not have done that, and he began to learn that I could be obstinate too.

'Perhaps that will let you know what treatment I had at his hands. I need not enlarge upon it: he was my husband, and he is dead. Let the matter rest. But oh, that I could speak to the inmost soul of every Scottish maiden, and bid her make her home in her own country, and marry one of her own nation! There cannot be happiness when ways and tastes and habits are so far apart as the French are from the Scotch.

'In time my baby was born. But for her, well, I should not be alive to-day. She was my very life, my all—my solace in home-sickness, in heart-yearnings for you, in sorrows of which I cannot write. Her name is Janet, but I called her Netta—that is the name she knows. She has received no baptism. When she comes home to Windyknowe, get Mr. Bourhill to christen her by the name which is

engraven on my heart.   I pray God, as I write,
that she may grow up something like the one
whose name she bears.

'Well, I am nearly done.   I am very frail in
health, and will not survive the birth of my
second child, I know.   I hope it will die with me
also.   I have with me here in Paris a faithful
soul, Marie Loufrois, a comparative stranger to
me, but who has shown me as much kindness as
I could have experienced among my own country-
women.   She has promised, and will perform what
I ask her, to take Netta home to Scotland when
I am gone.   You will see that she does not go
unrewarded.

'And now, my sister, best of friends, dear, dear
Janet, just one little word about my bairn and I
will finish.   Take her to your heart, if not for my
sake, for the sake of those who lie in the chapel-
yard of St. Mary.   As I write these words, what
memories throng about my heart!   But I must
not give way.   I daresay you will know how I
feel.   When she grows to be a woman, tell her
as much of her mother's life-story as you think
fit; it may be a warning to her.

'I cannot say anything to you, Janet, for my
heart fails me.   Not on earth do such as you
have their reward; but if there be a God, surely
He prepares a recompense for those who serve

Him as you do. Pray for me, Janet. Perhaps in some far-off time we may meet in a happier world, where the agonies of earth are forgotten.

'I feel very dark; it is so long since I have heard of holy things, or read a Bible. This is a terrible heathen land, where God is forgotten altogether, and each one lives for himself and this world. But I remember father used to read from the Book at Aldersyde, that Christ died to save sinners, and that though our sins were red like crimson, they should be made white as snow. I am trying humbly to trust in these words; perhaps at eventide there may be light for me.

'Good-bye, Janet, my sister. Oh, the love with which I write down these words, you will never know! Keep a little corner in your heart for Tibbie, and when you look at Netta, remember her mother only as she was when she was like her—that is all I ask.   TIBBIE.'

The paper fluttered from Miss Nesbit's hands to the floor, and her head fell upon her breast. At that moment there was in her heart a very different feeling from that which had prompted her gentle 'God's will be dune' little more than an hour ago.

All her life Janet Nesbit remembered with horror those minutes in that quiet, dimly-lighted room, beside the unconscious sleeping children. She tottered to her feet by and by, lowered the lamp, and went over to the window. The sky was dark and lowering, the moon hidden by low-hanging clouds; only right above the chapel of St. Mary shone, clear and bright, a solitary star.

It was a curious thing how that trivial incident went straight to the heart of the stricken woman who looked out into the night. It seemed to her a direct message from above. She fell down upon her knees, a wild rush of tears blinding her eyes, and stretching out her hands, those words fell from her lips in a low, sobbing cry:

'Lord, forgive; it is past. Thy will be dune!'

Then there came a great peace.

CHAPTER VII.

'My cup runneth over !'

EFORE eleven o'clock next forenoon, Mrs. Riddell of Ravelaw came in her coach to Windyknowe. Marget showed her gingerly into the dining-room, and went to seek her mistress, who was up-stairs with the bairns.

When Miss Nesbit entered the room, she was much struck with the change in the appearance of the lady of Ravelaw. Her attire was costly, but slovenly and negligent-looking, and the freshness of her beauty was gone. Her face was thin and sallow, and wore a look of discontent and peevishness painful to witness. She rose and bowed slightly to Miss Nesbit, who, for the sake of the Laird of Ravelaw, strove to be kind and courteous to his wife.

'I regret tae see ye lookin' sae ill, Mrs. Riddell,' she said gently.

'My health is wretched; my constitution has been utterly ruined by this vile Scotch climate,' said Mrs. Riddell languidly.

'I presume you will guess my errand to-day, Miss Nesbit. I have come to see my niece, Mademoiselle Reynaud, and to arrange matters with you regarding her.'

Miss Nesbit started. It had never occurred to her that Sandy Riddell's wife could have any claim upon Tibbie's bairn.

'Ye shall see her an' welcome,' Mrs. Riddell, she said slowly; 'but I hardly ken what ye mean by arrangements wi' me aboot her.'

'Oh! that is like you Scotch; you never see what you don't want to see,' said Mrs. Riddell with her unpleasantly sarcastic smile. 'I have come, then, to see how often you will desire to have my brother's child brought to see you, for I do not suppose you will come to see her when she is at Ravelaw.'

'I fail a' thegither tae understand ye yet, Mrs. Riddell,' said Miss Nesbit quietly.

'Now you are absurd. The child ought to have been brought to Ravelaw at once, as I told Sandy. Of course you cannot afford the additional burden of another child on your limited means; besides, she could not have the rearing befitting a Reynaud, so I am quite willing to take her to Ravelaw.

She will be a companion to Louis; my poor Marie, like her mother, has so poor health.'

Miss Nesbit looked steadily into the face of Mrs. Riddell, and made answer low and clearly:

'Ye ask a thing utterly oot o' the question, Mrs. Riddell. The bairn is mine, left a sacred legacy by my sister. Please God, naething on earth shall part us as long as she needs my care.'

Up rose the lady of Ravelaw in a towering passion.

'You are a greater fool than I thought you. Woman, are you blind to the advantages she would have at Ravelaw? It'—

'A brawer hoose, finer meat an' claes, she micht hae,' interrupted Miss Nesbit passionately, 'but I doot she micht come tae as waefu' an end as her puir unhappy mither. Ye hae brocht enough trouble on my nearest an' dearest already, Mrs. Riddell; an' as sure as I stand here, I'll keep my sister's bairn awa frae ye if it can be dune.'

In an instant Mrs. Riddell's manner changed, and she resumed her seat.

'May I see the child?' she asked smoothly.

Miss Nesbit touched the bell, and desired Marget to bring the little one down-stairs, which she did, and, placing her on the threshold of the door, retired very hastily to her own domain. In Mrs. Riddell's presence Marget was more than likely to forget discretion, so judged it best to keep out of the way.

Miss Nesbit held out her hand, and smiled at the slender little thing, who came running to her at once, but kept her eyes fixed on the face of the strange lady.

Mrs. Riddell put back her veil, ungloved her hands, and held them out to the child, saying coaxingly:

'Come, *petite;* come and kiss me!'

But Netta held back. Then Mrs. Riddell rose, and snatched her almost angrily in her arms.

'She has turned you against Aunt Honoré already, *ma chère,*' she said. 'Come with me, *petite*, and you shall have bon-bons and so many pretty things.'

But the child struggled in her arms, and held out beseeching hands to Miss Nesbit, screaming as she had done the night before. Then very deliberately Mrs. Riddell administered a smart slap on the child's bare arm, and set her roughly to the floor.

'Ugly little thing, that evil temper never belonged to a Reynaud. Well, Miss Nesbit, you have your work before you. Ah! I would not have her now at any cost; she would be a perfect plague in a house. Permit me to wish you good-morning. Good-bye, little fury,' she said, showing her teeth in a little scornful laugh; then she flounced out of the room.

'Is she away?' asked the child in terrified tones. 'I fitened, Auntie; hold me in your arms. Don't let her come in any more.'

The memory of that morning never faded from the mind of Netta Reynaud, and even when she no longer feared her black-browed aunt at Ravelaw, she shrank from and disliked her most thoroughly.

Miss Nesbit drew a long breath of relief when the rolling of Mrs. Riddell's coach wheels died away in the distance. The bairn herself had settled the matter beyond question, and again her heart was at rest.

Since Tibbie had quitted her roof-tree, Miss Nesbit had not required to work at her lace; but with the daily increasing wants of two children to provide for, she would need to return to her only means of adding to her slender income. Whatever happened, the revenues of Aldersyde must remain untouched.

She went very quietly about it, not saying anything to Marget, knowing what a grief it would be to her. She might have taken trouble by the forelock, and rendered herself unhappy with gloomy thoughts of the future, when there would be education to pay for and innumerable additional expenses ; but she took the wiser way, and left the future of her bairns with the God who had never failed her yet.

Grizel Oliphant of Yair had truly washed her hands of the Nesbits, for Janet had never seen her face since the memorable day succeeding Tibbie's flight. She had heard occasionally through the Scotts that she was still the same sour, cankered old woman, and that her bodily strength was failing every day.

Dear Lady Scott, who had indeed proved an abiding friend to Janet Nesbit, came over one day to give her tender sympathy in her new tribulation, and to see the little one who had found a home at Windyknowe. From her Miss Nesbit learned that Grizel Oliphant was even then lying hopelessly ill at Yair, unattended save by her grim serving-woman.

'If ye'll gie me a seat in yer coach, Leddy Scott, I'll jist gang back tae Yair wi' ye an' see the puir auld body,' said Miss Nesbit. 'Marget 'll mind the bairns brawly for ae nicht.'

'My dear, I'll be more than delighted, and if you could stay with us till Friday, you will see Marjorie. We expect the Earl and her from their Sussex home for a few days before they proceed to the north for the shooting,' returned Lady Scott.

'I'll see aboot it,' Miss Nesbit answered, her heart yearning for a sight of bonnie Marjorie, the blithe bairn she had aye loved.

Great was the consternation of the bairns when they beheld Auntie come down dressed to go away with the lady in her coach. Beyond a quiver of his red lip, Walter made no sign of his grief; but again, Netta stamped her small feet, and went into a passion of tears and crying.

Miss Nesbit took her up, and carrying her over to the window, took the little doubled-up fists out of the wet eyes, and looked gravely and sternly into her face.

'Netta, you must be quiet and good, or Auntie canna love ye ony mair. If ye mak sic a din, I'll be forced tae punish ye, an' shut ye up away frae Walter a' thegither.'

The child looked into her face in mute amazement. Hitherto she had been accustomed to rule those about her, to have her own way in everything, and did not know the meaning of being punished. But there was no smile on her aunt's face: she had never seen her look so nearly angry before; and in a moment the little will was broken, and Miss Nesbit's firmness had gained the mastery. There was no more screaming or stamping, but a very woful-faced little maiden returned Auntie's kiss, and then climbed up in the window to watch her drive away.

'I'm beginnin' tae hae some inklin' o' a mither's battle, Leddy Scott,' said Miss Nesbit with a smile. 'I couldna hae believed it was sic an ill thing tae guide bairns.'

'It takes a deal of patience, I know,' returned Lady Scott. 'And you are at a disadvantage, Janet; you have not the enduring mother-love to fall back on.'

'I couldna lo'e them muckle mair, tho' they were my ain,' returned Miss Nesbit.

Then they fell to talking in earnest about the best way to train children, a subject which was not exhausted when they reached the Brig of Yair. Miss Nesbit was set down at the door of Miss Oliphant's dwelling, and bade Lady Scott just go home. If she was not well received by her kinswoman, she would walk up to Scottrigg after the moon had risen.

Even in her sick-bed, Grizel Oliphant's sharp ears had heard the coach stop at her gate, and despatched her serving-woman Lisbeth to see who it was, before Miss Nesbit had time to knock at the door.

'Hoo's Miss Grizzie, Lisbeth?' asked Miss Nesbit. 'D'ye think she'll let me see her?'

'Lord only kens, mem,' returned Lisbeth, ushering her into the sitting-room. 'She's that thrawn, there's nae leevin' wi' her. She'll no dae a thing the doctor bids her, an' whiles she'll no let me open the door till him efter he's cam a' the way frae Aldershope tae see her.'

'Lisbeth Harden, ye aff-pitten body,' cried a shrill, wheezy voice, 'how daur ye bide there clashin' tae onybody. Fesh them in whaever they are, an' dinna staund there misca'in me thegither.'

Without more ado, Miss Nesbit, putting down her gloves and veil, went away into Miss Grizzie's bedroom. There was no fire in the place,—a whim of the sick woman's,—though the doctor had expressly ordered it, the autumn air being so keen and chilly.

Although unable to sit without the support of half-a-dozen pillows, Miss Grizzie refused to lie down; and there she was, propped up against the head of the bed, with a shawl about her shoulders, and a high, stiffly-starched muslin cap on her head. Beneath its full plaited border, the face was wofully thin and haggard and yellow, the long thin lips pinched and blue-looking, the bead-like eyes dim and glazed. But the old temper had not abated its sharpness a jot; for when she saw Janet Nesbit enter, she immediately went into a fit of passion.

'Hoo daur ye come here, Janet Nesbit, tae craw ower me wi' yer red cheeks and yer healthy step, when I'm brocht low on a sick-bed?' she screamed. 'Get oot o' my sicht! If it's my bits o' gear yer efter, or my twa three bawbees, I may tell ye aince for a' ye'll no get nane o'd; an' I'm no gaun tae dee yet,—I winna dee, I say, till I'm ready. I'—

She was obliged to stop through sheer exhaustion; then without ado, Janet Nesbit laid off her bonnet and shawl, and greatly to Lisbeth's amazement went over to the bed, and throwing all the pillows but one out on the floor, very deliberately took the shawl from Miss Grizzie's shoulders, and laid her down in her bed. She was too weak to resist, and I believe she felt the rest grateful to her weary body, though she would not have admitted it.

'Noo, Miss Grizzie, ye'll lie still, see. If ye're no gaun tae dee, ye're takin' the surest way tae yer end, sittin' up there shiverin' i' the cauld. Lisbeth, licht a spunk o' fire, my wummin; it's fair Greenland in here.'

'Ye winna waste my peats, Janet Nesbit; I'm no cauld,' Miss Grizzie began; but Miss Nesbit took no notice of her. 'I want tae ken what's brocht ye here, Janet Nesbit?' she said by and by, though in a quieter voice.

'I cam tae see ye, of coorse. Had I kent ye were ill, I wad hae been afore noo. Dinna be feared,' she added good humouredly, 'I'm no gaun tae bide. I'll just see the fire set, an' syne I'll be awa up tae Scottrigg.'

'Scottrigg, again!' groaned Miss Grizzie. 'Lord deliver her frae the flesh-pats o' Egypt. Weel, I suppose ye've gotten anither bairn hame. Ye'd better set up a puirshouse at aince.'

'I'm quite wullint, if the Lord ca's me tae the wark, Miss Grizzie,' replied Janet cheerily. 'Weel, I'll come and bide wi' ye till ye're better, if ye like. I'm a grand nurse, if ye'll but try me.'

'Oo ay, ye can get roon some folk; but ye canna get roon me, Janet Nesbit,' said Miss Grizzie sourly. 'I ken it's the bawbees; but ye'll no get them: ye needna build yer houps on that. The Kirk better deserves them than you.'

'Let the Kirk get them an' welcome,' smiled Miss Nesbit. 'Brawly ye ken, Miss Grizzie, that bawbees never entered my heid. But ye're jist the auld wife, I see, an' winna tak a kindness as it's offered.'

'Weel, awa ye gang up tae Scottrigg among yirls and coontesses, an' let auld Grizel Oliphant dee in peace. When she wants you, Janet

Nesbit, she'll no forget tae send for ye,' said the old woman grimly.

So Miss Nesbit put on her things again, and bidding her farewell, left the house, wondering, with a great pity in her heart, if she should ever look on the unhappy old woman in life again. No sooner was she out of the door than Lisbeth was ordered to carry the blazing peats back to the kitchen fire, which she did, being in great awe of her sharp-tongued mistress.

At Scottrigg, to her surprise and pleasure, Miss Nesbit found the Earl of Dryburgh and his fair young wife, they having arrived earlier than they were expected. Warmly she took the blithe bairn to her heart, looking lovingly into the happy face, and stroking down the sunny hair which even the dignity of wifehood and great rank could not induce to lie smooth and straight on the broad white brow.

Then the Earl came forward to be introduced to the lady of whom he had heard so much; and after one look into his noble, manly face and true eyes, Miss Nesbit spoke to him as a friend, because she said that Marjorie's husband was worthy of her.

A happy evening was spent in that dear home circle, and Miss Nesbit lay down in her bed thanking God for this sunny spot in her life, and for the blessing of such true friends. Having seen Marjorie, she did not require to stay another day at Scottrigg, much as they desired it; and her heart was at home with her bairns.

'I'm the heid o' a family noo, Marjorie,' she said as she tied on her bonnet, 'an' hae mony claims on me. When my bairns are awa tae hames o' their ain, I'll come and bide an' help ye to bring up yours.'

'All right, Janet; I'll hold you to it,' laughed Marjorie, and in after years she claimed and received part fulfilment of Janet's promise. Then Miss Nesbit took her to her heart again, and prayed God to bless an' keep her aye, for she was a glint o' His ain sunshine in a weary world.

Such a welcome awaited Auntie at Windyknowe! It was worth being away to see the look of perfect content on Walter's face, and to hear, too, the more boisterously expressive joy from Netta.

'She's been a wunnerfu' guid bairn,' Marget said. 'Never a cheep sin' ye gaed awa.'

So with gentle but firm management, Tibbie's passionate little girl might not be so ill to guide after all.

For some days Miss Nesbit heard no more of Miss Grizzie's state, Doctor Elliot having ceased to attend her. Drawing very near her end, Grizzel Oliphant's heart went out yearningly to Janet

Nesbit, whose sweet face and tender womanly ways would have made smooth her last hours ; but since she had turned her from the door, she could not humble herself to send for her again.　Curious as it may seem, Grizel Oliphant's heart was not dead yet, and it clung with what tenderness it possessed to Janet Nesbit.　Even in her frequent fits of anger which Janet's honest tongue had kindled, she had felt drawn towards her, though nobody, least of all Janet herself, could have guessed it.　But the old woman died as she had lived, trampling down all softer impulses, and showing to the end the grim exterior which had made her so unpopular all her days.

Her last act was to scold Lisbeth for lighting the fire when she found all other means inadequate to warm the chilled frame of her mistress.

One day, about a week after her return from Scottrigg, Miss Nesbit was surprised by a visit from Mr. Douglas, who brought the news of Miss Oliphant's death the previous morning.　He carried with him a document which he silently handed to Miss Nesbit for perusal.

It was the last will and testament of Grizel Oliphant of Birkenshaws, Yair ; and after making mention of a legacy to Lisbeth Harden, bequeathed to her well - beloved kinswoman, Janet Hay Nesbit of Windyknowe. the house of Birkenshaws, with all gear and plenishing within its walls; also all moneys pertaining to the said Grizel Oliphant, to be paid without reserve three days after her decease.

'Amounting in all to fully three thousand pounds, Miss Nesbit,' supplemented the lawyer when she folded up the document with a strange expression on her face.

'I had nae expectation o' this, Mr. Douglas,' she said.

'I believe you ; but Miss Grizzie, in spite of her scant courtesy, entertained for you a very profound affection and respect. She told me the day before she died there was not one in Ettrick Vale fit to hold a candle to you.'

'Puir Miss Grizzie !' said Miss Nesbit from the depths of her heart. By and by when the lawyer had gone, she sat down in the window to realize how great a change this bequest would make in her life. Henceforth she need have no anxiety, no fear concerning the future of herself or her bairns. It was assured.

'Auntie,' said Walter's earnest voice at her side, 'are you vexed about anything?'

She turned about and lifted him to her knee, and made answer, more to herself than to him :

'My cup runneth over.'

CHAPTER VIII.

AREFUL guidance needed Tibbie's bairn. Passionate, impulsive, self-willed, and headstrong, she taxed all the energies of Miss Nesbit. In the matter of right and wrong, it was vain to appeal to her reason or her better judgment. It was only by working upon her feelings that she could be won to obedience.

One attribute of her character occasioned Miss Nesbit much anxiety; namely, the sudden growth of her likes and dislikes. There was no middle course for her: she either loved or hated. Seeing what a hold the feelings of the heart had upon her in childhood, Miss Nesbit trembled for the womanhood of the bairn. It was possible that the very intensity of her nature might make shipwreck of her life.

She was indeed a child of many prayers.

Often Miss Nesbit longed to be able to keep her aye a bairn, because of the tribulation and care the later years might hold, and which she was not by nature fitted to come through unscathed.

But regardless of all, Time hurried on, the bairn grew apace, and Miss Nesbit continued to watch and pray.

It is no exaggeration to say that Netta Reynaud worshipped her Aunt Janet, and would have laid down her life for her. Next in order came Walter, whom she alternately teased and tyrannized over in a way Miss Nesbit did not altogether approve.

Walter was not without a will of his own, but it was marvellously subservient to that of Netta. His devotion to her, even in his boyish days, had in it something of the chivalry of the knights of old.

He had never occasioned Miss Nesbit a moment's anxiety in his life. Gentle and yet fearless, solicitous to obey and even to anticipate her slightest wish, true and honourable to the core even in the little things boys are so apt to regard beneath their notice, he did indeed promise to be such a Laird as Aldersyde had never seen before.

Both the bairns received lessons from Mr. Bourhill. Netta was a negligent, idle scholar; but

all her coaxing could not tempt Walter to devote
to play the time he owed to his studies. Mr.
Bourhill prophesied for him a glorious future at
the University, to which it was Miss Nesbit's
intention to send him in his sixteenth year.

She kept the word she passed to Mrs. Riddell ;
for when Netta was twelve years old, she had
never set foot in Ravelaw, and knew her cousins
only by sight. But there came a day when
the child claimed for herself a right to make
the acquaintance of her father's kinsfolk, and then
Miss Nesbit judged it best to let her have her way.

She had been to Aldershope one day, and came
running into the house to her aunt, her cheeks
flushed, and her eyes dancing with excitement.

'Oh, Auntie!' she burst out; 'I met Uncle
Riddell in Aldershope, and he asked why I never
came to see him, and said would I come to-
morrow, and bring Walter. Oh! may we, Auntie?
Say yes; I want so much to see the beautiful
house and all the fine things my cousins have
at Ravelaw.'

A pang shot to the heart of Miss Nesbit.
Was this the beginning of the end? Had she
inherited her mother's craving for the good
things of life? and would nature triumph at last
over the careful, prayerful training she had given
Tibbie's bairn?

These thoughts chased each other through her brain in an instant of time, and their seriousness made her answer grave, and somewhat cold.

'I'll consider it, Netta, an' tell ye in the mornin',' she said, and turned to Walter, asking him some question about his lessons.

Netta's under-lip fell ; but she knew her aunt too well to venture to dispute her words. But all the evening Miss Nesbit noticed how restless and excited she was, and her heart grew heavy indeed.

'Lord, keep Thy arm aboot the bairn,' was her inward prayer ; the last on her lips when she sought her pillow that night. In the morning her decision was made, and Netta heard with delight that she and Walter were to walk over to Ravelaw after their early dinner.

'Tak care o' Netta, Walter, lad,' said Miss Nesbit as she parted from them at the door.

'Of course I will, Auntie,' answered the boy, looking back with beaming, earnest eyes ; and as she went into the house, the hope which had lain in her heart for years found vent in another prayer.

'Lord, if it be Thy will, let him care for the bairn a' his days.'

The house was very empty without the blithe young presence of the bairns. She had bidden them leave Ravelaw before sunset, so that they might reach Windyknowe at the darkening. What was her amazement, then, when she was finishing her solitary tea, to hear a quick foot on the passage, and behold Netta bursting into the room. She did not look like herself: her eyes were wet with tears, and yet shone with strange brilliancy, her cheeks burning, her black locks all dishevelled. Little wonder Miss Nesbit started to her feet in affright at the apparition.

' Bairn, what is't ? '

'I ran away from that horrid place, Auntie,' fell thick and fast from Netta's lips. 'I could not even wait for Walter, I wanted so to get home.'

Here a wild passion of tears choked her utterance ; and drawing a stool to her aunt's side, she leaned her head on her knees, and wept sore. Miss Nesbit wisely let the tempest run its course, but wondered sorely what had happened at Ravelaw so to upset the bairn.

' Oh, Auntie, Uncle Riddell's wife said you were a bad, wicked woman, and broke my mamma's heart ; and she asked me would I not come and live with her, or you would break mine too,' said Netta through her sobs. 'And I got mad, Auntie. I could have killed her, I hated her so ; and I told her *she* was the bad, wicked woman, and that I would never, never come near her any more.   Oh, Auntie, it is not true, is it?'

'My bairn, my bairn, God forgi'e her,' fell very low from Miss Nesbit's lips.   Then there was a long silence.

'Tell me what you did at Ravelaw all afternoon, Netta,' asked Miss Nesbit by and by.

'Uncle Riddell met us at the gate, Auntie : he was looking for us ; and, oh, I do love him, he is so good and kind.   He said my eyes were very like mamma's ; and he said I must grow up like you, for you were the best woman on God's earth.   These are his very words, Auntie : I said them over and over, so that I could tell them right ; and he looked so solemn and sad when he said them, I am sure he must love you very much.   Well, he walked up with us to the house—how big and grand it is, Auntie !   I felt quite afraid in it ; but Walter looked as if he was quite at home in it, and smiled because I crept near to him and said I was afraid.'

A little smile crept about Miss Nesbit's lips. Young though he was, Aldersyde's laird could hold his own anywhere.

'Well, we went to see Aunt Honorè in her own room, and she kissed me.   I didn't like it, Auntie : I didn't love her, you see ; her face is so cross and strange looking.   Cousin Marie was with her.   She is very like her, and is not strong, I am sure, she is

so pale.   She is cross, too : just like her mother ; and
I was glad to get away out with Walter to see
Louis and the ponies.'

'I hope ye liked Louis better ?'

'Oh yes; he is the best, next to Uncle Riddell, and
he fears nothing under the sun.   He says he will
teach me to ride.   I would like it, Auntie, but not if
I have to go up there to learn.'

Again there was a little silence.

'Cousin Marie came out after awhile, and spoiled
all our fun.   Louis and she quarrelled all the time,
and he teased her, and tried to frighten her with the
horses.   I don't think they are so happy as we
are, Auntie, though they have so many nice things.'

'*They* canna mak happiness, my bairn,' said
Auntie softly, thankful that already Netta's shrewd
eyes had learned the great truth.

'We went in after a bit, and got our dinner ; then
Uncle Riddell's wife took me up-stairs, and showed
me ever so many trinkets and things, and said I
should have them all if I would come and live with
her and play with Marie.   I said no every time,
and then she got angry ; and Marie and she laughed
at my clothes, and said I was a pauper ; and then she
said all these wicked things about you, and I
screamed out at her, Auntie, and said I would kill
her, and then I ran out of the house, and ran all the
way home.'

'My bairn, ye'll hae tae learn tae hear in silence, an' bear an' mak nae sign,' said Miss Nesbit.

'Not if wicked people say such things about you, dear, dear Auntie,' cried Netta, in her impulsiveness flinging her arms about her aunt's neck. 'I couldn't love them. You don't want me to love them, Auntie ; for I couldn't, even to please you.'

Walter's entrance at that moment interrupted their talk. Miss Nesbit looked up anxiously, wondering what had been his experience of Ravelaw. He said very little, but Miss Nesbit knew from the firm curve of his lips that it had not been altogether pleasant. She hastened to begin a talk about something else, and soon the unpleasant memories of the visit to Ravelaw seemed to have faded from Netta's mind. Walter lingered in the dining-room after Netta had gone to bed, and finally said to his aunt :

'You will not let Netta go any more to Ravelaw, Aunt Janet ?'

He spoke with a grave earnestness strange to see in a boy.

'No, if I can help it, Walter,' she answered with a sigh.

'Oh, Auntie, I could not live as yon folk do,' he said by and by. 'I never thought Windyknowe was such a dear place before.'

'Ye'll mind, then, Walter that it's no great riches

nor a braw hoose that can mak happiness,' she said gravely, ' but a contented soul.'

' I'll mind, Auntie,' fell low and earnestly from the boy's lips. 'And when I'm a man, I'll try to live as you would like me to live, and never do anything you would be vexed to know.'

'I'm no feared for ye, my laddie. Ye hae the grace o' God in yer heart, young as ye are,' said Janet Nesbit from the fulness of her heart.

Then Walter moved to her side, and putting one arm about her, said with a break in his boyish voice :

'And if I ever forget you, and what you've done and been to me, Auntie, I pray God may punish me as I deserve, for I shall not be fit to live.'

For a moment Janet Nesbit let her head fall on the strong young arm, a song of thanksgiving echoing in her heart. Surely this was recompense indeed for all the years of toil and anxious care: already she could look to him for support and comfort.

By and by she laid her two hands upon his shoulders, and the solemn, beautiful blessing of Holy Writ fell tremulously from her lips:

' The Lord bless thee and keep thee, and lift up His countenance upon thee, and give thee peace ! '

CHAPTER IX.

N a golden August evening Netta Reynaud stood in the window of the dining-
room at Windyknowe, with her hands
idly clasped before her, and her bright eyes looking eagerly and expectantly down the road to
Aldershope. Six years had wrought a great
change; they had transformed the child into a
woman.

The sweet, gracious curves of cheek and lip and
chin, the changeful light of the lovely eyes, the
wealth of raven locks, and the nameless, indescrib-
able grace and charm which lingered about her,
and characterized her every movement, made her
indeed fair to see. In many respects she was the
Netta of old. The wilful, winning way, the loving
impulsiveness and quick exhibition of feeling,
were still her characteristics; but they were the

blossoms of her nature: the weeds had been rooted out.

Fitted to grace the highest rank, there was no more contented being in bonnie Scotland than Netta Reynaud, living simply and quietly in the muirland dwelling. She went through her daily round of duties with willing heart and hand, making labour light with gay snatches of song, and shedding God's own sunshine in the home she loved.

During Walter's absence at Edinburgh she did her utmost to make up to her aunt for his loss. The parting had been a sore blow to Miss Nesbit, for she knew that never again could Walter fill the same place at Windyknowe. When his college days were over, Aldersyde would claim its laird, and he would need to fill his place, and do his share of work in the world.

On this August evening they were expecting him home after his last summer term at Edinburgh. Miss Nesbit, in her arm-chair, thought of his future; and in the window Netta thought of him also, with a strange softening in the lovely eyes, and a tender curve of the sweet, proud lips.

'He's surely late, Netta?' said Miss Nesbit when the clock struck five.

'No, Auntie; the coach is only due at Aldershope, you know, at half-past four, and it is often late,' answered Netta. 'I see Louis and Marie coming up the road; I wish they had not come just now.'

A cloud flitted momentarily across the sweet face, and it was reflected also on Miss Nesbit's. Never since that memorable day six years ago had Netta Reynaud set foot within Ravelaw, but her cousins were constant visitors at Windyknowe.

They were riding to-day; and, like his father, Louis Riddell looked his best on horseback. He was a tall, manly fellow, strongly resembling his father in appearance, and not a little in nature.

A pale, sickly, delicate-looking being was the one daughter of the house of Ravelaw, with a discontented, peevish look on her face, which made it a perfect contrast to the brightness of Netta's. There was no love between the two girls, for each was the antipodes of the other.

But it only needed a glance at the face of Louis Riddell, when he entered Netta's presence, to tell even a careless observer that he loved her with the fierce, all-absorbing passion of which his nature was capable. He never took his eyes from her face; but she seemed unaware of his looks, for she chattered to him frankly and unrestrainedly, while Miss Nesbit inquired kindly for Marie's delicate health, and listened patiently to her grumbling about her want of strength and other ailments.

In the middle of their talk, a quick, firm step trod the gravel, and Netta's eyes drooped. Young Riddell saw it, and ground his teeth, knowing full well he had no power to bring that tender blush to the face he loved.

'Aunt Janet! Netta! where are you?' called out the deep, manly tones, the dearest on earth to at least two in that room.

Miss Nesbit rose and slipped out for a word with her boy away from strange eyes. When they entered together, Netta rose, and offered Walter her hand with the old, bright smile he had treasured in his heart since his boyhood. He held the slender fingers a moment in his manly clasp, then turned to speak courteously to the Riddells.

A red flush mounted to Marie's pale face when he touched her hand, and inquired gently and compassionately if she had grown stronger while he was away. It was Walter's way to be tender to all women, especially to those who were frail and delicate; but to Netta's imaginative mind, his greeting was needlessly warm. How had he so many kind words for Marie, and not even one for her? As for Marie herself, she read her own meaning out of them, and her vain heart beat high with hope.

'I hope we shall see you often at Ravelaw now, Mr. Nesbit?' she said as she gathered her skirts in her hand.

'I thank you, Miss Marie,' he answered courteously. 'I fear I shall not have much time for visiting for long; but rest assured, that when I am at leisure, I shall not forget your kind words.'

A chill seemed to strike to the heart of Netta Reynaud. A less sensitive, less imaginative nature might have seen nothing beyond ordinary courtesy in Walter's words; but when Netta's heart had awakened to the one love of her life, it had awakened also to the miserable, jealous fear which in some natures is love's inseparable companion. She was glad to rise and go with her cousins to the door, just to get away for a little from Walter's presence.

'Ah, how handsome the Laird of Aldersyde has grown!' whispered Marie while Louis went to adjust her saddle. 'It is not a month since we met in Edinburgh, and I could fancy an improvement almost since then.'

'You did not tell me you met in Edinburgh, Marie?' said Netta coldly, and added to herself, 'nor did Walter.'

'Did I not? Impossible! Ah, what a time

we had, driving, riding, sketching; and best of all, charming moonlight strolls round yon terrible cliffs in the Park!'

'I should not think that Aunt Honorè would have cared for the last mentioned?' said Netta, hating herself for asking the indirect question.

'You little fool!' laughed Marie coquettishly. 'Mamma had her comfortable after-dinner nap while we were out. Yes, Louis, I'm ready!'

Then Louis helped his sister to her saddle, and turned to bid Netta good-bye. She was conscious that he was murmuring some passionate nonsense about love, which she hastily interrupted, and nodding to Marie, ran into the house.

She had no intention of returning to the dining-room; but as she set her foot on the stair, the door opened, and her aunt called her. So she was obliged to go in and sit down, though she placed herself as far away from Walter as she could, and took not the slightest part in the conversation.

Any question or remark which Walter addressed to her, she either ignored or answered so stiffly as to dumfounder him. This was not the Netta of old!

They talked chiefly of Aldersyde, where Walter was to take up his immediate abode; and when

Miss Nesbit said to him jokingly he would need to get a wife to reign in the old house, Netta abruptly rose and fled up-stairs.

Then Walter changed the subject.

'Aunt Janet, there is something the matter with Netta,' he said in a troubled way. 'What is it?'

'Nonsense, laddie; she's only that gled tac see ye she canna speak muckle.'

'That's not Netta's way; but she is a young lady now, and I suppose I cannot expect her to fly at me as she used to do.'

'She's a dear bairn!' said Miss Nesbit warmly, 'the very licht an' sunshine o' Windyknowe.'

'Ay, I know that, Aunt Janet,' returned Walter in a queer, quick voice. 'Well, how do you suppose I'm going to exist at Aldersyde alone? Won't you and Netta take pity on me?'

Miss Nesbit smiled.

'Na, na; I maun keep my ain roof-tree, an' the day'll come when ye'll no be yer lane at Aldersyde. Eh, Walter, lad, my prayers are answered this day when I see ye come hame, ready and able tae claim yer ain!'

The young man rose, and began to pace restlessly up and down the floor. By and by he stopped in front of her, and looked down at her, his true eyes moist and tender.

'Aunt Janet, it was only to-day I learned from Mr. Douglas *all* you have done for me. I can hardly speak of it. It unmans me. There is nothing I can do, or hope ever to do, which could repay a tithe of it.'

'Ay, there's ae thing, my bairn,' said Aunt Janet with kindling face; 'serve yer mither's God wi' a' the strength o' yer manhood, an' lo'e Aldersyde as she lo'ed it, an' as I hae lo'ed it a' my days.'

'Aunt Janet, God helping me, I will try!' said he, bending his manly head in humility before her. 'With you to help me as you have done since you took pity on me when I was a motherless infant, I have no fear for the future.'

Again, as it had done many, many times before, Janet Nesbit's heart overflowed with the fulness and joy of her recompense.

Not many days later Walter Nesbit took up his abode at Aldersyde, which had been set in readiness for him by the hands which had laboured for him since his birth. The furnishings which had been bought for his fair young mother were as she had left them, and her sweet, gentle influence seemed to linger in every room and make it a hallowed spot to the son who cherished her memory with a most passionate devotion.

Janet Nesbit had not forgotten that part of her vow, for she had talked to Walter Nesbit about his mother, and, as Mary herself expressed it, kept her memory green in his heart.

It was lonely in the great house for the young man, and it was little wonder that his horse's feet turned very often in the direction of Windyknowe, where he was aye sure of a welcome from his aunt at least.

He could not understand Netta. The old frank confidence, the teasing, winning manner had entirely disappeared. She was shy and reticent, even to coldness, in his presence; and the poor fellow, not being versed in the logic of a maiden's heart, could not read between the lines, but fancied he was an object of aversion to her, and that Louis Riddell was likely to win the prize he would give a world to call his own.

Aunt Janet looked on, and saw them daily drift farther apart in sorrowfulness of soul. She did not know which was to blame; but when she saw how Netta's face brightened and her tongue loosed when her Cousin Louis came, and how she would sit silent or slip out of the room altogether when Walter paid his visits to Windyknowe, she began to fear her hopes were not destined to be fulfilled.

In the country side the young Laird of Aldersyde

was made much of, and nowhere did he receive a warmer welcome than at Ravelaw. For him, Marie Riddell donned her most becoming attire, and her sweetest smile; for him even the bad-tempered lady of Ravelaw had a courteous word, and the Laird a warm welcome.

Louis Riddell never failed to tell Netta when Walter Nesbit had been at Ravelaw, and laid special stress on his devotion and attention to Marie. And Netta would laugh her little clear, scornful laugh, and say he had soon tired of bachelor loneliness at Aldersyde.

Upon a certain afternoon about six months after Walter Nesbit took up his abode at Aldersyde, Mrs. Riddell of Ravelaw called at Windyknowe—a very unusual thing for her, as she had not crossed its threshold since Netta was a bairn. Miss Nesbit, however, received her courteously, and bade her be seated, knowing perfectly well the lady had some end in view. She had not very long to wait, for presently, after a few common-place remarks, Mrs. Riddell said abruptly:

'Well, Miss Nesbit, I have come over for a friendly and confidential chat with you about our young people.'

Miss Nesbit bowed, and waited for the rest.

'You must have seen, I suppose, how devotedly

attached to Nettie my poor Louis is,' said Mrs. Riddell with a little cunning smile.

'Maybe, an' maybe no,' returned Miss Nesbit drily.

'Well, it is the truth. So I have come to talk to you about it, as you stand in the place of a parent to my brother's child. I am very willing that they should marry, though Louis might have found a richer bride. Ravelaw is willing to give them Alderburn for a residence, and everything is charmingly arranged,—with your consent.'

'Has your son obtained Netta's word yet?' asked Miss Nesbit in tones which sounded cold and hard.

'My dear, I have never asked, but no doubt it is all settled between them. No girl could long resist Louis, he is so charming in every way. Well, I suppose you cannot have any objections?'

'Whatever the bairn thinks best for her ain happiness, I will agree tae, Mrs. Riddell,' returned Miss Nesbit in a low voice. 'She has come tae woman's estate noo, an' can judge for hersel''

'Umph! You do not even express any delight at such a splendid settlement in life for her.'

The ghost of a smile flitted across the patient face of Janet Nesbit; but she kept to herself the thought in her heart.

'I feel quite *distrait*, quite woe-begone, I assure

T

you,' said Mrs. Riddell with a pretty affectation of pathos. 'Marie will not be long behind her brother, and I shall be left childless at Ravelaw.'

'Indeed!' said Miss Nesbit. 'Is your daughter contemplatin' changin' her state also?'

At that moment Netta came into the dining-room, dressed for walking, and listlessly greeted her aunt, Mrs. Riddell of Ravelaw.

'I am going to the Manse for a little while, Aunt Janet,' she said. 'If Mrs. Ferguson and Bessie are in, I shall likely stay to tea.'

'Very well, my dear,' said Miss Nesbit.

'You look pale, Netta love,' said Mrs. Riddell. 'You mope too much, I fear. Come up to Ravelaw, and we will rouse you up.'

'Thank you, Aunt Honorè. I am very well content at home,' returned Netta—an answer which displeased highly the lady of Ravelaw.

'Marie will have a lot to tell you, I fancy,' she said, smiling, though her eyes gleamed slightly. 'I was just saying to your aunt I would soon be left childless at Ravelaw. I expect your young Laird of Aldersyde will soon be stealing my sweet Marie; he is seldom from her side, and she seems to have set her heart upon him.'

Miss Nesbit started and grew pale; as for Netta, she turned her face away.

'God forbid!' said Miss Nesbit, unable for the

life of her to keep back the words; but they did
not ruffle the composure of the lady of Ravelaw,
and even when Netta suddenly walked out of
the room without a word of farewell, she kept a
smile upon her face.

'I think you should have advice about the dear
child, she really looks so ill and behaves so oddly,'
she said, rising languidly from her chair. 'Well,
I will be going. Surely the happiness of our young
people will heal old sores and make us friends
once more?'

The words, *merely* words, found no echo in the
heart of Janet Nesbit, and she was too straight-
forward to make any pretence. Therefore without
remark at all she showed her visitor out, and,
returning to the dining-room, sat down by the fire
with her head on her hand, to face the complete
overthrow of all her hopes.

Coming in by and by to set the tea, Marget
Drysdale saw the despondent attitude, and mentally
shook the lady of Ravelaw.

'Confoond her! she never comes but, like the ill
east winds, she leaves trouble at her back,' she
muttered to herself. But somehow she could not ask
her mistress any question concerning the business of
Mrs. Riddell's visit. She knew from past experience,
that, if necessary, Miss Nesbit would tell her, and
was content to bide that time.

Before the tea was ready, Walter Nesbit came riding up to Windyknowe. He fastened his horse's bridle to a post Marget had driven into the ground at the door for that purpose ; then he strode into the house, bidding her a cheery good afternoon, and asking if his aunt were within. Miss Nesbit rose when she heard him at the door, and went out to the hall to bid him welcome.

His keen, affectionate eyes were quick to note the sad and anxious expression on her face ; but, like Marget, he knew that Miss Nesbit would tell the trouble if need be, and if not, well, she would bear it alone.

'Can I have a cup of Marget's tea, Auntie ?' he said, tossing off his gloves. 'I declare I'll never get used to solitary meals at Aldersyde. Every mouthful is like to choke me, when I remember our merry meals at this table. Where's Netta ?'

'At Mr. Bourhill's. His sister and niece frae Glasgow are staying at the Manse, an' the lassies seem tae hae taen tae ane anither,' answered Miss Nesbit. 'Eh, Walter lad, what a big chield ye are ! —six feet if ye're an inch, I'll be bound.'

'Six feet one in my stocking soles, Aunt Janet,' said the young giant, drawing himself up. 'And two-and-twenty years of age. Can I answer any more questions, mem ?'

Miss Nesbit laughed.

'No the noo. I hae haen a ca' frae Mrs. Riddell the day.'

Walter looked surprised.

'What in the name of wonder brought her to to see you, Auntie?'

'Ye may weel ask,' said Miss Nesbit with a sigh; then after a moment's silence, she added wistfully, 'Is't true that it's Marie Riddell that's tae be mistress o' Aldersyde?'

'Did she put that into your wise old head, Aunt Janet?' asked the young man in tones which might mean anything.

'Maybe.'

'Do you think Marie Riddell likely ever to be mistress of Aldersyde?'

'Oh, Walter! I dinna ken. What can I ken o' the ways o' young men? Ye hae paid her by ordinar attention, I hae heard, and surely, unless my prayers an' guidin' are tae fa' tae the ground, that can hae but ae meanin'!'

'Who said I paid her by ordinar attention?' asked Walter hotly.

'A'body; no mony meenits syne, Mrs. Riddell telt Netta an' me, ye are seldom frae Marie's side.'

'It is true I am often at Raveclaw, as I am at Drumkerr and other places. I am obliged to seek solace somewhere: I get so poor a welcome where I most desire it.'

'Walter!' said Miss Nesbit solemnly, 'I hope it'll never can be said o' ye that ye played wi' a lassie's heart. It is ane o' the cruellest an' wickedest sins a man can be guilty o''

'Aunt Janet, I swear that no man nor woman can with truth say it of me now, and promise you that my future will be as blameless in this respect as the past has been,' returned Walter as solemnly. Then he strode over to the window, and stood there in silence.

'Come here, Aunt Janet,' he said by and by.

In much amazement, Miss Nesbit joined him at the window.

Out in the garden, fastening up a refractory rose bush, was Netta, her fair young arm bare to the dainty elbow, her face flushed with the exertion, and beautiful exceedingly. Man's eyes never rested on a sweeter or more loveworthy maiden than Netta Reynaud in her gracious girlish loveliness.

'There is my wife, if she will have me, Aunt Janet,' said Walter Nesbit passionately and earnestly. 'If not, no other woman shall ever reign at Aldersyde.'

CHAPTER X.

NETTA REYNAUD had been making a call in Aldershope, and was walking slowly up the road to Windyknowe in the grey, solemn dusk of a September evening Her step was slow and listless, her head bent upon her breast, as if she had some care at her heart.

So absorbed in her own thoughts was she, that she did not notice the approach of a pedestrian from the opposite direction till he was close upon her. Then she raised her head, to see before her the figure of her cousin Louis Riddell. She offered him her hand frankly enough, without blush or other sign of embarrassment, and asked if he had been at Windyknowe.

'Yes, and your aunt told me you were in Aldershope, Netta,' he said, bending his dark eyes on her face, 'and gave me permission to meet you and bring you home.'

'It is very kind of you to think of me, Louis,' she said listlessly, and began to move on her way.

The young man turned also, and walked by her side.

'Are you glad to see me, Netta?' he asked abruptly.

'Yes, I am always pleased to see you, Louis. Is Marie well?'

'As usual. I left Nesbit at Ravelaw; he is becoming quite a member of our home circle.'

Swiftly Netta turned her head away, but not before Louis Riddell saw the grey shadow creep over cheek and brow, and the quiver of the sweet, proud lips. More than a week had gone since Walter had been at Windyknowe, and then he had stayed but a few minutes, pleading want of time. Probably he had an engagement with Marie Riddell at Ravelaw.

'Are you likely to have a good hunting season?' she asked, feeling that the subject must be changed and at once.

'Yes; when did you begin to feel an interest in the field?' asked Louis Riddell with the slightest perceptible sneer.

'You had better go away home, Louis, if you

cannot answer me more courteously,' said Netta with a flash of the old wilful way.

Then Louis humbly asked her pardon, and promised better behaviour in future. The talk was of general interest till they reached the gate of Windyknowe; then Louis Riddell placed himself up against the gatepost, as if he intended to make a stand there for a considerable time.

'Good night, Louis. I must not stand, or Aunt Janet will be out to look for me.'

The young man took her hand in that of his, and bent his passionate eyes upon her fair face.

'Netta, do you grudge me a few minutes here?'

'Don't talk nonsense, Louis,' said Netta sharply; 'I can't bide to waste even a few minutes. Good night.'

'Not yet; I swear you shall hear what I have to say. Netta, I love you. You must be my wife—must, I tell you. I'—

'Who are you that you should command me, Louis Riddell?' asked the maiden in her cool, clear, sweet tones.

'Netta, don't answer me like that,' said the young man hoarsely. 'It is life or death almost to me, I love you so dearly.'

Then a look of weariness and pain came on the face of Netta Reynaud.

'Don't talk in that wild way, Louis,' she said more gently. 'We are cousins, and I can be nothing more to you. Let me go, or we shall have Aunt Janet out.'

'Netta, it is impossible! I can't leave you without some little word of encouragement and hope. You must care for me; I can't live without you.'

'I have no patience to hear a man talk like that,' said Netta sharply. 'I do not care for you, and I shall never be your wife.'

Very dark grew the face of Louis Riddell, and he muttered something under his breath which it was as well Netta did not hear.

'Dear Louis, don't be angry with me,' she said by and by, her tone one of quiet wistfulness now. 'Let us be happy together as we have been.'

'You think that will satisfy me?' said Louis Riddell hotly. 'I don't need to be told that you have set your heart on Nesbit, who cares no more for you than for the meanest peasant girl on his lands. No later than yesterday, I heard him jesting about you to young Patrick Kerr and the rest of his set when we met at Drumkerr.'

'Louis Riddell!'

Clear, and sharp, and scornful the warning words broke upon his ear, and he saw his cousin draw herself up and felt the flashing of her indignant eyes.

'It is true,' he said sullenly. 'Any way, he is devoted to Marie.'

Without a word, Netta Reynaud turned from him and fled into the house, up-stairs to her own little chamber to let her passion have vent. Humbled, insulted, crushed to the very dust, she could only lie with her face buried in her pillows, writhing in her tearless pain.

By and by she rose, and laying aside hat and gloves, smoothed her hair, and went away down to the dining-room. The lamp was not 'set,' but the red glow of the firelight showed the figure of Miss Nesbit sitting in her arm-chair, with her hands idly folded on her lap. Sometimes now Aunt Janet would take a rest, knowing that willing young hands were aye ready to do what had to be done in the house.

'Bairn, when did ye come in?' she asked in some surprise.

'A little while ago, Auntie,' answered Netta, and moved restlessly about the room.

'Did ye meet Louis Riddell?'

'Yes, Auntie,' said Netta very low. And then, coming over to the hearth, she knelt down by Miss Nesbit's chair, and hid her face on her knee.

'Oh, Auntie, life is very hard!' she said brokenly, and instinctively the elder woman's arm stole protectingly about the drooping figure, as if to keep away all harm from the bairn.

'Are ye beginnin' tae find that oot, my bairn?' she asked tremulously.

No answer made Netta, but her aunt felt her trembling from head to foot. Was it possible that *her* life-story was to be repeated again in Netta's experience, and was one of the faithless Riddells to rob the bright young life of all sweetness, and make her desolate in the very spring-time of her days?

'Has Louis Riddell ocht tae dae wi' this, Netta?' she asked in tones which her thought made very stern.

'No, no; don't ask me, Auntie; perhaps I shall tell you another time. Just let me lay my head down here, where I know it's safe,' said Netta in the same broken way.

Then there was a long silence. Very softly Aunt Janet passed her hand to and fro on the bowed head, her heart yearning unspeakably over the bairn, who had at last crossed the threshold where womanhood and childhood meet, and who was finding the new path very thorny for her feet.

From that day Netta was changed. Her work

was deftly and willingly performed, as it had aye been ; but both Miss Nesbit and Marget missed the blithe singing and the merry laugh which had been the very sunshine of Windyknowe. She moved about the house noiselessly and listlessly, and never volunteered to go out of doors unless desired by her aunt. So the days slipped away till the last sheaf was ingathered from Yarrow braes, and the greyness of the winter began to settle down on the earth.

Very seldom indeed did Walter Nesbit visit Windyknowe. He could not bear to face Netta's coldness and pointed avoidance of him, and found it better for his own peace of mind to abide at Aldersyde. Peace of mind, did I say? Truly, when love enters into the heart of a man, he may bid farewell to his peace of mind, so long as he is uncertain of the issue of his love. So Walter was unhappy in Aldersyde, and Netta in Windyknowe, when a word would have set matters right.

But there was none to speak that word, for Miss Nesbit attributed Netta's melancholy to another cause altogether. Well for us that a higher hand holds the ravelled skein of life ; our poor fingers could never make its threads smooth and straight. Louis Riddell came no more to Windyknowe ; but Marie called sometimes alone, and made no secret of her expectations concerning the Laird of Aldersyde.

Then Miss Nesbit grew very wroth with Walter, thinking that he had wilfully misled and deceived her regarding Marie. She looked back with painful longing to the days when her bairns said their prayers together at her knee, and when she could shut her door at night with the feeling that all she loved were safe beneath her own roof-tree.

One afternoon, towards the close of the year, Walter Nesbit came on foot to Windyknowe. Miss Nesbit was in the house alone, Netta having gone out for a walk across the moor. Of late she had taken a strange fancy to roaming over the desolate waste, where there was not a living thing but wild fowls and bright-eyed rabbits. The utter loneliness suited her mood, and she could better battle with her sorrow at home after fighting with the wild nor'-easter which came roaring over the hills and swept across the moor in a perfect hurricane.

Walter did not ask for her, being accustomed to miss her from the house, as she seldom stayed in the room when he paid his brief visits to Windy-knowe. What a change from other days, when they were one in heart and purpose, and when each was nothing without the other!

'Ye are growin' tae be a fair stranger in yer auld hame,' said Miss Nesbit when the first greetings were over, trying to speak lightly, though her heart was very sore.

'It is true, Aunt Janet,' returned the young man. 'Many a time I wish I had never quitted its roof-tree.'

'What way that?' she asked sharply. 'Is Aldersyde no sufficient for ye?'

'Aldersyde?—ay, it is the very apple of my eye, Aunt Janet,' returned Walter almost passionately. 'But can't you see what a life it is for me in that great house alone with not a soul to speak to?'

'That'll be mended by an' by, when ye get the dochter o' Ravelaw hame,' said Miss Nesbit drily.

A hot flush mounted to the young man's brow.

'That's not fair, Aunt Janet. I thought I had settled *that* in your mind long ago.'

'Seein's believin',' she returned with increased dryness. 'An' Marie comes here often. She makes nae secret o'd, though ye dae. Is't honourable, think ye, Walter Nesbit,—is't richt,—tae keep me in the dark aboot your weddin'? I'm no askin' ower muckle surely when I ask tae be telt the truth concernin' this.'

Slowly Walter Nesbit rose from his chair, looking with dazed and dumfoundered eyes on his aunt's stern face.

'Aunt Janet!'

That was all but the sharp pain in his voice went to her heart and broke her down.

'Ay, I'm quick in my speech, my laddie ; but oh, it tries me sair tae see this waefu' gulf atween Aldersyde and Windyknowe,' she said through her tears.

'Aunt Janet, it is not of my seeking. God knows, my whole heart is here. I swear to you before Him whom you have taught me to honour and love, that there is nothing between Marie Riddell and me, and that if I cannot have Netta for my wife, I will live a single man at Aldersyde all my days,' said Walter with most passionate earnestness.

It was impossible to doubt him ; it needed only a look into the frank, true eyes to see his whole soul mirrored there. The scales fell from her eyes in that moment, and she wondered that she could have been so blind.

Sandy Riddell's wife was at the bottom of all this trouble, as she had been at the bottom of many another, and had done her best to blight Netta's life, and secure the Laird of Aldersyde for Marie.

What wonder that Netta had believed all that was told to her, when even *she* had been deceived. Although her own spring-time was past, she knew how little a thing can make a barrier in love, and how trifles are magnified till they seem insurmountable.

'Laddie, forgi'e me; I hae wranged ye sair,' faltered Miss Nesbit, and she took him to her heart as she used to do in his childish days.

So peace, an enduring peace, was made between them, and by and by Miss Nesbit began to unburden her heart concerning Netta, and to express her anxious fears about the bairn.

'Where is she?' asked Walter suddenly.

'Ower the muir. She's aye there when she's no i' the hoose. An uncanny place for a lassie tae be hersel'; but I canna pit her past it,' returned Miss Nesbit.

Then Walter rose up and took his hat from the table.

'I'll go and meet her, Aunt Janet,' he said hoarsely. 'I don't know what mad impulse this is which has come upon me, but wish me God speed.'

Ay, she wished him God speed with all her heart, and prayed for him and for Netta while he was gone.

Walter Nesbit strode across the bleak moor that afternoon like a man who had some end in view. The grey December twilight was already beginning to fall, the air was chill and damp, and the keen north wind had a warning of snow in its teeth. Upon a piece of rising ground he paused, and took a keen survey of the stretch of brown muirland. Away in the distance, battling against the winds, he beheld the slight figure he knew so well, and his heart leaped within him with the great love he bore to her. Surely this impulse was heaven-born, for there was nothing but hope in his breast as he took swift strides toward her. He was close upon her ere she was aware of his approach, and then she flung up her head and looked at him with startled eyes. Surely a deeper crimson than that brought by the rude caress of the winter wind mounted to neck and cheek and brow, and surely that shy drooping of the eyelids could have but one meaning. But these fled in a moment, and she lifted her little head proudly, and looked at him with clear, cold, unfaltering eyes.

'Surely you are out of your way, Walter?' she said. 'This is not the road to or from Aldersyde.'

'I have been at Windyknowe, and Aunt Janet permitted me to come and look for you,' said Walter quietly, using unconsciously almost the same words which Louis Riddell had used the last time Netta had spoken with him alone.

'I am accustomed to walk alone,' said Netta coldly. 'Aunt Janet knows I am not afraid.'

'Perhaps she does; but I do not choose that you should walk in this wild spot alone after dusk,' said Walter daringly.

In the intensity of her amazement, Netta could find no words to reply. Suddenly she became aware that Walter was standing in front of her looking at her, and she was compelled to lift her eyes to his. Little wonder they drooped immediately, for if ever true, faithful love was reflected in man's eyes, it shone in Walter Nesbit's at that moment.

She was conscious of no feeling of surprise or embarrassment, but an unutterable sense of rest and peace seemed to steal over her, and make her wish that moment might last for ever.

'Netta,' said Walter, speaking slowly and dispassionately like a man who had weighed his words, 'we were one in childhood, and I find it very hard to realize that we must live our lives apart. I love you, have loved you all my days, do love you now, as a man loves but one woman in life. If there is no hope for me, lift your eyes to my face, and tell me so, as you would answer to God.'

The slight figure swayed in the wind, and would have fallen, had not Walter's strong arm taken her within its shelter.

She did not shrink from its clasp, but moved nearer to him, and laid her head upon his breast. The only thought in her heart was a kind of wondering surprise, that she had ever doubted him for a moment; it seemed so natural to feel his arms about her, and to know that she was the one woman in the world for him.

'Am I to have no answer, Netta?' asked Walter by and by, scarcely daring to believe

she was his own, though he held her to his
heart.

It was a very shy whisper, but he caught it:

'I will be your wife, Walter, if you will take
me, for I have never loved anybody but you.'

Little wonder Aunt Janet grew anxious about
her bairns; and yet their long absence was a sign
of hope. When she heard their footsteps at the
door, she rose up, living again an agony of suspense
the like of which she had not experienced since
the night the Laird of Ravelaw brought Netta
home. They came straight to the dining-room,
and it needed only one look into their faces to tell
the woman, whose heart was still young, that they
had found the 'new world which is the old.'

'Aunt Janet, this is my wife,' said Walter fondly
and proudly, though there was a tremor in his
brave young voice.

Then Netta drooped her head, for her face flushed
like the deepest tint of the apple-bloom.

Slowly the tears gathered in Janet Nesbit's
grateful eyes, and folding her hands above their
bended heads, she said solemnly:

'God be wi' my bairns for ever an' ever,' and then
she added under her breath, 'Lord, now let Thy
servant depart in peace!'

CHAPTER XI.

‘ Beside the still waters.’

‘ NOO, Marget, is that a’, think ye ? ’

These words Miss Nesbit addressed to Marget Drysdale in the dining-room at Aldersyde, one glorious summer evening, when the old house lay bathed in the golden light of the sunset hour. Surely it was a gala day at Aldersyde, for Miss Nesbit wore a rich satin gown, with lace about the throat, which had not seen the light for many a day ; and Marget was attired in an old-fashioned brocade which had been bequeathed to her by Mrs. Nesbit on her deathbed. Ay, it was a gala day, indeed ; for within an hour, the Laird of Aldersyde would bring home a fair young wife to the home of his fathers, and Janet Nesbit would behold the desire of her life fulfilled in the happiness of her bairns, and in the building up of Aldersyde.

The table in the dining-room was, as Marget expressed it, 'a perfect sicht.' All the silver and china and crystal ware which had been the pride of the ladies of Aldersyde in other days, had been brought forth in honour of the occasion. Miss Nesbit had kept it a sacred trust at Windyknowe for the wife of Walter Nesbit ; and it was no sacrifice to her to let it out of her possession now, but an unspeakable joy to see it restored to its rightful place, and to know it would pass into worthy hands. Her eyes as she looked were moist and tender, and her lips quivered, though there was a smile about them too.

'Eh, mem, I'm perfect set up for life noo,' said Marget, making no secret of her tears. 'If it was na' for the shame o' the thing, me bein' a sober middle-aged wummin, I could dance a reel the nicht.'

'Ye'll get a chance the morn, Marget, at the grand ball,' answered Miss Nesbit with a smile. 'Wheest ! I hear the wheels.'

Ay, sure enough, and in a few minutes the high - stepping greys, which had been one of Walter's wedding presents to his wife, came prancing round the bend in the avenue, and drew up at the door. The hour of their home-coming had been kept a secret, in order to avoid the demonstration which would certainly have awaited them.

They wanted their first evening at home to be as quiet as possible; on the morrow the rejoicings would begin in earnest.

Marget hurried out to the door to welcome the bairns, but Miss Nesbit lingered in the dining-room, her feelings like to overwhelm her.

'Well, Marget, how are you? Where's Aunt Janet?' she heard Walter say, and in a moment more he was in the dining-room and had her in his arms.

'The wife's just at hand,' he said with an attempt to hide his emotion. 'Here she is! Now, Aunt Janet, haven't I taken good care of her?'

'Ye hae that!' answered Miss Nesbit, and turned to bid Tibbie's bairn thrice welcome to Aldersyde. By and by she held her at arm's length, and looked fondly and proudly into the sweet, winsome face with its crown of black locks, and at the slender, lissom figure in its faultless attire. Then she looked to Walter, and said with a smile, 'There never was a fairer leddy o' Aldersyde than oor Netta, Walter.'

'Nor a more contented laird than I, I'll be bound,' said Walter merrily.

Surely to see these two before her — such a handsome, well-matched pair — was recompense sufficient for all the anxious care of the past—

ay, more than enough; her cup was full to overflowing.

'Aunt Janet, this is just like home,' whispered Netta as she looked about the room, which had been set in order for her by hands which had found it a labour of love.

'What else could it be like, pray, when it *is* home?' asked Walter teasingly.

'I was speaking to Aunt Janet, sir,' said Netta with a dignity which seemed to amuse him immensely.

'Well, will ye come up the stair, Netta, and change yer goon? The denner's jist ready tae bring up; and as ye ken, there's naething upsets Marget like keepin' the denner waitin''

'You'll just need to hurry her, Aunt Janet, I tell you,' said Walter in the same teasing way. 'I had such a time of it at the hotel in London, in keeping the people at the table in good humour till my lady completed her toilet. I'—

'Never mind Walter's nonsense, Aunt Janet; come away,' laughed Netta. He talks incessantly, you see, and can't always be expected to talk sense.'

Truly this was the Netta of old, the sweet, blithe, winsome bairn who could make sunshine in the darkest place.

'I bade them make ready the west rooms for

ye, Netta; they were Walter's mother's, an' tae my thinkin' they are the dearest rooms in Aldersyde,' said Miss Nesbit as they went up-stairs.

'Then, if you think so, I shall like them,' answered Netta. And when the door was thrown open, she could not repress a little cry of admiration. Everything was of the best, and in exquisite taste, for Walter had spared no expense to make Aldersyde fair for his wife.

With a quick, sudden gesture Netta closed the door, and with all her old impulsiveness flung herself into Miss Nesbit's arms.

'Oh, Auntie, I am so happy! I never thought there could be such perfect happiness in this world,' she sobbed. 'I am not worthy—I am not worthy.'

'Ay, my bairn, ye are worthy a' the love bestowed on ye, an' mair,' answered Miss Nesbit fondly. 'An' it will be my constant prayer, no that ye may hae an unclouded sky a' yer days, for in this world that is impossible, but that through a' ye may cling the closer tae ane anither, an' keep the love o' yer young days fresh in yer hearts tae the end.'

Many sacred scenes had that chamber witnessed: in it Janet Nesbit had experienced some of her keenest joys and keenest pains; but never before had she seated herself there in such contentedness of soul.

The dinner was a pleasant meal, though poor justice was done to the viands. Walter teased Netta unmercifully when she shyly took her place at the head of the table, but his eyes followed her every movement with fond pride. She felt quite at home at the head of her husband's table, for, as I said before, Netta was fitted to grace any rank.

In the drawing-room by and by the three sat, too happy to speak much.

'Aunt Janet,' said Netta suddenly, 'who do you think we saw in London?'

'I never guessed onything in my life, bairn,' said Aunt Janet with a quiet laugh.

'Well, Marie and her husband; properly speaking, Mr. and Mrs. Patrick Kerr.'

'They hae mairried in haste,' said Miss Nesbit with a sigh.

'And unless I am much mistaken, they will repent at leisure,' said Walter. 'Patrick Kerr could never make a woman happy, unless one like his sister.'

'Have you seen Mrs. Riddell since the wedding, Aunt?'

'No; but I met the Laird o' Ravelaw ae day in Aldershope, an' he seemed sair against it. His bairns are a great heartbreak: Louis is gaun a' wrang thegither, he tells me.'

For a moment Netta turned her face away, shuddering at the thought of what a life might have been hers if she had married the heir of Ravelaw. And yet at one time, in the bitterness of her heart, she had felt tempted to recall him, just to show Walter Nesbit she was not breaking her heart for him. Oh, but it was a merciful God who had guided her feet, and set them on a rock!

'Aunt Janet!' said Walter by and by, 'if we knew how, Netta and I would thank you for what we are to-night; but when we have spoken about it, we find words fail us altogether. Can you understand how we feel?'

'Brawly, brawly,' she answered hurriedly. 'Dinna speak o'd.'

'But only one thing I want to say, Aunt Janet. It is to tell you what surely you do not need to be told, that this is your home at any and all times; but for you it would never have been mine, at least so freely and fully mine as it is to-night,' continued Walter, striving to speak calmly. 'And if Netta and I ever forget for a moment what we owe to you, I repeat what I said to you once before, may God visit us as we shall deserve, for we shall not be fit to live.'

'My bairn, I am mair than repaid,' was all Aunt Janet could say.

'And it will be our aim, Netta's and mine,' went on Walter gravely, 'not only to restore in some measure the honour of Aldersyde, but to do with our wealth all the good we can in the world ; for we both consider it only held in trust for God. You will help us to spend it aright, Aunt Janet ?'

'Lord, it is enough!' they heard her whisper under her breath, and beyond that she spoke no more. By and by she rose up, and stole out of the room, leaving husband and wife together to talk and plan for the future which was so bright with promise. She put a shawl about her, and went down to the head of the kitchen stair.

'Marget!' she called softly.

In an instant Marget obeyed the summons.

'Pit a shawl aboot ye, my wummin,' said her mistress, 'an' come oot efter me, an' we'll tak a turn i' the starlicht.'

Marget nodded violently, and while she ran for her shawl, Miss Nesbit softly opened the front door and stole out into the night. Oh, but it was fair, and calm, and peaceful! No sound broke the stillness but the whisper of the summer wind among the leaves, and the breaking of the tiny waves of the loch upon the pebbly shore. Slowly she wended her way by the familiar path to the little gate opening upon the edge of the loch. Her heart was full—full to overflowing with peace, and joy, and thankfulness unspeakable. The past had been dark oftentimes, and inscrutable to her shadowed eyes. She had missed the chief joy and completeness of womanhood, but she could look back without regret, nay, rather with gratitude, that it had been so ordered, for the crown of her life had come to her now in the consecration of her bairns to the service of the Lord, in the building up of the house of her fathers, and in the blossoming of lovely hopes for the future.

Marget found her with her arms folded on the wicket, and her head bowed down upon them—not in sorrow, Marget rejoiced to know, but in great joy.

'Eh, mem, my heart's fair like tae rin ower the nicht,' said the faithful soul, 'for your sake an' for the bairns'.'

'Ay, Marget,' said Miss Nesbit, and turning about suddenly, she took the rough hands in her firm, gentle clasp, and looked straight into the honest eyes. 'Eh, wummin, but ye hae been a faithfu' freen an' a pillar o' strength tae me a' my days!'

'Ye hinna regrettit, then, that I took the law intil my ain hands yon time when ye set me awa?' asked Marget bluntly.

'It was the Lord's dacin', Marget. But for you I couldna hae come through what I hae.'

'An' but for you, guid only kens whaur I micht hae been,' said Marget tremulously. 'Weel, mem, tae leeve a' my days wi' you at Windyknowe, an' dee in't if the Lord wull, is a' I seek; an' syne a buryin' up yonder aside them that's awa.'

Then a silence fell upon them, and the thoughts of each went back to long gone days which were fraught with most precious memories.

'The twenty-third was my mither's psalm,' said Miss Nesbit dreamily. 'D'ye mind hoo she lo'ed the words, "He leadeth me by the still waters"?'

'Ay, I mind,' answered Marget very low.

'A' this day, Marget, I hae heard her sayin't ower an' ower. I think she kens a' up yonder, an' sees the firm buildin' up o' Aldersyde,' continued Miss Nesbit with a strange, far-off look on her face. 'Efter the swell o' the warld's sea, we're anchored in the still waters at last, Marget.'

'Tae His name be a' the praise,' Marget answered reverently.

As they turned to go, the summer clouds cleared away beyond the chapel of St. Mary, and the first faint beams of the rising moon trembled on the bosom of the loch. And above solemn Bourhope many stars were shining.

THE END.

Crown 8vo, cloth extra, Illustrated, 3s. 6d.; plainer binding, without
Illustrations, 2s. 6d.,

'The Laird's Secret.' By JANE H. JAMIESON.

'To intelligent readers there is a charm in so genuine a story of modern
life and thought.'—*Athenæum.*

'It is long since we have read an equally healthy, pure, and bracing story.
The scene is laid in a country parish near Edinburgh. Mr. Scott, the young
"Laird," is vigorously drawn, and the handsome and attractive Dr. Blackburn is a careful study of character. There are also many glimpses of humble
Scottish life throughout the book, which attest the able hand of the writer.
It is emphatically good, alike as regards style and tone.'—*British Quarterly
Review.*

'The three girls are fresh and breezy as the heathery hills around them,
and many of the situations they figure in are powerfully exciting. Once
open the book, and you cannot lay it down till you have followed the fortunes
of the three sisters to the close.'—*Court Journal.*

'Exhibits a clear insight into human nature.'—*Public Opinion.*

'There is some love-making in the story, and the doings of all the people
in a Scottish village near Edinburgh are minutely chronicled with a simple-hearted jubilation at the superiority of all things Scotch. The plot mainly
turns on the machinations of the Popish factor, who is, of course, outwitted
in the end.'—*Daily News.*

'Deeply interesting from beginning to end.'—*Literary World.*

'A delightful story well told.'—*Christian World.*

'The characters are all graphically sketched, old Robbie Gourlay, Sir
John Maitland, and the handsome and attractive Dr. Blackburn especially
so.'—*Glasgow Herald.*

'Readers of healthy fiction will welcome a new edition.'—*Scotsman.*

'We will heartily welcome a new edition of "The Laird's Secret."'—
English Churchman.

'A first-rate story. The characters are boldly and truthfully sketched;
makes a most tempting prize or gift-book.'—*Perthshire Constitutional.*

'The story is not without pathetic touches, just as the happiest life is not
free from crosses; but the general tone is sprightly and exhilarating.'—
Daily Review.

'Pervaded by a fresh, pure, and healthy tone, which renders it delightful
reading.'—*Northern Whig.*

'Mr. Scott, the young laird, and Dr. Blackburn are sharply cut as
silhouettes, and will live in our literature. . . . An excellent work, cleverly
conceived, and showing unusual power.'—*Sheffield Telegraph.*

'A very fascinating tale; worth a hundred of the æsthetic and dolorously
tragical volumes, in which there is often so much fine writing associated with
mean sentiment.'—*Sheffield Independent.*

'Herein are combined a story of real life interest, characters which are
well drawn and fascinating, and adequate though not elaborate descriptions
of scenes and associations in rural Scotland; and while "The Laird's
Secret," with its love-making and love troubles, and its spice of sensationalism,
must have charms for readers in general, the quaint Doric speech of some of
the personages will endow the book with special attractions in Scottish
eyes.'—*Liverpool Courier.*

Crown 8vo, cloth extra, Illustrated, price 3s. 6d.; plainer binding, without
Illustrations, 2s. 6d.,

Preston Tower ; or, Will He no' come Back Again ?
By Jessie M. E. Saxby, Author of 'Ben Hanson,' etc.

'A capital story, with only so much flavour of religious teaching in it as to
give it that quality which many parents and others think essential in all such
works.'—*Scotsman.*

'Will be found specially interesting by those who are familiar with the
scenery of East Lothian, some of the local descriptions being particularly
good.   We have not forgotten Miss Saxby's story of "Ben Hanson,"
but the present volume seems to us full of greater power both in plot and
incident.'—*Liverpool Mercury.*

'The tone of the book is morally healthy, its spirit evangelical, and in a
quiet persuasive manner it inculcates lessons of the highest moment, and
offers to young men counsels and warnings whose observance will not only
save them from failure and disgrace, but insure to them success, honour, and
the infinitely greater boon of eternal life.'—*Baptist Magazine.*

'This is a romantic and pleasing story of family life and affection, which
reminds us of a sentence by Edward Garrett, to the effect that "there is a
certain misery which means, for the wise observer, that one of the other sex
has been at the making of it."'—*Christian World.*

'A very readable romance of real life.   .   There is plenty of incident as
well as character, and the author knows how to portray deep feeling in a
simple, natural way.'—*Liverpool Courier.*

'The author of "Preston Tower" possesses abilities as a story-teller of a
very high order. It is some time since we read a story of such good all-
round merit.'—*Ardrossan Herald.*

'A quaint story, opening with an exceedingly graphic description of the
village of Prestonpans, and presenting in the course of its clever plot a
remarkable variety of typical characters, some of them "racy of the soil,'
and all of them people worth knowing.'—*Kilmarnock Standard.*

'The plot is good, and the hero is successful in getting out of the toils, and
virtue is rewarded in the good old fashion.'—*Aberdeen Free Press.*

'The whole story throughout is beautifully told, and an exciting interest is
awakened at the beginning, which feeling becomes more intense as the story
proceeds, and which never flags till the last page is reached.'—*Huntly Express.*

'This is a Scotch tale of a very refreshing and wholesome nature.   The
interest of the reader is aroused by the introduction of a thread of love, which
takes its usual devious course, but ultimately triumphs.'—*Perthshire Constitutional.*

'The history of a young high-spirited youth, who engages in all kinds of
mad escapades, and becomes at last an exile from home, serving with distinc-
tion in the Indian army, supplies the authoress with plenty of material for
telling situations, thrilling scenes, and romantic incidents, and of this
material she fully avails herself.'—*Northern Whig.*

'There is abundance of incident woven together into a well-contrived plot,
and there is powerfully drawn character in this story, which is sure to interest
and can hardly be read without some advantage.'—*Spectator.*

Matthew Dale, Farmer. By Mrs Sanders.
Crown 8vo, Illustrated, cloth extra.

Doris Cheyne : The Story of a Noble Life.
By Annie S. Swan. Cr. 8vo, cl. extra.

**Additional Remains of the Rev. Robert
Murray M'Cheyne.** Extra crown
8vo, cloth. New Edition.

**Eastern Manners Illustrative of New
Testament History.** By Rev. Robert
Jamieson, D.D. Eighth Ed., cr. 8vo.

History of Joseph : Viewed in Connection
with Egyptian Antiquities, and the
Customs of the Times in which he
lived. By Rev. Thornley Smith.
Fifth Edition, crown 8vo.

History of Moses. By Rev. Thornley
Smith. Third Edition, crown 8vo.

History of Joshua : Viewed in Connection
with the Topography of Canaan, and
the Customs of the Times in which he
lived. By Rev. Thornley Smith.
Fourth Edition, crown 8vo.

Prayers for the Use of Families. By
Rev. C. Watson, D.D. Eighteenth
Edition, bevelled boards, red edges,
post 8vo.

**Memoir and Remains of the Rev. Robert
Murray M'Cheyne.** Extra crown 8vo,
cloth, with Portrait.

Rambles in Bible Lands. By Rev.
Richard Newton, D.D. Extra crown
8vo, cloth, Illustrated.

Rutherford's Letters. Cheap Edition.
Extra crown 8vo, cloth.

Princetoniana. Charles and A. A. Hodge,
with Class and Table Talk of Hodge
the younger. By a Scottish Prince-
tonian (Rev. C. A. Salmond, M.A.).
With portraits of the Hodges, and of
Dr M'Cosh. Crown 8vo, cloth extra.

Books at 3/6
OLIPHANT ANDERSON, & FERRIER